WIDOWS
of
SOMERSET

TIMELESS *Regency* COLLECTION

WIDOWS of SOMERSET

Rebecca Connolly
Jen Geigle Johnson
Heather B. Moore

Mirror Press

Copyright © 2020 Mirror Press
Print edition
All rights reserved

No part of this book may be reproduced or distributed in any form whatsoever without prior written permission of the publisher, except in the case of brief passages embodied in critical reviews and articles. These novels are works of fiction. The characters, names, incidents, places, and dialog are products of the authors' imaginations and are not to be construed as real.

Interior Design by Cora Johnson
Edited by Kelsey Down and Lisa Shepherd
Cover design by Rachael Anderson
Cover Photo Credit: Arcangel

Published by Mirror Press, LLC

Widows of Somerset is a Timeless Romance Anthology® book

Timeless Romance Anthology® is a registered trademark of Mirror Press, LLC

ISBN: 978-1-947152-95-3

Timeless Regency Collections:

Autumn Masquerade
A Midwinter Ball
Spring in Hyde Park
Summer House Party
A Country Christmas
A Season in London
A Holiday in Bath
A Night in Grosvenor Square
Road to Gretna Green
Wedding Wagers
An Evening at Almack's
A Week in Brighton
To Love a Governess
Widows of Somerset
A Christmas Promise

Table of Contents

An Heir to Spare _____ 1
by Rebecca Connolly

The Widow of Lavender Cottage _____ 109
by Jen Geigle Johnson

A Promise Forgotten _____ 231
by Heather B. Moore

An Heir to Spare

Rebecca Connolly

1

WHAT ARE YOU doing, Anna Allsbaugh?

The question would remain unanswered for the plain and simple reason that Anna had no idea what she was doing, and asking herself repeatedly was not going to make the situation improve itself in any way.

From the moment she had received the extraordinary invitation last week, Anna Allsbaugh, Lady Lyndham, had thought of little else. She'd debated endlessly over whether or not she would really accept, if she could dare to venture out so boldly in this way before her mourning period was complete.

Before she'd begun it, really.

She hadn't quite managed the mourning part of her mourning period yet.

Not that Anna had disliked her husband, Win, for she hadn't. There wasn't a soul in existence who could say they had disliked Winthrope Howard Allsbaugh, Lord Lyndham. He had been affable, proper, polite, and perfectly decent in all things.

He'd also been stuffy, boring, absent-minded, and entirely indifferent to the actions, interests, and all-around personage of his wife.

Considering the fight he had put up with her father to get her, that had proven quite the disappointment.

To her father, not to Anna.

One tedious man without affection was no different than any other, in her mind.

But what did she know? She had been married for four years, five months, and seven days. Now she had been widowed for six months, one week, and three days.

In anyone's reckoning of those numbers, she was rather ignorant, really.

And it was that ignorance that had her walking this lane at this moment, invitation clutched in her hand.

She hated her ignorance.

And Lady Joanna Kingswood had offered her a chance to change that.

Anna barely avoided a heavy sigh that would have revealed the degree of her worry. She'd kept it hidden for months now from her mother's querying letters, her housekeeper's innocent prodding, and her neighbors' prying interventions. Everything was fine, there was no cause for alarm, and she was perfectly situated for the time being.

Except nothing in her life was perfect. At all.

Win, for all his good manners and good upbringing, had a terrible notion of what a decent living for his wife would be in his permanent absence.

In fact, it appeared that he had fully intended to outlive his wife and had fashioned his will accordingly.

There had been no provisions made for her, save a hundred pounds a year. Nothing more. And a hundred pounds a year was a pittance compared to what Anna's dowry had been.

To marry a man and be poorer for it was simply cruel.

All she had was Laurisbee Park, and time alone would tell how long she had it for.

Why were there no safety measures in place for the widows of the world? Had she borne her husband a child, there might have been a bit more to live on. Had she borne him a son, he would have inherited the title and the house would have safely remained her residence until that son married and began his own family.

But she had no children to extend her living, and she had no son to inherit the title.

Laurisbee would go to the new Lord Lyndham, a distant cousin of Win's, and Anna had been assured that he would not have any interest in Laurisbee for some time. He was a respectable man, a gentleman, and one without any previous ties to any titles or the peerage, so he shouldn't have much by expectation.

She'd been told all of this by her solicitor, who was Win's solicitor, who assured Anna she had no need to read the will herself, for it was only more tedium and details.

He wouldn't budge on the matter, and she couldn't exercise any rights to force him to do so.

Poor, homeless, and desperate. That was where Anna was now.

All at the age of twenty-six.

If there were any decency in the workings of fate, Lady Joanna would have some ideas on how to improve Anna's situation. Anna didn't know the woman well, but Lady Joanna was well respected and much admired in Somerset, so the fact that she had deigned to invite Anna anywhere was nothing short of miraculous.

To be invited to take tea with her and other ladies of her acquaintance at Lady Joanna's home of Kingsberry was beyond anything.

Anna wasn't one to quake in the face of a challenge, but Lady Joanna was intimidating. She was likely not yet fifty, though age was wise enough not to trifle with such a woman, and she bore all the elegance and refinement one might expect from society. She was also rather inclined to express her opinion and held all of Somerset in her hand.

How Anna had attracted her notice was a mystery, but she was grateful for it.

She walked down the drive leading to Kingsberry now, her fingers flexing and releasing with some anxiety by her sides. The house was nearly white in its shade, adding to its splendor, and the magnificence had Anna feeling almost insecure about Laurisbee.

"It's just a house," she reminded herself, her fingers curling into fists. "Just a house and just a woman."

It wasn't as simple as that, but it did help the quiver in her stomach to fade.

Her quick strides had her to the house momentarily, and she was shown in with surprising deference.

The butler led her through the house, and she could hear the hum of a few voices ahead. The question rose in her mind: just how many widows would be there?

An imagined scene sprang into mind, that of a dozen graying ladies all taking tea together with Anna sitting in the midst and trying to find some commonality among them.

She blanched at the thought and hurried to follow the butler.

Luckily for Anna, when they turned into the sitting room, she saw a number of women that were around her age, give or take a few years, and some of them were even familiar by sight.

And then there was Lady Joanna, smiling with indulgent benevolence as Anna entered. "Lady Lyndham, what a delight to see you!"

All of the ladies smiled in welcome, while Anna looked

around the room curiously. "Am I the last to arrive?" she asked, returning her attention to Lady Joanna.

"You are," the lady replied without concern. "But only just." Her eyes drifted down to the edge of Anna's skirts, and one auburn brow rose. "Lady Lyndham, did you walk here from Laurisbee?"

Instantly self-conscious, Anna looked at her hem, faintly streaked with grass and dirt, though not filthy by any stretch. Still, to appear even remotely untidy in such company . . .

Anna raised her chin, smiling sheepishly. "I did, your ladyship. It is a lovely day, and the road isn't difficult."

Lady Joanna's expression didn't change, though she did raise her eyes to Anna's, and there was no sign of disapproval. "It is nearly four miles, my lady."

"Yes," Anna replied very simply, clasping her hands before her.

A corner of Lady Joanna's lips quirked, and her eyes narrowed as though she smiled. "Brava. A bit of hearty exercise has never hurt anyone, especially a fine lady. Do be seated. Do you know the rest?"

Without waiting for a response, Lady Joanna made quick work of the introductions. Lillian Hunter, a pretty, fair-colored woman with a quick smile and spark in her eye; Penny Fletcher, who inexplicably seemed on the verge of tears and clutched a handkerchief to her nose; Georgia Givens, a young woman entirely too serious for her age and a little thin for preference; Charlotte Ashford, dark haired, dark eyed, and haunting, as though a breeze might blow her away; and Lydia Steele, who was plump and cheerful, somehow looking at Anna as though she were proud to see her.

It was an odd grouping, to be sure. None of the ladies, apart from Lady Joanna, could be more than thirty.

A gathering of young widows? To what point and purpose?

"Tea?" Lady Joanna inquired, almost as though she were answering Anna's unspoken question.

Anna nodded quickly and took a seat beside Mrs. Ashford, determined not to be mousey and not to seem too eager either. Behavior was a delicate balance based on expectation, circumstance, and companions. Win had never given Anna direction on which version of her he preferred, and her parents had been so focused on her obtaining a well-situated husband that her behavior had been a fluid concept indeed.

Her identity, therefore, was a bit of a mess at the present.

"Ahem." Lady Joanna straightened and looked around at her gathered guests, her lips curved in a near smile. "Thank you all for coming to take tea with me today, and with each other. Not all of you have been to one of my meetings yet, but you will soon learn the way of them. For those of you who are new to my little gatherings, I must emphasize what brings us together: we are widows."

Mrs. Fletcher sniffled noisily into her handkerchief. Mrs. Givens rolled her eyes but patted the poor woman's back anyway.

Lady Joanna ignored them both. "This does not make us subjects for pity, but it can, in a way, render us powerless. Did any of you know of the provisions left for you by your late husband?"

Anna blinked and shook her head, looking around to see every other woman doing the same.

"And how many of you actually understood what those provisions were when they were made known to you?"

Not a single hand went up.

Suddenly Anna felt both better and worse about her situation. At least she was not alone in her clueless state.

Lady Joanna nodded, folding her hands in her lap. "This, unfortunately, is the common lot for widows of any age. It is not our business and not in our education. I myself have been widowed twice now, and after my first husband passed, I found myself at the mercy of his will, which left *much* to be desired. I determined never to allow myself such helplessness again."

"How?" Mrs. Givens demanded, her tone harsh in her eagerness.

"By my marriage to my second husband." Lady Joanna's smile deepened, becoming almost superior in nature. "It was entirely a marriage of convenience and cordiality, and I felt no qualms in asking Mr. Kingswood to show me his will so that I might better understand matters. He knew what I had suffered upon my first widowhood. He did better than what I asked; he brought in his solicitor and had the man tutor me."

A murmur of surprise rippled through the small group as they exchanged stunned looks. It was unheard of for a woman to be given such license and for her husband to have encouraged it . . .

"I was then," she went on, "permitted to make whatever adjustments to the will, regarding myself, as I pleased."

"Truly?" Mrs. Hunter asked, looking as though she might spring from her seat at any moment.

Lady Joanna gave her a sage nod. "Truly. I realize that Mr. Kingswood was a bit of a delightful aberration in this regard, which is why it is important to meet together before any of you venture for a second marriage."

Again, Mrs. Fletcher sniffled, this time accompanied by a whimper.

Anna gave the woman a pitying look. Clearly this was a woman in distress, but what was rather less clear was the reason why.

Lady Joanna glanced at Mrs. Fletcher but did not react to her behavior.

"Before we begin the topic of today's tea," Lady Joanna intoned, returning her attention to the rest, "I must state the rules for this society of ours. Those of you who have been before already know them, but bear with me. I believe they warrant repeating as a reminder."

Rules? How in the world could rules be applied to a group of ladies who occasionally met for tea?

"I do not give this information to all of the widows of my acquaintance," their hostess said, again answering a question Anna had not verbalized. "Only to those in whom I have taken an interest."

Lady Joanna looked at each woman in turn, her green eyes piercing in their careful assessment. "First, your husband must be well and truly dead."

Mrs. Fletcher wailed.

"Mrs. Fletcher, please do compose yourself," Lady Joanna snapped.

The handkerchief went to Mrs. Fletcher's full lips, and the sound was stifled for the moment.

Lady Joanna widened her eyes, clearing her throat. "Second, your reputation must be intact."

"Close, but just," Mrs. Steele quipped with a quick smile that made the others chuckle.

"Thirdly," Lady Joanna continued, "you must never do something so foolhardy as to fall in love again."

"I couldn't," Mrs. Fletcher hiccupped.

"Not an issue for me," Mrs. Ashford announced with a sly smile. "I didn't love the first one."

The almost matching smiles around the room bore a sad tale of their marriages indeed.

Even Lady Joanna smiled at the comment. "Finally, if you do enter into a marriage again, the groom must sign the Continuation of Care contract."

"The what?" Anna asked before she could help herself.

Lady Joanna looked at her calmly. Clearly, the question had been asked before. "A document my solicitor has worked up for my friends. It secures you and your future regardless of the husband's circumstances."

Anna frowned. "Did you not marry a second time, my lady?"

"You were not listening," Lady Joanna said without heat. "I did marry a second time, but I did not love him. Not then, anyway. I married a good man, and an intelligent one. It was after we had been married for a time when affection came into it. Love will make you behave recklessly if you are not secure."

Love *after* marriage. Was there such a thing? It did not seem likely, but she must take Lady Joanna at her word. She would know best, after all.

"Do you all consent to these rules?" Lady Joanna asked.

Heads bobbed all around the room, even from Mrs. Fletcher.

Lady Joanna smiled the first full smile Anna had seen from her yet. "Excellent. Then I will begin by introducing my guest." She lifted her chin and gestured to a servant in the back of the room.

A door opened behind the group, and they all turned to look at the balding man with white remnants of hair entering. His eyes twinkled, and a neatly trimmed mustache sat above his upper lip. Under one arm, he carried a stack of papers, and his suit was simply tailored, but tidy.

Clearly a man of business, but what business was that?

"Ladies, this is my solicitor, Mr. Norton. He is here to discuss the legal verbiage that may have escaped your education, and how such language might be used in a will."

2

Lord Lyndham.

IT SOUNDED PRETENTIOUS. It *was* pretentious. He was now a viscount. A peerage for a man who had only ever known a mediocre life was a recipe for the most pretentious of pies, and no one in the world would fault him for cutting himself a rather large slice of it.

A pity that Ned Richards didn't care about that, apart from the increase to his salary and the freedom from preparing weekly sermons.

Religious orders had never suited in that regard. He was a good Christian and had been raised by good Christians, but he had only become a clergyman for the ease of it. He was no soldier, had no head for the law, and would have been positively hopeless in anything trade. As his family did not come from money, the church had been his only viable option.

Being of use was more his calling than any actual holy orders or responsibility. He thrived upon assisting with home repairs, bringing goods to those in need, and generally being a comfort to those who had nowhere else to turn. It all sounded very grand and saintly, but really, it wasn't all that honorable.

He hated boredom.

And now Ned was Lord Lyndham. Officially.

Preparing the move from Surrey to Somerset in order to take up his seat at his new estate had been change enough for him, what with the loss of his parish and spending the first few months of his new status ensuring a smooth transition for his flock. He had been assured repeatedly by the late Lord Lyndham's solicitor that there was nothing immediately requiring his presence or assistance and that he should take whatever time he needed before taking up his new estate.

For a man who had only ever lived in a simple house, an estate sounded rather grandiose and impressive. He was a fairly simple man, so he would undoubtedly rely on his estate manager and housekeeper to keep the details in check.

Ned chuckled to himself as he rode his horse along the country road. Details. He'd never really had details in his life, and now they would be everywhere.

It was a daunting thought, taking over an estate with tenants and farms. The solicitor had insisted that the previous Lord Lyndham had been a good master and that he had been well-liked, but there was no way to know that for sure from his word alone. Ned would need to speak with the estate manager and with the tenants themselves. Provided the tenants would want to talk with him at all.

That would take time and trust.

He would be an active lord and master. He could not sit, or stand, idly by when there was work to be done or concerns to be addressed. Strange as it might seem for them, that was the only way he could see this working well.

He slowed his horse as he passed through the village, trying to ignore the stares of nearly every passerby. He'd experienced the same thing when he'd first arrived in Surrey; a single gentleman of youngish years will always attract a certain amount of attention simply by existing.

Nodding at people absently, he fixed his face into a polite smile. He might not have the dress or appearance of a man of local influence yet, but first impressions would be important. And once he'd settled, he would certainly want their good opinion and willingness to associate with him.

Once safely on the other side of the village, Ned exhaled heavily in relief and relaxed his position, nudging the horse on faster. A good ride across this wild landscape was what he needed, the more rugged the better.

Just a few miles more, and he would be at his new estate. He hadn't thought to notify the staff of his arrival, but he had been repeatedly assured that they would have all in readiness for him no matter when he took his position there. Would they have been notified of his identity prior to his inheriting the title? Or had the family line been well-known and discussed in advance of him?

The facade of a grand house was suddenly visible, tucked as it was at the base of some lovely hills, the present view almost a vista in itself with a glimpse of gardens behind the house. Wildflowers dotted the expanse of ground between his present position and the house, and they added to the charm of the place. The hills that extended from the house itself grew more forested the further they went, and he suddenly itched to explore the lot of them.

It was grand without being excessive, romantic without being unfashionable, and stately without being imposing.

It was, in a word, perfection.

If a little old.

He frowned as he rode nearer, signs of age making themselves known here and there, though he was still a good ways off. He'd wanted action to jump into the moment he arrived, and it seemed he'd need to see to his own estate sooner than he might have anticipated. No matter; surely the staff would know what would be the best course and which issues were the most pressing.

The road curved away from the house to follow the slope of the hills, and a wagon in the road suddenly caught his attention, because of its resting position but also because of the expanse of dispersed items that seemed to have once been aboard it. An older gentleman and his wife were in the process of retrieving the scattered items, and a young woman helped them, a widemouthed basket under one arm. She seemed intent on the various apples that had gone to and fro in the accident.

Ned reined in his horse and dismounted smoothly, stripping off his gloves as he strode towards them. "Good day," he called. "Can I be of some assistance?"

The man smiled almost sheepishly at him. "That would be most appreciated, sir. I'm afraid the lot of our goods went awry when the wagon hit a rut in the road. Can't have fastened them down properly, but I can't think how . . ."

"No matter," Ned assured him as he approached, grinning and clapping a hand on his shoulder. "Anything lost or ruined?"

"Not that we can see," the man said with a quick glance around. "All seems well enough. It's just . . . everywhere."

Ned nodded, casting his own eye about the mess. "I can help with that. Leave it to me."

Without waiting for another comment, Ned moved to the nearest barrel, which had somehow miraculously avoided damage. He tested the weight of it with a quick tilt, then gripped the ends and hefted the moderate weight atop one shoulder. He turned and walked it over to the wagon bed, setting the barrel near the edge. Then he pressed himself up into the wagon bed and turned the barrel until it was safely tucked in the far corner.

He repeated almost the exact same measures with the second barrel, then made a start on rather large sacks, each one fitting neatly atop his shoulder.

The heat of the day began to make itself known, though it had seemed fair enough on his ride. But laboring in the weather was a good change from riding in it, and soon enough, he would neither look nor smell like a gentleman. How would that be for a first impression for his new staff?

"You're making neat work of those things, son," the man said when Ned hopped down from the wagon bed after his third sack.

Ned offered a swift smile as he shrugged. "It's been too long since I've really felt worked to the bone. I've missed the sensation."

"Clearly not that long," the young woman said in a dry tone, surveying him with remarkable green eyes, the bushel of apples propped on one slender hip.

Something about her made him want to smile and raised his defenses at the same time. Impertinent woman, but a remarkably pretty one.

Quite remarkably, actually.

"I try to keep my strength up," he muttered as he wrenched his attention back to the remaining items. "That's all."

After hefting two smaller sacks, one under each arm, Ned turned and strode to the wagon without another word or look at any of them. He handed them to the older man, now standing in the wagon bed.

"Now let's take some of those blankets, Mother," the man instructed. "Our friend must bring us the items from the blacksmith now, and we shan't want them touching the oats."

Ned smiled to himself as he picked up the tools, bridle, a set of horseshoes, and a bag of nails, pegs, and hooks. Then he took the handles of a spade and shovel and propped them on one shoulder, sighing as he made his way back to the wagon.

The bushel of apples had been placed, and now his load would finish the thing, apart from whatever fabrics the ladies seemed to be checking around the front of the wagon.

"I don't know how to thank you," the man said as he took the items from Ned. "I'd have been here a good long while if not for you."

"Think nothing of it." Ned held out his hand to shake. "Glad to have happened upon you in time to be of service."

That earned him a sincere smile and a firm handshake. "What's your name, son?"

"Ned Richards," Ned replied before he could stop himself. Hastily, he added, "Lord Lyndham."

The older man's eyes widened. "My . . . my lord . . . I had no idea . . ."

"I did not introduce myself," Ned overrode him kindly. "You couldn't have known, and it would have made no difference to me. The actions would remain the same."

"Arthur Cotter, my lord," came the shaky reply. "At your service."

Ned smiled and put his hand on the man's shoulder and squeezed. "Not today, Mr. Cotter. Today I am at yours." He nodded firmly, then strode alongside the wagon, tipping his hat to Mrs. Cotter and her daughter, though neither of them had the awed expression Mr. Cotter had worn.

Likely they had not heard the conversation, but it could be quite the story to tell at supper.

Mounting his horse, Ned dug his heels in and galloped away, nodding again at the Cotters as he passed them.

Well, that was one way to meet his tenants. Perhaps word would spread to the rest, and he'd have done his part to assure them of his dedication.

Feeling slightly invigorated and even more than slightly motivated, Ned pushed his horse harder, rounding the road to Laurisbee as though he already knew it by heart. The closer he got, the more welcoming it appeared, and while he would not yet call it home, he could easily see it eventually becoming so.

Home. What a concept.

A footman emerged hastily from the house as Ned reined in his horse just in front of it.

"Thank you," Ned told him after he'd dismounted. "I'm . . . Lord Lyndham, I suppose."

The lad's eyes widened, and his throat moved on a swallow. "My lord." He snapped a sharp bow before turning to look towards the house. "I'm sorry, sir, I don't know where Mr. Allens has gone."

"Never mind that." Ned grinned in what he hoped was a consoling manner. "I didn't send word ahead, and he'll likely be ruffled enough by that."

"I don't know, my lord," the footman replied, his eyes sober. "Mr. Allens doesn't ruffle easily."

Ned felt his smile turn lopsided. "Neither do I." He tapped the brim of his hat and jogged up the two stairs into the house.

The entrance hall was cavernous. There was no other way to describe it, and Ned could not avoid outright gaping. It belonged in a cathedral, not a residence, and, short of a few stained glass windows, might well have come from an actual cathedral. As it was, the gilding above him combined with the plaster medallions and painted frescoes seemed to illustrate with great emphasis just how far from his previous status he had come.

All because one man he had never met had died.

"May I help you, sir?"

The cultured, practiced tone in such a deep voice left Ned

in no doubt of the speaker's identity. His eyes lowered from the ceiling above to the impressive and imposing height of the middle-aged man before him, formal and cautious while avoiding being off-putting.

The man had perfected his role, there was no mistaking it.

"Mr. Allens, I presume," Ned greeted him, sweeping his hat off of his head. "The lad out front mentioned it."

"Yes, I am Mr. Allens," the butler acknowledged with a furrowed brow. "May I inquire as to your business?"

His business. Ned was so new to the thing he wasn't entirely certain what his business was. Meetings with the Lyndham solicitors had failed to clear that up for him, though they had gone over endless documents. He had farms, he had land, he had tenants. Beyond that, he couldn't have guessed.

"I'm Ned Richards." There was nothing to do but smile as he admitted that and watch as Allens's eyes widened, his jaw slackening. "Lord Lyndham."

"My lord," Allens managed, his words barely a breath, horror seeping from every fiber of the man's towering being. "We hadn't received word ... I am so ashamed, we have nothing in readiness for you."

Ned shook his head and took a step towards the man. "Allens, I am well aware I am upending everything in Laurisbee by showing up unannounced. I can assure you, my expectations are minimal. I need no apologies and should probably extend several of my own."

Allens blinked and straightened somehow, lifting his chin. "Not at all, my lord. We will make all of the arrangements immediately. You must meet the staff..."

"Tomorrow," Ned insisted with a wave of his hand. "Please, all formalities tomorrow. I'm ..." He chuckled wryly and shrugged. "I'm not used to formalities. Or finery. Or protocols."

The butler's expression was downright comical, and Ned would have laughed harder if he felt able.

"I see, my lord."

Ned swallowed the rising laughter. "I have always been a gentleman, Allens, but one of only moderate means. I was a clergyman for a few years, in fact."

Allens seemed to sigh in relief without actually exchanging air or shifting expression. "A modest living, I imagine."

"Fairly," Ned agreed. "This . . ." He gestured to the house around them, shaking his head. "This will be quite the adjustment."

"Indeed, my lord."

Oddly, Allens just stared at him, a hint of consternation in his features behind all the deference and calm.

Perhaps Ned had managed to ruffle him after all.

"Mr. Allens, have you sent for the gamekeeper yet?" an older woman asked, her dark, graying hair neatly tucked into a cap as she strode into the entrance hall. "Mrs. Garvins would like a brace of pheasants, if he can manage it." She paused a step when she saw Ned standing there. "Oh! Forgive me, I did not know we had a visitor."

"Mrs. Riggin," Allens intoned, puffing out his chest, "this is his lordship, Lord Lyndham. He has come to Laurisbee unexpectedly. See that all is prepared for him, please."

Mrs. Riggin might have been walloped over the head with one of the shining sconces on the walls. Her dark eyes went almost entirely round, and she looked at Allens with them, her jaw tightening, exchanging some secret message Ned hadn't a hope of interpreting.

Allens only dipped his chin, which sent Mrs. Riggin almost stumbling to one side, though somehow without losing her balance at all. She might have only stepped to one side, but for the dipping of a shoulder that belied her lack of stability.

"My lord," Mrs. Riggin said, her lips barely moving as she curtseyed.

"Mrs. Riggin." Ned nodded, smiling kindly. "I do apologize. I was just telling Allens, I hadn't meant to cause a fuss. I've never lived in a house as grand as Laurisbee nor had such a staff, and it never occurred to me that there would be so much to prepare."

He could see his housekeeper try for a smile, and he suspected she was usually quite a cheerful woman, though she seemed to struggle to be so now. "It isn't that, my lord. It would only take a moment, to be sure. It's just..."

"Mrs. Riggin..." Allens warned, shaking his head.

Ned frowned. What in the world would his butler stop his housekeeper from saying to the master of the house when he had only been there ten minutes?

"There might be some confusion," Mrs. Riggin went on, shifting her tone, though not in a way that seemed to please Allens.

"About?"

The woman's fingers began knotting with each other before her, though her arms never moved from her sides.

"The rooms, my lord," she said simply, again trying, and failing, to give him a smile.

"Mine?" Ned asked, raising a brow. "Why? Surely the master rooms..."

"Are already inhabited," a crisp and distinctly feminine voice answered from behind him. "By me. That is the material point, my lord."

Ned turned in surprise, then felt his jaw drop as the woman from the wagon stepped into the entrance hall. She removed her hat and coat, revealing a fine gown, though the hem was stained, and even finer features than he had granted her earlier. Her hair was the exact color of honey, and the green of her eyes was the same in his recollection, no less striking now than before.

She handed her things to a nearby maid that Ned hadn't noticed, barely acknowledging her as she did so. "You didn't introduce yourself earlier."

"Should I have?" Ned queried mildly, a sinking feeling hitting his stomach.

The cool smile quirked just a little. "Yes. It would have cleared up a great deal. My name is Anna, my lord. I am Lady Lyndham."

3

Thunderstruck was a description Anna thought was overused, and rarely accurate when it was, but it was truly the only word that came to mind.

"How?" Lyndham demanded, finding his voice once more. "How?"

"How what?" Anna inquired as mildly as possible, forcing her tense frame to at least appear serene. "The question will require some context before I can answer."

Lyndham's chin dipped, and his look turned colder. "How are you Lady Lyndham?"

Oh, he'd asked the easiest question of them all, and Anna was only too willing to answer.

"Simple enough. I married Lord Lyndham."

Something in the man's strong jaw twitched, and Anna wanted to flick an impertinent smile at it. "*I* am Lord Lyndham."

"So you've said," Anna conceded with a nod. "Now. But you were not Lord Lyndham five years ago. My late husband was. I believe he was a cousin of yours."

"Second cousin," Lyndham grunted. "Once removed."

As if that mattered.

"Lovely." Anna allowed herself to smile now, very politely. "Congratulations."

Lyndham stiffened at the word, his chin rising to a less direct position. "My condolences. Of course."

Anna's smile felt as lifeless as her knees presently. "Of course," she murmured.

That caused a furrow in Lyndham's high brow, his blue eyes squinting. "What are you doing here, Lady Lyndham?"

Anna tilted her head, feeling rather coy. "I live here, Lord Lyndham."

He exhaled roughly and shifted his weight. "Yes, so I understand, Lady Lyndham, but this is my home now. It cannot be both of our homes."

"Naturally," she replied with her limited patience. "But as I had no notion of your arrival, I could not very well remove myself prior to your coming."

"No, of course not." He exhaled again and ran a hand through his dark yet sun-kissed hair, ruffling it slightly. "It would seem I've made more of a muck of this than I'd considered." He shook his head and smiled at last, forcing Anna to blink in surprise at the warmth in it. "Forgive me, Lady Lyndham."

Anna's smile faded, not out of consternation but confusion. "For what? Lord Lyndham—"

"I'm sorry," he interrupted, his hand coming up in a halting motion. "Pardon, again, but it is so tiresome, not to mention complicated, for us to reference each other by our titles. Would it completely abandon principle for you to call me Ned? Even Edward is preferable to the title, though I rarely answer to my real given name." He smiled, but it faded quickly. "I don't mean to encourage any particular familiarity; it would just simplify matters infinitely."

He had a point.

"I'd go by another name if I had one," Anna admitted with some apology.

"It would be no trouble for me to return to being Mr. Richards for a time."

"I cannot ask that of you." She gave him a scolding look and moved towards the drawing room, indicating he follow her. "You have inherited; there is nothing you or I can say or do to change that. You have earned the right to be referred to by your birthright."

He laughed once behind her. "I think you'll find I did nothing to earn all of this. I was born, and that is all that can be said for me. I have done nothing great, nor was I raised with any sort of prestige."

Anna peered over her shoulder, glimpsing his charming smile yet again. "And I was born into a respected family line with minimal prospects and thus have earned, and possess, nothing." She reached a settee and turned, gesturing for him to sit on the couch opposite. "I was fortunate to marry Win at all. Lord Lyndham, I mean."

Lyndham looked amusingly suspicious again. "And yet you do not sound as though you feel fortunate."

"Fortunate in my prospects," she clarified as she sat, managing an almost real smile. "Though the reality now is anything but."

"Meaning?" He sat, crossing one foot across another, his tall riding boots enhancing what seemed to be rather strong legs. That would have fit well with the work she had seen him perform earlier, impressive as it was.

Anna eyed him for a moment, sensing a kindness in him, and a genuine nature, but he remained her late husband's heir, and thus the exact manner of her present ruin.

"I have lost my identity," she told him plainly.

Deep furrows dug into Lyndham's brow again. "Surely not."

"Have I not?" Anna shot back. "I was Miss Denning prior to my marriage, and Lady Lyndham after. I have no children, no son, more specifically; therefore I will never be the Dowager Lady Lyndham. I was married to Lord Lyndham, but now I am not married to Lord Lyndham. By this logic, I should no longer be Lady Lyndham, yet my name cannot change." She gave him a rather frank look and held her hands out in surrender. "So who am I? What am I?"

Lyndham seemed bewildered by the situation Anna had just spun for him. "I haven't the faintest idea."

For some reason, that made her want to laugh, and she let herself smile without reservation. "Thank you. It is oddly comforting to be validated."

He returned her smile. "But it does little for our situation, does it not?"

Anna's face fell as the reality sunk in. He was the heir to her husband; Laurisbee was his home.

Which meant it could no longer be hers.

"No," she murmured, her attention returning to her fingers as they gripped at her skirts. "No, it does not."

Silence filled the space between them, and the words were on Anna's tongue to offer to leave as soon as possible, but she bit them back.

She had nowhere to go, even if she could leave.

"I don't want to force you to leave, my lady," Lyndham said softly.

Anna glanced up, feeling young, small, and powerless. "Your presence here requires that I do."

His smile was sympathetic, which meant something, she supposed, though it was possible for men's faces to say one thing while their words said another. "But not necessarily this moment."

"What?"

Lyndham chuckled and uncrossed his feet, sitting forward to gently rub his hands together. "My lady, I'm not going to send you upstairs to pack your trunks and rid my rooms of your belongings. I'm not about to turn you from Laurisbee onto the streets as I claim lordship here. Was that what you expected?"

It seemed almost ridiculous to hear it aloud, but she had expected something of the sort. Some burly, toxic version of Win with a cruel scowl and crueler manner, who would see Anna as worthless and insignificant. A miniscule obstacle to be overpowered and then ignored without concern.

Ned, it seemed, was not that sort of Lord Lyndham.

Ned. Not Lord Lyndham.

Just Ned.

It suited, now she looked at him. It suited rather well.

She could have burst into tears, were she not still paralyzed with apprehension. "Yes," she managed, struggling to swallow. "I had little reason to hope . . ."

"I may not bring hope with me," Ned insisted with a laugh, "but I daresay I bring a head filled with good sense. Or at least not foolishness." He smiled, then sat back again. "I will stay at the inn in the village until you are settled elsewhere."

"Thank you, Ned," Anna murmured. "Truly. Thank you."

Ned smiled, this time a lopsided one that made Anna want to smile in return. It was infectious and entirely unlordly.

That, too, suited him well.

"How long do you think that will take?"

The warmth in Anna's stomach suddenly turned cold and hard, her expression falling into one of dubious regard.

The man was an idiot and a bore, and there was nothing that could convince her otherwise.

"Unbelievable," Anna muttered to herself, shaking her

head and rising. "And yet entirely believable. So like a man. So very, very like a man."

"What?" Ned asked, gesturing helplessly. "What? What did I say?"

Anna threw him a glare. "How long will that take?" She snorted softly, stomping towards the doorway. "How long will that take. Well, Ned, as my husband's will, if you read a word of it, made no provisions for a wife, let alone one without children, I have only what remains of my dowry to live on. I have no brothers to turn to, nor are my aging parents in any position at all to support me, should I return to their care. So unless you have a generous stipend you are willing to give your forerunner's widow, it could very well take me ten years to have enough saved up to afford a cottage on the outskirts of the village." She smiled very flatly, skewering the man with her eyes as though they had the power to do anything of the sort. "Unless you wish to keep me as a mistress under your roof, which I don't recommend."

"I never meant . . ." Ned protested as he shot to his feet, his volume rising.

"No one ever means anything," Anna cried, laughing without humor as she backed out of the room. "I doubt Win meant to leave me with nothing at all, though I'd be very surprised if it ever occurred to him that I might need something. My father didn't mean it when he said my husband would care for me—that was rubbish and simply his way of washing his hands of me. My husband's solicitor didn't mean it when he told me that he would see me generously settled, knowing full well there is nothing generous about being left nothing."

Hysteria began to well up within her, but she couldn't stop it. She saw the widening of Ned's eyes, knew her voice would carry elsewhere, couldn't help this outpouring of words and emotions any more than she could stop herself breathing.

It was long past time.

"And now," Anna went on, whirling around and striding to the stairs, her voice rising in pitch, "I mean to go up to my rooms . . . Excuse me, to *your* rooms, and pack up every pitiful thing I own. Perhaps I can sell what remains of my trousseau and anything that has ever been left to me to supplement my meager funds. Or else there's the poorhouse. I've been generous there in the past." She strode up a few stairs, gripping the railing as she suddenly felt unsteady.

Inhaling sharply, she turned to look down at Ned, Allens and Mrs. Riggin having fortunately departed the entrance hall. "I can no more believe that you meant what you said just a moment ago, that I may remain for a time." Her voice broke, and she gripped the railing harder. "That I may yet call Laurisbee my home until I find someplace else. Because the truth of it is, I have nowhere to go, and no one to go to. I am as pitiful as a widow comes, and your coming here means that I have nothing now. Nothing—"

Sobs caught in her throat, and Anna's knees gave out, sending her sinking to the stairs as tears rolled down her cheeks. Her lungs were racked with every cry, shaking her frame as she clung to the railing still. Her legs shook as they curled beneath her, one free hand covering her face in shame, in embarrassment, in fear. Every loathsome, dark emotion she had felt that could never be considered grief over Win surged through her veins, along with the guilt she had spent months burying them with.

It was over now. She was out of time.

"Anna . . ." A voice broke through the haze of her panic and her tears, though she did not have the power to look, to move, or to do anything more than hear it.

She hiccupped on a pair of sobs, praying the voice would count it as an acknowledgement.

"I never meant to cause this distress ... Please, stay as long as it takes. However long it takes. I'll take my leave of you now and ... call tomorrow." His voice was earnest, genuine, concerned, but possessed the hesitation and awkward cadence known to every man's voice when faced with an onslaught of female emotions he did not comprehend.

Clipped footsteps echoed in the entrance hall, and then a great door creaked to a close, leaving only her sobs to bounce from wall to wall and up into the arches of the room.

"My lady."

Anna whimpered a weak cry and felt her fingers being gently pried from the railing, an arm wrapping around her back.

"Come, my lady, let me make you some tea, hmm?" Soft fabric dabbed at Anna's cheeks and under her nose, another body sitting beside her on the stairs. "There, there, my lady. Don't think me impertinent, ma'am, but I'm going to hold you now."

Anna laughed a watery sound as Mrs. Riggin pulled her close, encircling her in her arms like she might a daughter. "I'd never think you impertinent."

The woman chuckled and rubbed Anna's back. "Then you've never heard me at my best, my lady. Hush now, all will be well."

"Will it?" Anna sniffled and exhaled weakly. "I don't know how. And I've just dissolved myself in front of the new heir. Lady Joanna will castigate me for that."

"If Lady Joanna has never lost her emotions in a difficult state, I'll eat my own apron." She dabbed at Anna's cheeks again with a square of white linen. "I don't think his lordship will gossip, my lady. He seems a good sort, and he was rather terrified by your outburst."

The thought made Anna giggle sheepishly. "Anyone

would have been." She sighed, took the handkerchief from the housekeeper, and swiped at her eyes again, then offered it back. "Thank you, Mrs. Riggin."

Mrs. Riggin smiled warmly, but with a twinkle in her eyes. "That isn't mine, my lady. His lordship offered it to me for you before he took his leave. That's why I don't believe you've anything to fear from him in this."

Anna looked down at the linen in her hands, half expecting it to burst into flames in her palms. The monogram was simple, without much refinement or embellishment, but clear enough.

E.G.R.

Edward Richards.

She ran her thumb over the blue embroidery with a sniff. "Tea would be lovely, Mrs. Riggin."

4

"It is a simple enough matter, my lord. As you can see here..."

"Yes, I can see there, Margett. I can see every word on this page, and what's more, I understand them with some level of comprehension. What I don't see is why the house has been let to fall into such a state when, in every other regard, matters prosper."

The man gave Ned a perplexed look, then returned his attention to the documents on the table. "The state is not so terrible, my lord. We meant to begin repairs on the north wing in the spring, but the late Lord Lyndham had not settled on the builders nor the materials."

Ned propped an elbow on the table and heaved a would-be patient sigh. "It's a repair, Margett, not a renovation. What could possibly need settling?"

Margett shuffled and shifted his weight loudly. "Well, his late lordship thought it might be a good time to consider renovation..."

"I am not his late lordship," Ned overrode him firmly, giving the older and more rounded man a serious look. "And there is no need at all to consider renovation."

"But my lord..."

"When we cannot properly care for our people, Margett, it is a poor time to consider enhancing one's estate for the sake of finery." Ned looked up at him and raised a brow.

Margett sputtered, his face blotching. "His lordship would never have let his tenants suffer for his own vanity. Never. He was a good master to them."

"I see no signs of neglect," Ned assured the affronted man. "Only a lack of attention. Whatever his thoughts on enhancing Laurisbee, forget it. Only necessary repairs until the estate, as a whole, is settled. Not just our own coffers. Understood?"

"My lord . . ." Margett squawked, apparently not understanding at all.

The entire morning had been like this, and Ned was exhausted. If his predecessor were alive now, Ned would have killed him without a second question. As far as he could tell, the man had never done anything one way or the other. He had been a man of inaction, and likely inattentiveness—leaving matters he did not understand to those who understood only part, and therefore preventing any real improvement.

It was a maddening mess, and he had only dipped his toe in thus far.

"Margett," Ned said suddenly, breaking into the man's continuing stream of plaintive protests, "have you an assistant estate manager?"

"I have, my lord," came the quick reply. "Thomas Wooler. Fine man, barely thirty. He will be very good one day, I assure you."

Ned nodded and sat back in his chair. "Send for him, will you? Let's see if the two of you can figure something out together."

Margett bowed repeatedly. "Of course, my lord. Right

away, my lord." He hurried for the door, which had never fully closed for their meeting.

"Thank you," Ned muttered dryly as he watched the man go. Shaking his head, he rubbed at his brow and exhaled a low, rough growl.

If he had known this was what he would inherit, he might have changed his name the moment he'd been approached with the will.

Ignorance was not a crime, but apathy ought to be. And there was no doubt that Winthrope Allsbaugh, Lord Lyndham, had been as apathetic as they come.

A soft knock at the door brought him up. He feared for his sanity if that idiot Margett was back with another question or point.

It was Anna, however, who pushed the door open further, a pink-muslin dress giving her the appearance of the dawn. Her hair had a looser hold today, barely seeming held aloft at all, and a few honey curls trailed along her shoulders. She bore a hesitant smile, her green eyes having a distinctly bronze sheen at the moment.

"Good morning," was all she said, though there was clearly more in her thoughts.

It would be gentlemanly to be cordial, but Ned was exhausted. "Is it? I hadn't noticed." He forced a smile that could barely be called one, and only did so for effect.

"Margett was Win's man, through and through." Anna wrinkled her nose up and shrugged. "I cannot pretend either of them did anything much, but I'm afraid I wasn't particularly involved with decisions or the process."

"I don't think anybody was particularly involved with decisions or process." Ned rose, very belatedly, and bowed. "Sorry, I didn't . . ."

Anna scoffed and waved him down as she took a seat. "I didn't even think of it. Sit down, Ned."

He did but looked her over with some concern. "How are you? Recovered?"

Her cheeks colored, and he wished he hadn't said anything. It likely wasn't right to ask a woman about her health, but as a clergyman, he had asked it regularly of his parishioners. And they had told him, most of the time truthfully, of their feelings and conditions, which he made it his duty to attend to.

It had become a habit, really. And that habit was not about to change now.

"Some," Anna admitted, surprising him with her honesty. "My circumstances have not changed, but I do not expect to melt into unbecoming hysteria again, if that was your fear."

"It wasn't." Ned offered a far more natural smile now. "This is still your home, and you may feel however you wish."

"No, this is *your* home." Anna gave him a scolding look. "And I am a guest."

Ned scoffed and waved his hand. "Look at it however you like; it all means the same." He looked down at the pages before him, laughing to himself. "This is a mess. A right, honest mess. No wonder your husband did nothing for the estate—the details and terms have not been updated for at least fifty years. I have no experience in managing an estate, and still I can tell you that."

Anna laughed again, this time in derision. "I don't think Margett has any experience either."

"Evidently not." Ned chuckled louder and let himself sigh again. "Oh, heavens, Anna. What have I gotten myself into?"

He paused, realizing she had not actually given him permission to call her by her first name, though she was calling him Ned now.

"Apologies," he said quickly. "May I call you Anna?"

The woman smiled so easily it was difficult to believe she was the same woman from yesterday. And oh, what a sweet smile she had! "Of course. I thought we had agreed to that yesterday."

He cleared his throat sheepishly. "I believe it was suggested yesterday but not entirely agreed upon."

"Was it?" Anna quirked a brow and nodded. "Well, I agree. You were very kind to me yesterday, all things considered, and you were quite right; it would be difficult for us both to be called Lyndham at the same time."

"I was not that kind," Ned assured her ruefully. "I was panicked and recovering badly."

Anna laughed once. "Not casting me out of your rightful estate? Indulging my hysteria without using it against me? I call that very kind." She waited a moment, then smiled in an almost impish manner. "The delivery left something to be desired, I grant you . . ."

"There it is." Ned leaned his head back against the chair, groaning to himself. "Thank you. You give it a far more polite name than I could have. It was an outright butchery of a delicate situation that I did not comprehend. Still don't, but it's really none of my affair."

"Isn't it? I'm still under this roof." She pointed to the ceiling above them as if to prove a point. "I have no right to be here."

Ned rolled his eyes and gave her a hard look. "Do you want me to kick you out? Send you into the village so that you may beg for bread in the streets?"

Anna clasped her hands in her lap, shrugging her slender shoulders in a way that made her hair dance. "All I am telling you is that you could. By rights, you could."

"Well, having the right to do something doesn't actually make it the right thing to do," he pointed out. "And exercising a right that isn't right isn't something I have any interest in doing." He smiled at the awkward pattern of words, his brow furrowing with it. "All right?"

She snickered, looking away from him to do so, unwittingly displaying a perfect turn of throat and only enhancing her general air of loveliness, let alone perfection of figure.

"And now you're mocking my inelegant speech," he grumbled playfully as he pushed up from his seat, moving towards the lone window in the room. "It's not my fault I was not blessed with a great command of words."

"Were you not a clergyman?" Anna shot back, draping one arm across the rest of her chair. "I thought I understood from Allens and Mrs. Riggin that . . ."

Ned turned to look at her, smiling once more. "Oh, I was. My sermons were short but heartfelt, and no one would find me particularly learned after hearing them. I was very good at the manual, physical aspects of being a clergyman. Terrible at the scriptural, teaching aspects."

"You must have been delightful at weddings and funerals."

"Actually, I was quite favored there." He flashed a quick, wide grin. "Nobody wants those services drawn out. At any rate, back to my comment: do you want me to send you away?"

"Of course not." Anna turned more serious as well, a wrinkle briefly creasing her fair brow. "But what I want . . ."

"Kindly do yourself, and me, a favor," Ned interrupted with as much gentlemanly behavior as an interruption allowed, "and stop telling me how little you matter in this. Or how much I do."

Anna's green-and-bronze eyes widened, her lips parting in surprise. Then her mouth snapped shut, and she swallowed. "That is the way it is, though."

"I do not care." Ned moved back to the table and pressed

his palms into the surface, staring at Anna without hesitation. "I have no interest in exploiting the differences in our present situation for my own benefit. I'd like to think that any decent man would do the same, but I know enough of men and the world to know that's fairly naive. I am a gentleman in breeding, but breeding is no sign of good manners."

"True enough," the woman before him murmured absently, her eyes still on him.

He nodded in acknowledgement of her statement. "The point of it is, Anna, that I want to help you. I don't care if I hold all the rights. As far as I'm concerned, so do you. I refuse to inherit at the expense of your downfall."

Anna wet her lips carefully. "Are you certain?"

Ned raised his brows and straightened, folding his arms. "Do I look like a man who is uncertain to you?"

She shook her head, the corners of her mouth pressing into her cheeks in an almost smile.

"Good," he grunted. "Because I'm not." He smiled again, easing his stance. "So stop insinuating that I am going to throw you out. That isn't happening. Don't thank me for letting you stay, don't feel guilt for remaining here, and don't act as though this is some very great favor or momentous act of kindness. I'm just trying to be gentlemanly, and that is all that can be said for me. Understood?"

For a long moment, Anna was silent, staring at him. It was unnerving, the power she could hold in her eyes; it left one feeling somehow exposed and examined without any shame in it. At once he felt seen, not just acknowledged, and somehow seen down to his soul.

But what was she seeing? What was she *thinking*? Her face was a beautiful, elegant mask, giving nothing away of what lay beneath or what to expect.

It was far and away more unnerving than the frank awareness in her gaze.

"You're an unusual man, Ned Richards," Anna finally told him, her head tilting to one side as if for additional consideration.

"So I've heard," he replied, a pocket of tension coiling somewhere behind his navel.

She smiled at last, seeming to relax into her seat without losing a modicum of her perfect posture. "Why do you look as if you consider that a compliment?"

The tension released with what would have been an embarrassing rush of an exhale, had he not covered it with a sort of laugh. "I take anything that distinguishes me from other men as a compliment." He glanced down at his papers, then made a point of piling them up and pushing them aside. "This is ridiculous." He looked at Anna, smiling. "What should I know about Laurisbee and its tenants, Lady Lyndham?"

Anna straightened her position, lifting her chin, and adopting a more formal expression. "Well," she began, her tone playfully haughty and clipped, making his smile spread, "there isn't much to be said for high society, but the turnout for harvest supper is the finest in twenty miles."

"Is it really?" Ned asked with genuine surprise. "I wouldn't have thought my cousin the sort to host those, given what I've discovered so far."

"Win didn't have much of a choice," Anna told him as she returned to her natural voice. "It's a long-standing tradition, and he couldn't disappoint anyone. We don't have the highest number of farms or tenants in the area, but come harvest supper, that matters little. And then there are the orchards, of course."

Ned jerked in his seat, fingers freezing in their absent drumming against the tabletop. "Orchards?" he repeated. "What orchards?"

Anna stared silently in disbelief. "Oh, Ned," she murmured finally with a sympathetic laugh. "Did nobody tell you about the orchards?"

"Evidently not." That seemed to be a massive omission on the part of Mr. Margett, and there was no indication in this paperwork that orchards even existed.

How did anyone keep any estate afloat with so much carelessness?

"The orchards were not part of the original estate," Anna informed him, taking pity on his confusion. "My late husband's father purchased them during his time, from a neighboring estate that wished to retrench. I believe he made some great improvements to them. The care of the orchards, however, was mostly left to Lady Lyndham, Win's mother. It was her own special project of sorts, and when I married Win, she bequeathed them to me, so to speak."

Ned shook his head and lifted the pages of incomplete information for emphasis. "What is the point of examining all of these if they don't have the details I need? Heavens above." He snorted in disgust and set them back down, slumping back against his chair. "This is a mess, Anna."

"Is that why you sent for Wooler?"

He nodded. "Margett needs to go, that much is evident, and if Wooler is even halfway capable as an estate manager, he can take over. I need some vigor and energy in this area, and Margett is clearly lacking both."

Anna laughed quietly, drawing his eyes back to her. "Planning on uprooting all of the old ways, Ned?"

"If I must." He tilted his head, observing her carefully. "Will the tenants object?"

"I shouldn't think so." Anna lowered her eyes in thought, the faint wrinkle in her brow appearing again. "I make regular visits to them and know most of them well. Though they never said so, I believe they were growing weary of Win, or perhaps of Mr. Margett. I don't believe anything has really changed since his father's time, and while that may have suited then, it isn't likely to suit now. But I'm not all that informed."

Ned grunted in acknowledgement, though the sound wouldn't indicate his feelings one way or the other. "You seem well-informed enough."

Anna's eyes shot up to his, and something in her expression hardened. "I'm not. At all, as it happens. I visit the tenants and take a basket where it is suggested I do so. Beyond that, I know nothing."

"You answered my question, though," Ned pointed out.

"I have eyes and ears," she snapped with a flash of her brilliant eyes. "And I use them well. I am almost entirely ignorant as to anything regarding Laurisbee, as every matter of the estate down to the groceries for the kitchens was taken to Win and not me. He took no pains to give me responsibilities or occupation, and, other than existing as lady of the house, I had no role in his life."

Ned stilled in his chair, watching the display of emotions in her, his mind reeling. Certainly a wife would have the run of the household in the typical home, but to be denied that? What in the world did his cousin think that he had married for?

"But ..." he started, wondering at the wisdom of interjecting at all.

Anna, however, knew his question. "What of the last six months?" she finished for him. At his nod, she scoffed under her breath. "I have been repeatedly informed that I do not need to worry myself about the affairs of the estate. That all would be in readiness for the new Lord Lyndham, and it would all be too tedious for me to undertake. Even when I insisted, I was rebuffed, and so in my widowhood I am as ignorant as I was in my marriage."

"Who?" Ned demanded in a low voice, the word clipped by his rising irritation. "Who was denying you?"

"Mr. Margett," she informed him, her indignation seeming to fade with the admission of it. "And Mr. Knotts, the solicitor. I've done what I can with the tenants in spite of my ignorance, but..."

"Will you walk with me tomorrow?" Ned overrode her without thinking.

Anna looked at him, consternation flicking across her features, no doubt at his rudeness. "Will I what?"

He winced, not bothering to hide that he was doing so. "Apologies. I was listening to you, and my thoughts spun at the same time. What I mean is, will you walk with me to visit the tenants? You've made connections with them, it seems, and I'd like to continue whatever familiarity you've started there. Also, I'd like to see the orchards."

"Did you not...?" Anna trailed off, pointing towards the door to the room absently. "Did you not just send Mr. Margett to fetch Mr. Wooler so that you might learn all of this?"

Ned tugged at his cravat, making a note to avoid such a fastidious style in the future. "I sent for Wooler because I am in desperate need of intelligent conversation with regards to the estate. I'm asking to walk with you tomorrow for the same. Wooler can tell me what he knows, and so can you. Seems a shame to not take advantage of every knowledgeable resource available to me while it is so." He folded his hands across his torso, allowing himself to smile at the beautiful woman looking at him with such confusion. "If I am to improve upon this estate, and I intend to, I mean to start now. Today. With my own two hands when I can, and upon the advice of those who know better when I must."

"Starting with renovations to the house?" Her eyes narrowed slightly, and Ned had the distinct impression she was surveying him as much as he was her.

"Heavens, no." Ned shook his head firmly. "None are needed, and it would be a waste of the estate's resources. I only mean to take on the essential repairs to the house itself and devote the rest of my attention to the farms and tenants. And the orchards too," he added as an afterthought with a nod in her direction.

Anna stared at him still, unmoving, the thoroughness of her gaze almost flattering. "You're a very unusual man, Ned Richards."

Ned smiled slightly. "When I believe you are complimenting me instead of expressing confusion, I'll tell you my thoughts on you."

"What?" She laughed and seemed to snap from her observational state. "Why not now? First impressions, after all . . ."

"Impressions are fluid, but no one ever admits that." He continued to smile, pleased to have found a sort of comfort with her so early in their acquaintance. It would make everything so much easier. "I look forward to what your input will do to my impressions of Laurisbee and the village."

Anna's lips twitched before spreading into a smile that sent a jolt of feeling into his right foot. "I shall endeavor to prove a useful source, then."

He opened his mouth to reply, though what he would counter with hadn't occurred to him yet, when a knock at the door brought them both round.

"My lord," Allens intoned, "Mr. Margett has returned with Mr. Wooler for you."

"I'll leave you to them," Anna said quickly as she rose.

Ned was not two seconds behind her in rising himself. "You can stay, Anna. Really, do."

She smiled at him but shook her head. "That's very considerate, Ned, but Laurisbee isn't going to be my home for much longer. It's yours now. It would serve no purpose for me to stay." Nodding to him, she slipped out of the study without another word.

Why did her response leave him so filled with annoyance?

"My lord," Margett announced as he reentered the room, a younger, taller man striding in behind him. "May I present my assistant, Mr. Wooler?"

Ned extended a hand to the man, feeling much better seeing a fit, tanned assistant to his hopeless estate manager there. Wooler shook his hand hard, grip secure, calluses scratching against Ned's palm.

This man would do very well indeed.

"Pleasure, sir," Wooler said, his voice low as he stepped back.

Ned nodded to himself. "Wooler, I'd like to promote you to my estate manager and agent in full. Margett, you are thanked for your years of service and dismissed. My solicitor will be in touch to settle the appropriate severance for you."

Both men's mouths fell open, though Wooler slowly began to smile. Margett, however, looked as though he had been struck across the back of his head.

"My ... my lord ..." Margett stammered, stepping forward.

Ned took pity on the man but gave him a firm look. "Margett, you've done your best, and I thank you. But it is time. Please." He gestured for the door, leaving his arm extended.

Margett blinked at him and looked at the door, then reluctantly left the room.

Ned exhaled with some relief and resumed his seat. "Right. That's done, so ..."

"My lord," Wooler interjected, stepping forward. "I

promise to serve you well and work for the betterment of Laurisbee. I'm a good worker, sir, and an honest one. You won't regret this."

"I know." Ned looked up at the man, grinning. "I'll make good use of you, Wooler, and fully expect you to partner me in an ambitious plan for this place. We'll set up your new salary and situation as soon as we can, but for now, I need to start over on everything with regards to the estate. I hope you didn't have any plans for the remainder of the day."

Wooler grinned back. "I'll just need to send word to my wife, sir, or she'll hold my supper until dawn."

Ned chuckled and gestured for the man to sit. "I'll send her word myself, with a profound apology." He pulled the stack of pages back from where he'd pushed them earlier, straightened them, and then paused as he returned his attention to Wooler. "Before we begin, though, I need your advice. I'll be in need of a new solicitor after we finish here. Know of anyone capable enough yet foolish enough to take us on?"

5

NED RICHARDS WAS handsome.

This was not new information, but it felt significant at the present.

It made having to look at him both more interesting and more challenging. And it made being looked at *by* him almost unbearable.

Maddening.

Nerve-shattering.

Ticklish.

She didn't quite understand how that last word fit with what she was feeling, but there was no other way to describe it. *Ticklish* was entirely appropriate, and the sensation of it rippled across her entire expanse of exposed skin, of which there was very little. Then, of all things, it settled in her kneecaps.

Ticklish kneecaps were incredibly disconcerting to a lady.

Particularly when one was walking alongside a handsome man who was looking at her, and at whom she was required to look on occasion.

But *must* he be so very attractive? She'd thought so when he helped the Cotters with their dispersed goods, before she knew his identity, and even when she'd been furious to discover he was the man to evict her, she'd acknowledged his attractiveness. Of course, at that moment it had been an unfortunate truth, but after he had become better known to her, his appearance had become a benefit once more.

Now, however...

Her cheeks began to heat as she walked beside him through the rows of apple trees. He'd come to Laurisbee very early this morning, eaten breakfast alone, and then met with a solicitor, though she wasn't certain Mr. Knotts had truly made the journey from London. By the time Anna had risen and breakfasted herself, Ned had been ready to commence their walk, if she was still of a mind.

And so they had walked, Anna dressed in her plainest calico with apron, her hair loosely plaited but pinned up. Ned matched her in his country attire, relaxed and well-fitting but hardly lordly. No one seeing them would guess them to be the former mistress and current master of a grand estate.

Strangely, Anna didn't mind in the least. Win had always made it clear that she was to appear the lady regardless of situation, though he never gave an opinion on the specifics. She had taken to continuing the trend out of habit after his death and only recently had begun to relax her approach entirely.

She had never permitted anyone to see her so informally attired as this.

But with Ned, she didn't mind.

His attractiveness aside.

"I'm impressed," Ned was saying as he walked beside her, grinning at the trees for the time being instead of at her. "Very impressed, actually. This is a fine operation."

"I can't take any credit for it," Anna laughed, embarrassed by the praise. "I did not plant the trees, nor do I tend them. Much of the improvements were done before I ever set foot here."

Ned swung his head around to look at her, and the color of his eyes nearly matched the sky above them. "There is something to be said for maintaining improvements once they are made, you know. And being responsible for the decisions about this orchard is as important as the day-to-day care of it."

Anna looked away, running her hand along the bark of the nearest tree as they passed it. "I come out here when I can, sometimes to speak with Hawking about updates or problem spots, other times just to see it. I was out here every fine day this spring. The blossoms were beautiful, and so fragrant. It was the most soothing experience I have ever known."

"It must have been a relief," Ned remarked softly. "In your grief, to have such a beautiful place to find solace in."

"Grief." Anna smiled a little at the taste of the word, the feel of it. "I suppose it was grief, but not in the way most people expect. I grieved the life I had known. I grieved the identity I had taken on. I grieved the comfort of my life, knowing it would all change. I grieved never having children . . ." She paused at this, true emotion rising and forming a lump she fought to swallow back.

"Anna . . ."

She shook her head and sniffed once, looking heavenward and letting the warm sun graze her cheeks. "Yes, I came here to grieve, but, I am sorry to admit, not for my husband."

"You did not care for him?"

The question was an honest one, and asked without judgment, but still she hesitated to answer.

"Win was a husband of distance," Anna finally admitted, choosing her words with care. "He had his roles, and I had mine, and it suited him that we remain in those roles throughout. He had little interference in my daily life and actions, and I had even less in his. It was as comfortable a marriage as I could have expected. I am sorry he is dead; I am well aware my circumstances could have been much worse in a marriage, and I am thankful they were not."

Ned made a soft, noncommittal, unreadable sound, sweeping his hands behind his back and looking at each tree they passed. "Shall I tell you what I think? Purely from my recent observations, of course."

Anna glanced at him with interest, smiling softly. "If you like."

He nodded, pursing his lips for just a moment.

Odd what a distracting motion that was on a man. She'd never noticed before, but looking at him now . . .

"I think your husband was a fool."

Anna blinked. "I beg your pardon?"

Ned did not so much as twitch in her direction, continuing to gaze at the trees without concern. "A fool," he repeated clearly, as though she had not heard him. "I presumed so after seeing the documents for the estate and how little he paid attention to them, but after hearing you . . . There is no question now that he was a fool, God rest him."

"How could you know that?" Anna demanded, more amused than indignant, not particularly caring that he would know. "You didn't know Win, did you?"

"No, I had no idea of his existence until I received word of his death and my subsequent inheritance." He gave her a quick look, smiling in an almost mischievous way. "But you don't have to know a man to know he's a fool."

"Don't you?"

Ned shook his head, still smiling playfully. "Not at all. I believe that I have enough evidence to suspect that your husband was as indifferent in all other parts of his life as he seemed to be with the estate itself. I have no doubt he wanted it to be successful, but I find he took very little personal interest in it. Correct me if I am wrong, Anna, but he seems to have treated his marriage in the same regard. With indifference."

Nearly all of the air left Anna's lungs with that single word. *Indifference.*

Indifferent to their marriage, to their life, to Anna herself...

Anna had hated indifference.

"And so I ask myself," Ned went on calmly, though he had to have noticed Anna's change, "what is the good in living with indifference in anything? What a waste. What a perfectly miserable waste of a life."

"I hadn't thought of it in that light," Anna said softly, a bittersweet pang pinching at her stomach.

Poor Win.

She frowned at herself for the thought. *Poor Win?* The man had everything he had ever wanted; it was not her fault that he had not wanted much. It *was,* however, her fault that he had not had a son.

And he had wanted that very much.

But in everything else, simple indifference.

Ned inched a tad closer, almost nudging Anna with his elbow. "Of course—you wouldn't. You were living with his indifference as a usual part of your life. But the more foolish is the fool who cannot see what is right before his face."

Anna sighed, nodding in agreement, then paused, the faint brush against her arm sending shocks into her frame. "What do you mean?"

"For a clever woman, Anna, you can be remarkably..." Ned trailed off, shaking his head. "It would be better if I didn't finish that statement. The point is that any man with a woman such as you in his life would be the fool's fool for behaving with anything less than undivided attention."

There were no words for such a statement. There were only heartbeats. Fervent, profound, fully alive heartbeats—and they pulsed in at least twelve points across her body.

Never, as far as she could recall, had she felt this vibrant, this aware, or this new.

Surely that was significant. For a widow with no prospects to suddenly wake from shadows she hadn't known surrounded her, the dawn was both breathtaking and terrifying.

Her fingers began to tingle, and she found herself blinking hard, earning a quick rush of tears that easily dissipated.

"So," Anna ground out, her voice rough, "was Mr. Wooler more helpful, as you hoped?"

"Infinitely so," Ned replied in the same easy tone from before, clearly not at all affected by his own words. "He'll put me through my paces shortly, and he'd likely be a better Lord Lyndham than I could hope to be."

"I don't know about that," Anna found herself muttering, averting her face a little to do so and praying he wouldn't hear her.

"He told me something very interesting about these orchards of yours," he continued. He turned to walk backwards, eying the rows behind them and the branches above. "He said that presently the orchards are the estate's largest source of income."

Anna returned her attention to him. "You're not serious."

Ned raised a brow, giving her a crooked smile. "I'm too new at all of this to be anything but serious. There's a lot of work to be done to bring the farms up to scratch, but you should have a look at the numbers before they change. You'd be amazed."

"I would love to," she admitted, surprising herself and beaming. Then she wrinkled up her nose. "I won't understand much of them . . ."

"Oh, I think you'll make a quick study." Ned nodded in approval, his smile both charming and fetching. "Come and have a look at them tomorrow. Wooler and I will be working at them still. You're more than welcome."

If she were to smile any further, her face would crack in two.

She might not have cared if it did.

"I would love to," she said again, this time with far more meaning.

The tone of his smile shifted just the slightest, and genuine pleasure radiated from it.

And the pit of her stomach clenched in primal approval.

"How are you finding your stay at the inn, Ned?" she heard herself ask, and she could have kicked herself for sounding like such a simpering miss.

If he noticed, he mercifully did not react. "Oh, it's comfortable enough. Better than most places I've stayed."

Anna picked up a small branch that had fallen to the ground, likely due to recent storms, and began absently fiddling with it. "Oh, I doubt that very much. Mrs. McKenzie does a well enough job managing things now that her husband has passed, but it can hardly be called comfortable."

Ned chuckled softly, and the sound rippled across Anna from her toes up. "Have you ever stayed there?"

It was disarming, but she quite liked the difference from other gentlemen, who would dance about a question or statement without any sort of clarity. She didn't have to decipher what Ned was saying at any point in time. There was no mistaking anything.

Refreshing. That was what it was. Ned's manner was entirely refreshing.

"No," Anna said in answer to his question. "No, I've never stayed at an inn. We never traveled enough to require that I do so, though we have stopped for a change of horses at one or two." She laughed to herself, realizing just how sheltered and spoiled that could sound. "I am in no position to state an opinion on anything of the sort, am I? I haven't the faintest idea what an inn should or should not be like, so it is in very poor taste to comment at all. Forget I said anything."

His laughter was loud, and it was infectious. "I will not. You're not to be faulted for a lack of experience or knowledge of inns, Anna. I don't consider such things a mark of refinement or necessary for one's life lessons."

"I am relieved to hear it."

"But," he continued, ignoring her statement, "as someone who has spent quite a bit of time in various inns over the years, let me assure you that Mrs. McKenzie does better than most. Excellent service, clean rooms, and good meals, and that is really all anyone can ask for."

Anna shook her head, laughing at him. "You've not had a single meal there outside of the first night, have you?"

Ned grinned back. "It was a very good meal, and it was hot."

"You're ridiculous." She swatted him with the branch she still held, and he snatched it away with a laugh.

"To a man who works himself to the bone, a hot meal is never to be taken for granted," Ned insisted, emphasizing each word with a flick of the branch. "And oftentimes, meals at an inn are better than meals at a great house."

Anna darted ahead a few paces, turning to face him as they walked, a strange, giddy playfulness filling her. "And what of the meals at Laurisbee, hmm? Does that meet with the high and mighty standards of his reluctant lordship?"

Ned's grin lit into Anna's heart, matching her childlike antics near perfectly. "Reluctant?" he repeated with mock effrontery. "I'll have you know I am eager in taking on my responsibilities, and the very, very trying task of living in a grand house with a hoard of servants, including and possibly most importantly, the most remarkable cook to ever grace a kitchen."

Beaming at the extravagant praise, Anna tossed her head back and laughed. "She will be delighted to hear it. I have no doubt she'll root out your favorite dessert and have it served to you this very night."

"Oh, it shouldn't be too difficult to discover," Ned said on an exhale, squinting into the sunlight above them. "I'm terribly fond of trifle, and I would never turn down sugar biscuits alongside cocoa."

Anna gaped, somehow still finding more laughter at hand. "My Lord Lyndham, you do surprise me. And you express your opinions rather decidedly, do you not?"

"Shouldn't I?" he retorted, swinging the branch he still held as though it could be a walking stick. "Shouldn't everyone?"

"In a word, no." Anna shook her head, hooking her fingers together behind her back. "Nobody in the peerage does. It's not at all the fashion."

Ned wrinkled up his nose, then shrugged. "Ah, well. I've never been particularly fond of following the fashion. I'd much rather make a mark."

Anna cocked her head to one side, suddenly wanting to ask him a hundred questions, interrogate him on anything and everything, find out his every plan and every secret for no other reason than because he was fascinating. And she was curious.

Vastly curious.

Insatiably so.

"What kind of a mark, Ned?" she asked, her playful streak fading just enough to let genuine interest shine through.

He slowed a step, his smile becoming a smirk that begged for more questions. "Do you really want to know?"

Anna nodded repeatedly, forgetting to be proper, distant, or aloof, as the lady of the estate was always supposed to be. "Yes. Tell me."

Ned's brows quirked playfully. "I could. Or . . ." His eyes narrowed in apparent thought and suspicion, looking Anna over.

"What?" she demanded on a laugh. "Or what?"

"Or I could show you." He stopped his progress entirely, prompting her to stop as well.

Anna was nearly breathless with her curiosity. "How?"

He only smiled and tossed his branch to one side, taking two steps closer to her.

Rearing back, breathlessness increasing, Anna swallowed. "How?" she asked again.

Ned's smile remained. "Walk me to the village," he said, his voice somehow lower. "Any tenants we pass, introduce me. And by and by, I'll show you."

It was an invitation she couldn't refuse, even if she had been so inclined. For one, she had offered to do so already. For another, she desperately wanted to do exactly as he asked.

She wanted to see the sort of man he was.

The sort of master he would be.

How Lord Lyndham behaved now.

And if she could ever think of anyone else bearing that title again.

"All right," she agreed, unhooking her fingers and anxiously brushing at her apron. "There's a path we can take just up here. Shall we?"

Ned nodded, smiling at her as though something amused him. "We shall, my lady. Lead on."

6

What in the name of high heaven was he doing?

Anna—Lady Lyndham—wasn't some country miss he could charm away from her chores, not that he'd ever been accused of any such thing. She was a fine lady, his predecessor's widow, and he should be respecting her widowhood and making her life comfortable.

Instead he was grasping at any excuse to spend the day with her.

Oh, he needed to see the orchards, and he needed to meet the tenants, and he could use a more concentrated exploration of the village, but none of that needed to be done at this moment and in her company.

He didn't care. He wanted to do this. Wanted to see what she knew. How she saw things. What made her laugh, light up, and linger. Anything and everything that amused or inspired her was of great interest to him now.

He should offer to help her. His solicitor was looking over the will, but there wasn't a reason to inform her of that. Besides, that was his solicitor. *Ned* should do something.

But what? He hadn't had much success with discussing her stay at Laurisbee in the past, and he wasn't entirely eager to try again.

Ned found himself looking over at the woman walking beside him, watching her as she surveyed their surroundings with a smile. He had never seen beauty like hers before, in the honey color of her hair, the blend of shades in her eyes, the healthy, rosy complexion that was somehow still as fair and unblemished as any society lady could wish. She stood no higher than his shoulder, and his hands could have spanned her waistline without any difficulty, so slender was she. Her motion was graceful, her posture perfect, and every step she took could have been part of a dance.

Something Anna saw must have amused her, for her lips pulled into a small, almost laughing smile, bringing his focus there.

Artists would weep over the perfection of her lips, which were full enough to draw attention without being outright distracting—and their shade weakened at least one knee at any given time. They curved with the right amount of invitation and pressed into a firm line that sent a chill straight to the base of one's spine. Somehow, those lips held more expression and emotion than any pair of eyes or set of features Ned had ever seen in his entire life.

No, there was no mistaking the beauty of Anna, Lady Lyndham, and he fully appreciated it.

But that wasn't why he had done what he had thus far, nor why he would continue to do it.

It might have been the tears he had witnessed on the Laurisbee stairs. It might have been the conversation they had shared the day before, when he had first suspected her late husband of being an imbecile. It might have been that she had taken time to help the Cotters and their wagon issue, though it had involved the menial motions of retrieving apples and small objects.

There was no saying why he *was* doing as he was, or what he intended to do, but he could freely say why he was not.

Decidedly, it was not because she was the most beautiful woman he had ever seen.

What would she have done if her husband had been more intelligent? More caring? What sort of life would she have wanted for her widowhood?

And why did it matter to him? Because suddenly, it did matter.

It mattered very much.

"What if Win had left you money?" he blurted without any sort of preparation or thought.

Anna gave him a strange look, her brow creasing. "What?"

Somehow he managed an apologetic smile. "The will," he explained, though he doubted she needed the clarification. "Had Win left you an adequate, or even reasonable, stipend, what would you have done with it?"

Her surprise seemed to clear but was only replaced with an expression of reflection. "I don't know," she admitted almost at once. "Win's death was so unexpected, there wasn't time to think or to prepare . . ." She trailed off, looking away.

Ned held his breath, praying that would not be the end of it. He liked Anna; she was clever, witty, kind, and entirely unpretentious—a rarity for a woman in her position, and he knew it well. It was early in their acquaintance, but Ned felt certain that, if she was being genuine with him, they could be friends.

Possibly good friends.

Even . . .

"I think," Anna said slowly, lowering her voice, "I would have found a house somewhere in the country. Something small and within walking distance of a village. A small staff, perhaps just a maid and a cook, and I would tend my own garden." Her perfect lips curved into a whimsical smile.

"Perhaps I would become the village busybody and know absolutely everything about everyone."

Ned laughed at the thought and shook his head. "No, that I cannot allow, even in imagination. You might be well-informed about your neighbors and such, but you cannot go to the extreme."

Anna only shrugged, her smile growing more amused. "You never know. Perhaps in my lonely widowhood, I shall."

Though her tone was not at all serious, Ned found himself sobering somewhat. "Is it lonely?"

She seemed to consider the question a moment. "Not for me. Win left me to myself more often than not, and I hadn't many friends to start with when I moved to Laurisbee. I have recently made some new friends through Lady Joanna, though, who keeps me from dwelling overly much."

Ned nodded slowly in thought. One could not breathe in Somerset without hearing of Lady Joanna Kingswood, if not meeting her, and it was imperative that anyone wishing to maintain standing in Somerset's society kept her good opinion.

"Does she, indeed?" Ned murmured, smiling to himself. "How so?"

"She's collected widows," Anna told him, running her hand across the tops of tall growing wildflowers beside their walking path. "Young widows, I mean."

That was an interesting hobby, make no mistake.

"Intriguing," was all Ned could think to say. "Socially or . . . ?"

"And educationally, as it happens." Anna gave him a sidelong glance, her smile turning coy. "We are learning the sort of matters a governess could never instruct us in. Contracts, wills, and inheritances. Entails, ledgers, and accounts. How to manage our own affairs and understand the affairs of others. Only yesterday we practiced remaining firm and rational in the face of emotion."

Ned laughed once, only to find himself staring into a coldly disapproving expression. "What?"

Anna shook her head, her jaw tight. "Why is any of that amusing? Should we not learn such things?"

"Of course," he insisted immediately. Seeing her disgruntled manner, he cleared his throat and exhaled before continuing. "Of course you should. Well-informed should be hand in hand with well-educated, and yet they seem so separate where ladies are concerned. I applaud Lady Joanna's efforts. I only laughed as I imagined a room of ladies trying to sway each other through heightened emotion." Even the memory of the imagining made him smile, laughter ready for the taking if he could.

But he wouldn't; he'd cough each laugh into seriousness if he had to.

If it would assure Anna he was taking her seriously.

He was taking her seriously, after all. He saw no fault in being educated in such things, and he thought it would have helped a great many widows he had known while a clergyman. Undoubtedly, it would have helped Anna.

That sobered him considerably.

It would have changed everything for Anna.

"It was rather awkward," Anna admitted reluctantly, turning back to walking beside him, the irritation apparently fading. "At first, it was very awkward. But then I recalled my interactions with Mr. Knotts and Mr. Margett, and how I felt being so patronized." She frowned a little, shaking her head. "It wasn't so awkward or embarrassing after that." Her expression cleared, and she stunned Ned by laughing herself. "Though I can only imagine what any of the servants or a passerby would have thought had they happened upon us!

Mrs. Fletcher in particular struggled to maintain her emotions."

"Ah." Ned felt safe enough to smile at this, and he nodded as though he understood completely. "Trouble staying serious? I would have struggled myself."

Anna looked at him again, this time her eyes wide. "No. No, Mrs. Fletcher could not stop weeping. The poor dear was very much in love with her husband, and feels his loss keenly." She shook her head with a heavy sigh. "I do not believe she is ready for the widows' society. She can barely accept that she is a widow, and her emotions overwhelm her so. It makes one understand all too clearly why we vow not to fall in love again."

"I can imagine so."

Ned took two steps, then stopped as his mind replayed what he had just heard and responded to, the dissonance between statement and response jarring him belatedly.

"Wait, what?"

Anna, perfectly at ease with what she had said and how Ned had replied, had kept walking, and only now stopped, turning to face him. "Pardon?"

Ned blinked, wondering how she could be so calm, so lovely, so breathtaking in the morning light after having just admitted something as earth-shattering as she had. "You vowed . . . what?"

"Not to love again," she repeated, solidifying her madness, in Ned's mind. "Lady Joanna insists that we never behave rationally when in love, and therefore, should any of us marry again, it must be without love. Else we may find ourselves in the same dire straits our first marriages have left us in."

He'd have gaped had his jaw loosened enough to even open his mouth at all. He could only clear his throat and fight for the ability to say something, anything, in response to the extraordinary statement.

"How?" he finally managed, though the single word was nearly strangled by his protesting throat. "How can you promise that?"

Anna did not look at him, only shrugging her slender shoulders. "Easily, as it happens. I did not marry for love, and having already been married once, I feel no rush to do so again. I did not give my husband children, so there is hardly an inducement for anyone to marry me. And, if Mrs. Fletcher is any indication, the loss of one's love is excruciating. Why should I submit myself to it?"

This was just getting worse and worse. There was nothing she had said that he could agree with, but he could not, in good conscience, argue against her. She was fully and freely entitled to her opinions, but the more she expressed, the more he ached.

Had her marriage to Win left her so scarred that she truly felt all of this?

"But what of joy, Anna?" Ned found himself asking. "I'm sure that if you asked Mrs. Fletcher, she would tell you of the great joy she felt in the love of her husband. Of the beauty it brought to her life. And I believe she would not regret having done so."

"She agreed to the vows, same as the rest of us," Anna pointed out. "No great testament to love there."

Ned placed a hand on her arm and gently pulled her to a stop, looking at her with all the sincerity he could muster. "Not wanting to love again is not the same thing as wishing one never had. Love could be the making of one's life when everything else has been bleak. Can you really wish for a life without it, knowing what you have had before?"

Anna's stunning eyes searched his, and slowly his breath

began to fade from his lungs, tightening squarely in the center of his chest. She held no anger, no disdain, no defiance as she looked at him. Yet there was nothing eager in her expression, no wishing to believe him, no lingering trace of whimsy from years gone by.

Whatever she was thinking, Ned had no insight into it. He could only continue to hold his breath.

"Have you ever been in love, Ned?" The question was clearly asked, the tone simple and inquisitive. Her perfect lips had formed the words, yet he barely heard them.

He took a minute before replying. "No, I haven't."

Anna offered a slight nod. "Nor have I. So neither of us can truthfully say one way or the other whether it would improve matters or not. It could feel rather ghastly."

"You don't believe that, do you?" Ned asked, the question more of a plea.

Her eyes turned almost hard. "I couldn't believe a husband could care so little for his wife before my marriage either. Yet my husband did not care for me. It wasn't abuse, neglect, or hatred that shattered my illusions of marriage. It was apathy."

The pain in her voice tightened his hold on her arm, bringing him closer to her. "Love is the opposite of apathy."

"I don't want the extreme of what I've known," Anna said, her voice breaking. She shook her head, swallowing. "I only want improvement."

Ned cocked his head, releasing her arm, though his hand remained close to hers. "Would love not be an improvement?"

Anna took his hand, not seeming to realize she had done so. "I don't know. Once, I might have said yes. Now, I truly don't know." She squeezed his hand, smiling; then, just as the heat from it raced up his arm and into his core, she released him and turned back to the road.

Her expression brightened almost at once. "Good morning, Mr. Ames!" she called out, waving to a man standing on a nearby barn roof. "How are the repairs coming?"

The man wiped at his brow. "Slow, my lady, but well enough."

Ned's eyes darted over various parts of the building, tracking where the man was and what still needed to be done. He followed Anna into the farmyard and began removing his coat, grinning to himself.

"What are you doing?" Anna nearly squawked as she watched him. "Ned, what are you doing?"

He tugged at his cravat and slid it from his collar. "Going to help my tenant. What does it look like?"

"You're not a clergyman any longer," she hissed as he folded his coat and set his cravat on top. "You are lord and master. Act like it!"

"I am." Ned chuckled and folded his sleeves back. "Clergymen aren't the only men on the earth who should serve by the labor of their hands. I am able, and I am willing; therefore, I will serve." He quirked his brow and started towards the ladder leaning against the barn.

Anna's barely restrained screech erupted behind him. "Ned! Lord Lyndham does not climb onto barn roofs!"

One foot on the ladder, Ned turned back to give her a look. "Am I Lord Lyndham?"

She scowled darkly. "Yes . . ." she grumbled, her hands fisted at her sides.

"Then it would appear that Lord Lyndham does." He shrugged and turned back to the ladder, scaling it easily.

"Mr. Ames!" Anna bellowed, her tone far less congenial than before. "The new Lord Lyndham is on his way up to assist you. Kindly do not let him fall off and break his neck. It took long enough for him to be found, I cannot even think what it would take for the next heir to be notified."

Ned barked a laugh as he reached the roof summit and stared up into the face of his shocked tenant. "I happen to have excellent balance," he replied, though his words were more for the benefit of Mr. Ames before him than Anna beneath them.

"My lord . . ." Ames said in surprise and consternation. "Are you certain you should . . . ?" He gestured to the roof.

"I'm certain I'd like to," Ned told him as he cautiously stepped off of the ladder onto the roof. "Whether or not I should is probably up to you once you see what kind of help I can offer."

Ames grinned and wiped at his brow again. "Well, if you're fool enough to try, my lord, I'll take any set of hands you've got." He inclined his head in a semi-bow. "Charles Ames."

Ned nodded. "Pleasure. Now, what can I help you with up here?"

7

"Ned! Ned, where are you? Ned!"

It was unthinkable—how could Anna have forgotten this? How long had Ned been at Laurisbee? And it had not occurred to her until this moment that, because Laurisbee was not hers, the guests that would shortly arrive might not be as welcome as they would have been previously?

Ever since Ned had arrived, time had become a muddled and indifferent thing. Often, she could not countenance the length of time that had passed, yet it also seemed to have been swift enough to steal her breath. Everything had changed, both for her and for the estate, and the notion that she would eventually have to leave Laurisbee was even more painful now than it was the day Ned had arrived.

She shook her head as she ran towards the north wing, her long plait of hair clapping against one shoulder and then the other as she ran.

The man was utterly maddening. Handsome, witty, charming, kind, impetuous, and unconventional, to be sure, all of which seemed to add up to the culmination of a maddening man.

One whom Anna was growing unbearably fond of, distracted by, and attracted to.

It hadn't helped that Lady Joanna Kingswood had continually given Anna smug and approving looks when she had invited them to a gathering at Kingsberry for supper and cards. Her ladyship had made it very evident that the new Lord Lyndham fascinated her, and meaningful glances towards Anna after Ned had uttered something particularly clever or done something especially charming had made the whole evening rather uncomfortable.

Did the woman want Anna to avoid falling in love again or not?

She knew she was in dangerous territory here. Every time Ned worked alongside his tenants, Anna felt her heart flip. Or when he mended fences with them. Or rolled up his sleeves with any workers employed for improvements on Laurisbee. Lord Lyndham would never have been found to do those things before, but Lord Lyndham had done them all now.

Seeing that same man of respectability cleaned up and dressed in perfect finery that same evening had done something to her knees and her toes.

If only something would happen to her mind and her heart, she would be ever so grateful.

Neither of those things was behaving at the present.

Anna cleared her throat as though she could clear her mind in the same way, lifting her chin as she entered the area of the north wing that was being repaired today. "Ned?" she called, wondering if he would be dressed in the same simple fashion as the workers or if he would somehow be distinctive in appearance. "Ned!"

"Up here," a now-familiar voice called out.

Turning to look at the landing, though not seeing anyone there, Anna put her hands to her hips. "Where?"

"Wherever you think up would be from where you are, I'd reckon," came the laughing response.

Anna scowled and shook her head. "Can you make yourself visible, please? The stairs don't seem a wise option for me, given their current state."

"Point taken." With a grunt and groan that seemed to echo in the open space, the tousled and dust-strewn head of Lord Lyndham appeared on the landing. He leaned his arms on the balustrade in front of him. "What can I do for you, my lady?"

Her eyes narrowed at the teasing formality before recollecting that there were other workmen about and that some form of respectability should be demonstrated.

Should. She had already tossed that away by hollering his given name through the house, so she might as well give it up entirely.

"I'm terribly sorry," Anna began, unable to keep herself from wincing, "but we will be receiving some guests today. I invited my friend to stay with me for a few days, and she accepted before you came to Laurisbee. It never crossed my mind to write her and inform her of the change."

Ned's brow creased as he looked down on her. "Why would you have needed to?"

"Laurisbee isn't mine anymore. I cannot extend invitations." She managed a weak smile, her fingers plucking absently at her skirt. "I can only offer my apologies. I'll tell Matilda they cannot stay long when they arrive."

"They?"

Anna nodded, now grimacing fully. "She will be traveling with her two sons as they move to their new home. They are but four and five years of age, and as their father has passed on, there is no one else to entrust them to while she . . ."

"Enough," Ned broke in with a quick flick of his hand. "I refuse your apologies, and you won't tell this Matilda anything."

"But . . ."

He silenced her with a look. "Do you really think I would send away a woman and her sons simply because I did not invite them myself? Utter nonsense, Anna. Until the day you leave this house with no intention of ever returning, Laurisbee remains your home, and you can and should invite whomever you like to stay here. What is the family name?"

"Jessop," Anna managed, though her throat was rapidly closing on grateful emotion.

"Mrs. Jessop and her boys can stay as long as you would have had them before I showed up," Ned said simply. "Longer, even. What time do you expect them?"

She desperately needed him to cease requiring answers from her, for soon none would be possible. "Luncheon."

Ned straightened as he pulled a pocket watch out and examined it. "Very well. I'll relieve Mr. Wells of my pathetic attempts at assistance in time to be presentable for their arrival. Perhaps you'll put the boys in the east blue bedchamber rather than the guest rooms. Excellent views of the pond, especially in the morning when the ducks come to feed. They'll love it." He nodded at her as he slipped his pocket watch back to its place, then grinned at her. "Best warn Allens and Mrs. Riggin to hide away anything fragile, Anna. The boys will find and break whatever they can, mark my words."

Anna couldn't laugh, couldn't do more than smile a watery smile at the amusing statement. "Thank you, Ned," she squeaked, blinking rapidly. "I'll . . . I'll be sure to tell them."

He softened his smile, clearly not fooled by her attempt at diversion. "Good." He leaned on his arms once more, continuing to smile at her in a way that only encouraged her to cry more and sent sparks through the tips of her toes.

She'd have told him to stop, had she the words to do so. The disconcerting, ticklish sensation he instilled in her would only get worse, and she knew what a comfort he would be if she'd let him—the gentleness in his expression would melt her into a weeping mess.

His handkerchief still sat in her pocket for such occasions, but something told her he wouldn't keep his distance this time.

That would end everything—and begin something else entirely.

Mustering whatever strength she had remaining, she gave him a scolding look, though her tear-filled eyes likely did nothing to aid her.

Ned's smile grew briefly, and then, of all things, he winked at her before pushing back from the balustrade and disappearing back to his work.

Anna exhaled very slowly, almost silently, and hurried out of the north wing with as little sound as possible. She needed to find her sanity, and that was not going to be found in the north wing.

"Is he always like this?"

Anna shook her head, exhaling in reluctant amusement as Ned roared even louder than he had yet, cantering on all fours after Henry and Charlie as some unidentified creature. "I haven't the faintest idea. This is the first I've seen him with children." She widened her eyes with exasperation as she sipped her tea.

He had been like this all afternoon, bearing the boys on his shoulders and daring them to touch the wood carvings above them or examining the railings of the stairs as possible slides. If this was any indication of what Ned had been like as a boy, his parents must have been delighted and relieved to have him go into the church after all they had endured.

"He's marvelous."

Anna nearly choked on her tea and looked at her friend in bewilderment. "He's what?"

Matilda's eyes were soft as she watched her sons interact with a grown man, Anna's squawked words not in any way ruffling her. "Look at him. Look at *them*."

"I have been," Anna muttered as she carefully set her tea back in its saucer, safely away from her gown or her fingers. "It's impossible to miss."

"And yet you are missing it."

Shaking her head, Anna gestured at the scene before them. "I am seeing it here and now, Matilda. He's being completely ridiculous, and he's always doing this. He never does as he should."

A would-be patient sigh emanated from her oldest friend, prompting Anna to glance over. Matilda shook her head, her chestnut curls dancing only just, and her gray eyes surveyed Anna with a somberness unlike her warm character.

"What?" Anna asked, fighting concern at seeing her friend so serious.

"You have no idea," Matilda murmured for her ears alone, "how much joy it brings me to see my boys playing like this. Just like this. I know that your marriage was not blessed with children, and even if it had been, Winthrope would not have played like this."

Anna coughed at the very thought. "No, indeed not."

Matilda nodded once. "But Anna, this is how life was with George before his illness set in." She indicated her boys, her lips both curling and trembling as she returned her attention to their giggles. "This is how they were with their father while they had him. They have been without this for a year now, and, try as I might, I cannot do justice to their father's antics. Charlie is destined to forget soon enough, but I hope Henry will remind him." She blinked rapidly, shaking her head quickly. "I'll never be able to thank Lyndham enough for this."

"Call him Ned," Anna told her softly, reaching over to squeeze her hand. "He already told the boys to do so, and he really doesn't stand on ceremony."

"He wouldn't, would he?" Matilda sipped her own tea, humming a laugh. "If ever you marry again, Anna, marry a man who will play on the floor with children."

Anna looked down, her attention suddenly fixed on the blue flowers embroidered into her muslin skirts. "I cannot have children. You know that."

"Doesn't matter," her friend replied at once, squeezing her hand in return. "A man like that will make you the most wonderful husband, and heaven knows you deserve that."

Did she? After the marriage she had, there was no great inducement to try for another. She'd never had a purpose as Lady Lyndham, which had made her marriage, such as it was, rather meaningless. She could not bear a meaningless arrangement again, and, after Lady Joanna's tutelage, she would not have to.

What would a wonderful husband be like?

"Higher, Ned!" Henry Jessop called out, doubling over in mirth as the man tossed his younger brother high into the air.

"Aye, higher it is," came the grunted reply. "Ready, Charlie?"

Charlie, torn between terror and delight, nodded, though his chocolate-brown eyes were wide.

Ned brought the boy closer to him, nearly touching his brow to the lad's. "I will not let you fall, Charlie. I promise to catch you. If you don't want to go higher, just say so."

Anna felt her heart give a mighty crack in adoration as the boy put his hands on Ned's cheeks, looking very serious indeed.

"Higher," came his now-firm response.

Ned grinned a grin fit for a rascally boy. "Yes, sir." Without another word, and without so much as a peep of effort, Charlie was launched high into the air, squealing the same mixture of fear and fun his face had borne moments before. True to his word, Ned caught him with the same ease and took a moment to hug the boy tight to emphasize his safety.

"You were almost to the rafters!" Ned chortled, pulling back to grin at Charlie. "I should have you clean the tapestries for the maids while you're flying like a bird up there."

"Did you see me, Henry?" Charlie cried, looking down at his brother. "Did you see?"

Henry nodded frantically, tugging on Ned's coat in excitement. "You almost touched the ceiling! So much higher than me!" He looked up at Ned, his smile wide. "What next, Ned? What next?"

"Boys," Matilda warned gently, sitting forward. "Let's not tire his lordship so soon into our visit."

Her sons and his lordship in question looked at her in matching bewilderment.

"Nonsense," Ned insisted after a moment's pause. "I've never felt so exuberant, except for when Anna comes around to pay me a compliment." He tossed a wink at her that made the boys giggle, while Anna only rolled her eyes.

Her cheeks did flush in pleasure, though, and there was no way that Ned would not have seen.

Matilda could see it also, if her present smirk was anything to go by.

"But perhaps we could find something else to do." Ned frowned in thought, swinging Charlie around in his arms as he pretended to think. "Let's see, let's see . . ."

Charlie laughed wildly, clinging to Ned's shirt as he was swung harder and harder.

"I simply do not know," Ned went on, grunting in apparent pain when Henry latched onto Ned's free arm. Tightening his hold, Ned began swinging Henry as well, taking on the strange appearance of a weighed-down maypole of sorts. "What could we do?"

Matilda giggled, her hands clasping before her lips as her boys continued to laugh and swing.

Anna watched Ned, smiling more and more as he continued to play. How had an already-attractive man grown somehow more irresistible in the space of a few minutes?

Marvelous, Matilda had called him. Yes, that was a rather fitting word for him. His tenants would agree, his servants would agree, and she had no doubt his former congregation would agree.

Anna agreed too. Wholeheartedly.

Ned Richards was marvelous, and the longer she watched him, the hotter the fire in her heart became, pumping its heat throughout her body with ever-increasing beats.

"Ah ha!" Ned exclaimed, bringing his swinging to a crashing halt that caused uproarious laughter in his young charges. "What say we take out a wagon and go into the village? Your mama can stroll the shops with Anna, and we ..." He paused, looking at both boys in serious consideration. "We could stop into the bakery and cross our fingers that there is a fresh batch of pastries."

The boys cheered, Charlie slipping down from Ned's hold and racing with his brother around Ned in excitement.

"Are you mad?" Matilda laughed as she looked up at him. "They're wild."

Ned propped his hands on his hips, grinning, and shrugged. "Boys their ages are always mad. Bit of fresh air and the open wagon will do us all good, and they can take turns helping me drive the team. You don't mind?"

Matilda shook her head. "Not in the least. I would love a good walk about your charming village after being cramped in the coach."

"Perfect." He scooped both boys up and put them over his shoulders. "I'll just load up the wagon for you, Mistress Jessop, with these bundles."

"Mmm, many thanks," she replied, cracking a smile as her boys wriggled in their place. "Do be sure they are secure. We don't want bundles rolling about the wagon."

"Right you are. I'll get the rope." Ned nodded, still grinning, and strode by them towards the door.

Anna couldn't help but to smile at him, the heat still swirling within her. "Ned . . ."

He paused a step, his smile softening just a touch. "Can't stop, Anna. These bundles must get loaded."

"I . . ." She shook her head, then reached out to him. With no hand to take, no arm to easily touch, she pressed her hand to his chest, looking into his eyes with a directness she hadn't dared before. "You're an unusual man, Ned Richards."

She felt his exhale as much as she heard it, and she could feel the beat of his heart where she touched him. It intensified as she noticed the rhythm, sped just a touch, and soon the feel of it pounded through her fingers and up her arm.

Anna could barely move, hardly breathe, everything attuned to the sensations beneath her hand. Ned's smile deepened, and his chest moved on another soft breath.

"I'll have to wait for a more appropriate time to tell you how I feel about you," he told her, his voice dipping low. "But I think you get the general idea."

A shaky inhale passed through Anna's lips, and she nodded shakily, unsure what she meant by doing so.

Ned's lips curved into a more crooked smile, and he cast a slight wink at her. "Don't be long, Anna. I've got plans in the village for you too." Hefting the boys more securely, he continued on.

Her hand shook in the now-cold air around it.

"Well, Anna," Matilda mused behind her, "what were you saying about Ned never doing as he should?"

Anna's mouth was suddenly dry, and she fought to moisten it. "I . . ."

"Because if you were to ask me," her friend continued, "Ned is doing everything as he should. Absolutely everything."

NED HATED DANCING. He could do it, but not as well as a gentleman should, and he took great pains to avoid being forced into dancing whenever he could.

Which made his current presence at the assembly rooms all the more mysterious.

He'd been planning it for several days, as it happened, never considering until he had entered the rooms that he actually hated the primary activity engaged in at a ball. Fortunately, it was a very relaxed evening, what with the relatively small numbers, and no one expected much when there were younger and more eager men present.

None of them were the master of a great estate, but Ned was enough of a mystery to not be especially plagued.

Yet.

So long as he continued to drink the ever-available spirits or ale, courtesy of some of his more generous tenants, he would be fine.

He swallowed a bitter gulp of weak wine, then glanced over to the source of his present discomfort and idiocy.

Anna laughed as his eyes fell upon her, the sound evaporating the air in his lungs. She was more beautiful than he had ever seen her, which was saying a great deal, as she was beautiful at every moment, and every effort he had and would continue to put forward was suddenly worth it all. Their jaunt into the village the other day with Matilda Jessop and her boys had held a particular errand for Anna: that of procuring a new gown especially for tonight's dance. Her protests had been fairly weak, he'd been told, which gave him confidence in his decision.

She was far enough into her mourning period to be permitted some joy, and their local circle was not stodgy enough to expect her to remain apart for a full year.

Had it been a society event, it would be different. But this was not society. This was a gathering of good, honest country folk, and they had welcomed them both with open arms.

And here Anna laughed with women she had only ever met on business or in passing. She talked and danced without care, every artifice stripped away in the face of honest pleasure. While dressed in an elegant and arresting shade of green, her remarkable hair plaited, pinned, and curled to perfection, Anna surpassed every other creation in existence in her majesty and loveliness, but her status remained the least interesting part of her.

The least important.

This was Anna the woman, no matter what her title, surname, or fortune afforded her.

And Ned was falling in love with her.

They could not stay much longer, not with guests at home, but he could not go without dancing with her.

As though heaven willed it, the musicians struck up one of the few tunes that Ned could comfortably dance to, and his feet obeyed his wishes before he instructed them, taking him the short but congested distance to Anna.

"My lady," Ned heard himself say as though from a distance. He bowed and extended a hand. "Will you dance the next with me?"

Anna beamed at him, her hand sliding into his without hesitation. "Always, my lord."

Always? What in the name of holy creation did she mean by that?

"Such a fine couple, the Lyndhams," someone nearby uttered, sending Ned's heart crashing against his ribs in a mix of pleasure-pain.

His hand closed around Anna's as he led her away. "Do they think . . . ?"

"They do," she said on a laugh, nearly erupting into giggles. "Apparently, the general public have a short memory, and many here believe we are husband and wife."

It was ridiculous, it truly was, and yet the sound of it was the very opposite of ridiculous.

It was at once everything Ned could have wished for himself.

But he had to laugh. For Anna's sake, he had to.

A stuttering grunt was all that emitted, and he covered his poor response by bringing her gloved hand to his lips for a kiss before stepping back in line with the other men.

Anna gave him a quizzical look. "What was that for?"

He managed to shrug. "I'd hate to disappoint anyone. The Lyndhams, you know."

She chortled a quick laugh, smiling at him as though she were the sun herself. "Oh, Ned . . ."

Laughter suddenly filled his chest, extending up into his face, allowing him to smile with true joy at this remarkable, enchanting, captivating woman who had upended his world. "Just wait until we dance, my lady."

Anna playfully curtseyed, and they took each other by the hand, as all the couples did, moving into the jaunty dance in unison.

A country dance did not exactly allow a couple to

converse with his partner extensively, particularly with a tempo such as this, but Ned didn't care. Couldn't have cared. Anna was dancing merrily, her feet barely seeming to touch the floor, and skipping about with her was the only thing he could imagine himself doing at the present. He had talked with Anna, and extensively at times since he'd arrived. Conversation had its place, but they'd talk themselves in circles soon.

He needed Anna to *feel* something, not hear it.

The dance ended shortly thereafter, the small number of couples limiting the length of time the dance could continue, but he would forgive them that. After all, his time with Anna was not limited to only this event. He'd escort her home, stay for a nightcap, the pair of them reveling in the delirium of high spirits for a time before they'd recollect their positions and relationship, and then, only then, would the evening end for him.

The couples all clapped for the musicians, and Anna's wild grin at Ned made him wish for a daring deed to accomplish in her honor.

She seemed to read his thoughts at once, her smile fading, though the brightness of her expression remained. "I suppose we'd better return to Laurisbee."

Ned smiled with some sympathy. "We could remain. There's nothing that says we must stay or go; we are masters of our own fate."

"Hardly," Anna said with a laugh. She looked around the room, sighing in what he hoped was delight. "This was marvelous, Ned. Thank you for insisting we come. I had forgotten how much I love dancing purely for the joy of it." Her smile flashed back into place. "It has been so long, and I feel so much younger than I was only this morning."

Touched beyond his ability to express, Ned had no

course but to take her hand and gently squeeze it. "Then it was an evening well spent." He swallowed, then managed a returning grin. "And we had better leave before either of us begin to feel our actual age and regret our impulses of youth."

Anna flicked a sharp smack against his chest, laughing in protest, but she turned and moved towards the doors of the room, nodding and taking the hands of several guests as she did so. Ned followed with an amused smile, hands clasped behind his back up until they reached the cloak room. Then, and only then, did he offer an arm to her, which she took with a coy nod.

He was just about to assist her into the coach when a sound to his right caught his attention.

A man whistled sharply at his companion driving a cart, though the rut the cart's wheel was presently stuck in was not one to manage alone. The horses were already pulling at their full strength, but no progress was being made.

Ned shucked off his coat and tossed it into the coach. "One moment," he told Anna as he strode away.

"Ned?" she replied in confusion behind him.

"Ho there," Ned called out, raising a hand. "Need some help?"

"Aye," came a relieved response. "It's no' budging. Shoulda minded tha storm t'other night."

Ned shook his head and rubbed his hands together. "No matter. Shall we?" Placing his hands on the bed of the cart, he lifted and shoved his shoulder against the wood while the other man pushed at the wheel.

Again and again they worked, settling into a strange rhythm with the driver, who soon jumped down and pulled the horses by hand.

A shift somewhere sent a ripple into Ned's frame, and he grunted. "It's going!" he bellowed, forcing his body harder into the effort.

The cart groaned a deep creak as it heaved, then moved, breaching the ridge of the rut with nearly as much relief as the men around it did.

Ned exhaled in a rush, wiping his hands together, finding wood dust and mud streaking his palms. He chuckled and glanced at his companions. "All right, then?"

"Aye," they replied as one. "T'anks, milord."

He nodded and turned back for the coach, grinning at Anna's agape expression as she stood by, her wrap weaving through her folded arms. He held out his hands to her. "Will you dance with me now, Lady Lyndham?"

She squawked a protesting laugh as she hastily backed away. "Don't you dare touch me with those filthy hands, Ned Richards!" She pointed at the coach, though her eyes twinkled in the evening light. "You fetch yourself a handkerchief and clean up before you do anything else."

Ned pulled a linen square from his pocket and dangled it before her. "I have one here, see? I'm not so removed from a gentleman that I cannot carry one on me." He pointedly began to clean off his hands, smiling at nothing.

"I don't think you're removed from being a gentleman at all," Anna murmured, making him pause in the action while his heart skipped.

He looked at her for a long moment, all sensation settling into each heartbeat as she met his gaze squarely.

She swallowed once. "Shall we go home?" she asked softly, a breeze dislodging a curl at her temple.

His hand clenched as he resisted the urge to tuck it back into place, to touch her at all. "Yes," he said roughly. "Let's go home."

How long could she bear this overwhelming tension?

Every beat of Anna's heart felt thunderous, every inhale difficult, and every exhale shallow. Yet she felt no distress. On the contrary, she felt alive, aware of every ridge of her fingertips and attuned to every strand of her hair. And she simply wanted to smile.

The confined space of this coach would not help matters. Blessedly, Laurisbee was not far, and release would soon be upon her. Release, space, and sanity.

She hoped.

The dance had been an impulse she could not refuse, and the evening had delighted her in a way very little had since her marriage. And dancing with Ned had felt . . .

Right. It had felt so very right.

And that frightened her.

They pulled up to Laurisbee before her thoughts could venture too far. Almost as if he, too, was anxious to breathe freer air, Ned hopped down before they had fully stopped. He turned and held out a hand for her, and, not thinking, she took it for assistance, forgetting that she had already removed her gloves.

The contact of skin against skin shocked her, and she barely managed to contain the gasp at the heat racing into her arm. Ned's grip on her hand was sure, but there was the slightest tremble to it as his fingers curved around hers.

Heart racing, Anna let him lead her into the house, leaving her hand safe in his hold, though the rest of her felt anything but safe.

There was no fear, only anticipation.

But for what?

Silently the servants took their things, and silently the pair of them moved into the drawing room, where a large fire had been built up for them. Anna immediately went there, holding her hands out for warmth, though her entire frame felt flushed at the present.

"What a night," she murmured to the room. "Now that we are here, I feel quite fatigued."

"I don't doubt it," Ned replied, his voice almost rough in its timbre. "Did you dance every dance or only most of them? I lost count, there were so many."

Anna threw a wry look over her shoulder. "Says the man who danced only five. Why did you insist we go if you care for dancing so little?"

He tilted his head at her, his lips taking on a curious smile. "Because I wanted you to go, and I wanted to go with you."

Her throat dried at once, and she blinked unsteadily, then turned to look back at the fire, unable to manage a word.

"You once asked me what you were, now that your husband's title was mine," Ned said softly, his voice somehow distant yet perfectly clear.

Anna nodded. "I remember."

"I believe I've figured it out." She could hear him move, though without haste, his direction unclear. "You are Anna. Goddess of the earth and sky, giver of light, mistress of all you meet. Gracious in your manner and generous in your attention. The picture of grace, beauty, and goodness, and defiant warrior of your own fate."

Heavens, he was coming towards her. He was nearly to her, and she couldn't breathe. "How much wine have you had, Ned?" she asked, forcing herself to laugh, the sound strained even to her.

"Just enough to tell the truth," he murmured, coming to her left side and leaning against the mantel beside her, "and not enough to have lost my faculties."

Anna shivered at his tone, feeling his eyes on her and unable to meet them. "I think you may need to say good night, Ned."

"Do I?" he asked with a deep, rumbling tone. "Why?"

"Because I'm afraid," she whispered, her voice catching.

"Of what?"

She struggled on a swallow. "I'm afraid you aren't flattering me, and what that means is frightening."

"Is it?" He was smiling now, she could hear it. Couldn't look, but it was there.

"Terrifying."

He leaned closer. "Why?"

"Because . . ." Anna couldn't help it; she looked up at him now, her legs beginning to quake. "I'm beginning to forget who I am. Who you are. Why . . ."

Ned searched her eyes, his slight smile warm and powerful. "Why what?"

"Why . . . we can't."

"Can't we?"

The heat in his question raced down her spine, and her lashes fluttered. One hand flitted to his shoulder for balance, though the action brought them closer still. "Ned . . ."

It was unbearable, incredible, and utterly incendiary, this feeling between them, and she arched into him, inhaling the scent of him as it enveloped her. Ned dipped his head close to her, his nose grazing against hers, one hand finding her cheek and stroking against it in the most hypnotic motion known to man.

Anna's lips parted. She sighed as he continued to nuzzle her, driving her wild and stirring up sensations she'd long thought herself incapable of.

Ned chuckled very softly, his nose brushing hers once more, his lips dusting across her cheek with the motion, their destination explicitly clear.

"We can't," Anna breathed, surprising herself.

Ned stilled, his mouth a breath above hers.

She swallowed, dropped her hand, and leaned away. "I can't."

"Because I'm me?" Ned asked as he straightened, his tone clipped. "Or because you're you?"

Anna shivered, suddenly cold, and stepped back. "Because I can't. That's all."

Ned stared at her, expression unreadable. She watched as his chest moved on an exhale, as he looked down at the floor, hands at his hips, as he finally looked back at her. "I think you'd find you could. If you wanted to." He inhaled sharply, then exhaled in one rush of breath. "But as you don't, I'll bid you good night." He bowed formally, then strode from the room without a second look at her, no doubt returning to the inn for the night.

A weak, pitiful whimper combined with a sigh as Anna gripped a nearby chair for balance. Her legs, never quite steady, trembled worse than ever before and threatened to give out entirely now.

Oh, Ned...

Tears welled within her eyes, and she turned back towards the fire, squeezing her eyes shut against the flood of moisture. She covered her mouth with one hand, a sob escaping before she could stop it.

If you wanted to.

She *had* wanted to. Couldn't he see that? She was wild about him, desperate for him, ached to be held by him.

It was just that she was terrified of wanting him.

She was a coward. That was all.

9

"My lord, you have a visitor."

Ned grunted, not even looking up from his desk. "I'm not at home."

"Erm..."

Though he hadn't known Allens long, he knew him well enough to understand that any sound of hesitation, uncertainty, or argument was momentous.

Slowly, Ned glanced up at his blank-faced butler. "I am at home?"

Allens nodded once, his shoulders nearly sagging in relief. "I think it would be best if you were, my lord."

Ned set his pen down and groaned, grinding his palms into his eyes. "Why?"

"It is Lady Joanna Kingswood, my lord."

That made Ned pause, and slowly his hands lowered. "For me?"

Allens dipped his chin. "Yes, sir."

"Not Lady Lyndham?" Ned swallowed the bitter taste that uttering Anna's name gave him. He'd asked after her every day, but he had yet to see her since...

Well, since everything had changed, really.

"No, sir," Allens confirmed. "She asked for you specifically."

Ned sat back roughly, staring off at nothing. Lady Joanna was here to see him, and the only reason he could think of was the one topic he had no wish to discuss.

He had no choice but to face her. Keeping her waiting was not an option.

Groaning, he pushed himself up, then, on second thought, grabbed the document he had been examining. "Very well. Where did you put her?"

"The east parlor, sir. It is the finest."

"Thank you, Allens." He nodded and passed his butler, heading down the corridor for the room in question.

He was not dressed finely today, even for the country. He was not poorly dressed, but any other gentleman likely would have changed before seeing a woman of Lady Joanna's station. Ned had no interest in pretending to be anything but what he was, even for her.

He entered the room, managing a small smile when Lady Joanna rose. Her finery was understated today, compared to what he understood her to wear usually, but there was no mistaking the quality of her cream ensemble. It likely cost more than he'd ever have seen as a clergyman.

Now he was of her station officially. The irony was not lost on him.

"Lady Joanna."

The lady dipped her chin regally. "Lord Lyndham. I've come to inquire as to your intentions regarding Lady Lyndham."

Ned lifted a brow. "Yes, I'd rather thought you had. Please." He gestured to her seat and moved to take one opposite her.

"I take a special interest in the young widows of

Somerset," Lady Joanna said as she clasped her hands in her lap. "A concern, if you will. I trust you are aware of this."

Ned nodded, fighting a reluctant exhale. "You don't need to be concerned about me, my lady. See here." He handed over the document in his hand, then sat back, watching as she read.

Her eyes widened as she read. "Well, well, Lord Lyndham, this is rather tidy, is it not? Rather tidy indeed. And a little sentimental, if I'm being honest."

Ned ignored that implication. "But will it be enough?"

Lady Joanna's eyes flicked to his. "Enough for what?"

He sighed, forgoing any and all pride, and gestured to the document. "I have been poring over documents for weeks now trying to find a way to get Anna the funds and support that she deserves and needs. Would it be enough to see her settled?"

"Settled? My dear Lord Lyndham, this will be enough to make her quite rich." Lady Joanna laughed once, seeming truly delighted by what she had read and what she was hearing. "The orchards at Laurisbee are the finest for several miles. Anna will find herself with quite a fortune, and it will make her quite a catch for any future suitors."

"Good," he grunted with a nod.

"Good?" she repeated, her brows rising. Her lips pursed, and she sat forward. "Lord Lyndham, may I be impertinent?"

Ned only smirked. "Probably."

She ignored him. "Are you in love with Anna?"

"Yes."

Lady Joanna blinked once, then again before her mouth curved into a smile. "So simple, so straightforward. No hint of demurrals."

Ned shrugged a shoulder. "I see little point in denying the truth."

"Is Anna aware of this?"

"Not in so many words," he admitted, letting a bitter note seep into his voice. "She doesn't feel the same. And I know about her vow not to fall in love." He smiled a very flat, patronizing smile at the influential woman. "She seems to be staying true to that, so you may be proud."

"Does she, by heaven? Well, well." To her credit, Lady Joanna did not look remotely ashamed or embarrassed, and she did not seem particularly gratified either. Her expression was one of pure interest, if not amusement. "Does she know about this?" She hefted the papers in her hands.

Ned shook his head, his shoulders slumping. "No, but she will soon. I send this in today, and the solicitor will notify her how her situation presently stands before she leaves. Whenever she leaves."

Lady Joanna stared at him steadily, and he stared frankly back. "This could change everything, you know. For you both."

Disgusted, more by his situation than by anything that had been said, Ned pushed to his feet, shaking his head. "I didn't do it to change anything for myself. My lady, if that's what you think . . ." He bit back a curse and ran a hand through his hair. "I did it for no other reason than to make sure Anna could live comfortably, however she wished, as though my cousin had actually had a care for her."

Lady Joanna snorted softly. "This is more generous than he would have been had he had a care."

"Good," he shot back. "Anna deserves no less. This is how it should have been."

Her eyes narrowed, and she cocked her head at him, then held the papers out to him. "She may know it was you orchestrating this."

"She may." Ned nodded as he took the papers back, looking down at them feeling as though he was holding his heart. "But it was only righting a wrong. I don't mean this to make her love me in return. I've already done what I can there with the time we've had. More time would give me more chances, but there is no more time."

"More's the pity."

Ned stiffened, the wry note in the woman's tone irking him and reminding him that he did not have to explain himself to her. He owed her nothing.

Only Anna deserved to know everything, and only she would.

"If you'll excuse me, my lady," he said with a slight dip of his chin, "I have several tenants waiting upon me this morning. If you wish to see Anna, please make yourself comfortable and send for her. Otherwise, I bid you good day." He bowed with all due politeness and deference, then left the room, feeling as though he had been denied by the woman he loved yet again.

Anna gaped shamelessly. It wasn't ladylike, it wasn't respectable, and it wasn't like her, but there was nothing else to do.

How was this possible? It couldn't be—she had been told time and time again that there was nothing that could improve her situation based on Win's last will and testament.

And yet...

"I beg your pardon?" she managed, her voice not entirely steady.

Mr. Norton smiled indulgently, chuckling to himself. "We have found a way to get you a thousand pounds a year from your late husband's will. I take it you did not think I would find anything when you asked me to examine it."

"No," Anna murmured softly. "No, I did not. I was told..." She shook her head, laughing breathlessly. "It doesn't matter what I was told, as it is apparently irrelevant. A thousand pounds a year? That's incredible."

"Steady, my lady," Mr. Norton replied, patting her hand and smiling still. "A thousand pounds is not a great living. You will still have to be careful with your money."

Anna grinned without hesitation. "Mr. Norton, I have been under the impression for the last seven months that I would have nothing from my late husband. Compared to nothing, I can assure you that a thousand pounds is a fortune."

Mr. Norton's eyes crinkled with a warm smile, and he nodded, giving her hand another pat. "I suppose it is, my lady." He pulled his hand back and turned one of the pages facedown, pushing it aside. "Now, I do believe we have also found a little something to make your life infinitely more comfortable."

"More than a thousand pounds?" Anna laughed merrily, clapping her hands. "I'm not entirely sure I can bear more, sir."

"I pray you will try." He flicked a quick smile, then looked back at the new page before him, his eyes scanning. "It has been brought to my attention, ma'am, that the orchards at Laurisbee have only been acquired within the last fifty years. Prior to that, they belonged to the Norris family. Is that correct?"

Anna stared at the solicitor warily. "Yes . . . Yes, that is true. Win's father purchased them."

Mr. Norton nodded in satisfaction, and she suspected he was well aware of the details of the Laurisbee estate, far more so than he ought to have been for simply looking into matters as a favor to her. "Well, as it happens, the orchards were never allotted as part of the estate in perpetuity. Your late husband made no alterations to the estate that his father had left to him, which also had not included the orchards as part of the estate. The details are somewhat complicated, but the fact of the matter remains: the orchard rights and profits were left by Lord Lyndham, your late husband's father, to Lady Lyndham. Her identity was never specified as being his wife. As your husband made no alterations . . ." He trailed off, raising his eyes to hers knowingly, smiling again.

"I can have the orchards?" she gasped, unable to believe that she could be so fortunate. "Are you sure? What about . . . what about Ned? He needs to know, this changes everything." She blinked, her heart slamming against her ribs, and she shook her head. "No. No, Mr. Norton, I cannot take the orchards from the estate, no matter what the will says or does not say. Ned needs them to remain. The profits need to funnel into the estate as a whole, or he may not have enough."

Raising a brow at her, Mr. Norton removed his spectacles. "Lady Lyndham . . ."

"No," Anna said again, more firmly. "No. I will take the pension from Win's will, but I will not take from Ned. I can't."

Mr. Norton tapped his spectacles into the palm of his hand, then sat back slowly. "My lady, the present Lord Lyndham is well aware of both of these issues. The pension is simple enough, but the orchards . . . He fully approves of this. I have his signature here."

Anna would have gaped again had her heart not leapt into her throat. She blinked once. "Were the orchards your idea, Mr. Norton? Or were they his?"

"His," the solicitor said without shame. "I've recently been hired on as his lordship's solicitor as well, my lady, which made this entire situation much easier. We negotiated the pension easily, and he came forward with the orchards on his own. I simply made it possible."

Anna's mind spun on the revelations, and the implications of them. All of this would have begun before she had spurned Ned's attentions, but he could have put a stop to them, if he'd chosen to.

He hadn't. He'd let it continue despite the disappointment.

But of course he had. That was who Ned was.

Hope fluttered its wings within her, and Anna grinned despite the breathlessness she felt.

"Thank you, Mr. Norton. If you'll excuse me." She dashed from the room and was almost immediately assisted into her carriage.

It was not far from the city of Wells to Laurisbee, but at the moment it could have spanned the whole of England. Every minute was agony, and every mile a lifetime.

Ned had done this. *Ned* had . . .

Anna laughed merrily, falling back against the cushions of the coach as the laughter became tears, the feelings behind them so very mixed. Her days had been filled with emotions: how much she loved him and how she had missed him. Their separation had been of her making and the pain self-inflicted, but the time apart had only solidified her resolve.

She wanted Ned, nothing more or less.

Nothing had been done that could not be undone, and she would see to it that he knew precisely how she felt about him. What he meant to her. Where her heart lay.

The ride to Laurisbee was intolerable when she felt so much, when she could think so long, when she could imagine scenario after scenario of her going to him. All it had done was make her anxious, trembling, and uncertain, though she was determined to move forward regardless.

She had been cowardly before; she could not be so now.

Would not.

The house was before her, and this time she would not wait for it to stop. She bolted from the coach before she could be helped down, racing into the house.

"Allens!" she bellowed. "Where is his lordship?"

"In the garden, my lady!" came the response, though the butler was nowhere in sight.

Flinging off her bonnet, Anna tore through the house until she reached the terrace, which provided the best view of the garden and her best chance of finding Ned. Her breath caught as she saw him digging at the roots of a bush that had failed to bloom this year, all signs of finery gone.

Ned as he was. As he always and ever was.

Her heart could have burst, and tears were close at hand, but she forced them all back as she darted down the terrace steps, moving into the garden without a care for her hemline, her hair, or anything but getting to that man and confessing all that was in her heart.

He heard her approach; she could see him pause in his action, his eyes glancing back though neither his frame nor his head had moved.

Anna slowed and tried to gather some semblance of breath as she neared him, plucking a stray twig from her hair and flicking it away. "Ned," she panted.

She saw his throat work on a swallow, then watched as he forced the shovel into the ground around the bush. "Anna. Are you well?"

She frowned at the question, then recalled that he had not seen her in days. "Yes," she managed. "Yes, I'm well."

"Good." He continued to work as though he had no further interest in her or her words.

Pain lanced through her. How he must have ached with her silence! There would be much to atone for when this was over, if only he would give her the time to do so.

"I've been to Wells," she informed him, clasping her hands together to keep them from shaking.

"Have you?" He grunted as he continued to hack at the roots. "What took you there?"

Anna hummed a humorless laugh. "My new solicitor. Who, as it happens, is your new solicitor. And he told me that not only do I have a pension after all but the orchards of Laurisbee are mine."

There was only the slightest hesitation before his next strike at the bush. "Good. It was time you knew."

"Ned," Anna scolded, wishing he would look at her. "Why did you do that? I know that was not part of Win's will, I've spent months fighting for anything. Why would you give so much to me?"

"Just trying to be gentlemanly." He shrugged and pried at the handle of the shovel, intent on the bush.

"Gentlemanly?" Anna barked another laugh and stepped closer. "That would have been the stipend alone, Ned. You gave me the orchards! That's the estate's largest source of income, you said so yourself!"

He exhaled and straightened. "And?"

Maddening man, he would be the death of her. Anna shook her head. "Why would you give them to me? Why?"

Ned raised his head and looked at her at last, his bright eyes clashing with hers. "Because they should be yours. Because I don't want to walk through them without you. Don't want to spend the rest of my life wandering the rows of trees thinking about you. Because profiting off of your work when I don't have you does not interest me."

A lump formed in her throat, and it would not budge. "Ned . . ."

"I love you, Anna," he told her simply, his eyes and expression clear. "But I didn't rework the will because I love you. I did it because you deserve everything. Absolutely everything." Again, his throat worked and he looked behind her at the house. "And I'm going to hate Laurisbee when you leave it. Maybe I'll pull the whole thing down and rebuild it so nothing reminds me of you."

Impossibly, Anna began to smile. "You said renovation would waste resources."

Ned didn't seem to notice the change in her, still staring at the house as he was. "But it would save my soul. I may be selfish enough for that." He shook his head and stuck the shovel into the ground beside him, his eyes falling to it. "Don't think of me, just go on with your life as you please. You're free to do so now."

"I love you."

There it was—all she could say, and it seemed so lacking for all its significance. It should have been more, but it was everything she had.

Slowly, Ned's eyes rose to her, his body stilling completely. "What did you say?"

Anna smiled fully, though it wavered with her pent-up emotion. "I love you. I'm in love with you, Ned." She swallowed hard, a hand going to her heart. "So much. So much I couldn't look at you after the assembly, so much that I am terrified of leaving you, so much . . ."

Her words faded as Ned dropped the shovel and marched over to her, his mouth crushing to hers, his arms cradling her and keeping her from stumbling with the force of him. She sobbed and sighed into his mouth, gripping his shirt. She pulled him close to her as his lips took hers again and again, almost punishing in their attentions yet poignant in their taste.

"It's enough," he rasped against her mouth, the rough stubble of his jaw rubbing the skin of her face into almost painful sensitivity. "More than enough."

His lips took hers again, now tender and lingering, layering kiss after kiss into a never-ending foray of exultant caresses.

Anna sighed, and Ned chuckled, his arms shifting around her in an almost awkward manner.

"What?" she demanded, pulling back only enough to ask.

He slid his arms from her, his hands raised and clearly never having touched her as they were stained and speckled with dirt from his work. "I've kept my hands off of you," he admitted, replacing his arms without using his hands. "I know how you feel about dirty hands, but it's not easy."

Even now, in the middle of this, he was thinking of her. Thinking of someone else. Helping someone without a thought for himself.

How could she not adore this man?

Anna's jaw tensed against rising emotion, and she locked her fingers behind his neck, pulling him closer still. "I don't care about dirty hands, Ned," she told him firmly, her tone dipping. "I want you to hold me. Hold me tightly and don't let me go."

His eyes darkened, and immediately, his hold on her tightened. "Yes, my lady," he growled before kissing her again, one hand latching into her hair while the other lifted her just enough for the fit of them to be utterly perfect. Electrifying and perfect.

Anna reveled in the feel of his mouth against hers, folding her arms about his neck, deepening the kiss into something ethereal. Something that shattered who she had been and illuminated who she could be. She felt herself soaring in his arms, and she arched into the sensation, desperate to bind herself to him, to lose herself in him.

For in him, through him, she had found herself.

He had found her too. And she would not let him go.

"Marry me," Anna whispered when Ned let her breathe.

His lips paused, hovering above hers. "What?"

Anna pulled back just enough to touch her brow to his, sliding her fingers into his hair, cupping his face. "I don't want to leave you. I don't want to be anywhere without you. Marry me, Ned."

Ned exhaled in a rush, the air tickling her now-sensitive lips. Softly, gently, he brought his lips back to hers, the tenderness breaking her into a thousand brilliant, glowing pieces. "Yes," he murmured against her lips. "Yes, yes, and yes. Marry me. Stay with me. Stay forever, my love. Yes."

Laughing, the sound nearly lost into the mouth of the man she loved, Anna curled into Ned, letting him lift her from the ground and spin her around like some giddy illustration of lovers in a garden.

For, after all, that was what they were.

Just as they were.

Epilogue

THERE WAS A great deal of confusion and fuss when Lord Lyndham married Lady Lyndham, and it was revealed that Lord Lyndham had in fact been living in Mrs. McKenzie's inn for several weeks. Mrs. McKenzie assured anyone who would listen that his lordship was a model guest, always very polite, and never spoke a harsh word under her roof. Indeed, she was most distressed to lose him as a patron, but she agreed it was for the best.

The confusion was not in any way cleared up when the Laurisbee harvest supper was held and his lordship announced that her ladyship was in the family way, for it had long been known that Lady Lyndham was barren.

Lady Joanna Kingswood prided herself on making the match, which all agreed must have occurred, and made several remarks about holding his lordship to his contract, which his lordship took with all good graces and agreement.

The truth of the matter as regards the Lyndhams may never be fully understood, but when the dear little Miss Matilda Richards was born, all else seemed of little consequence.

When, however, Lady Lyndham was found to be with child at the subsequent harvest supper, a request was discussed and submitted to his lordship that he perhaps temper his attentions where his wife was concerned, for the assembly rooms had a great need for Lady Lyndham's presence and dancing ability.

Shortly after the Right Honorable Edward Geoffrey Richards was born, the request was flatly denied.

By her ladyship.

Rebecca Connolly writes romances, both period and contemporary, because she absolutely loves a good love story. She has been creating stories since childhood, and there are home videos to prove it! She started writing them down in elementary school and has never looked back. She currently lives in the Midwest, spends every spare moment away from her day job absorbed in her writing, and is a hot cocoa addict.

THE WIDOW
of
LAVENDER COTTAGE

Jen Geigle Johnson

To every woman who learned out of necessity to be brave.
And to chocolate-covered cinnamon bears.

1

HER HUSBAND, OLD Mr. Hunter, had meant to do well by Lillian in his will. Just like he'd meant to do so many other things. But a person's intentions had come to mean less to her than the breath that was required to express them. And she would have laughed at her lot, if it were not to be her living for the rest of her known days.

Lavender Cottage.

In Somerset—a place she'd never stepped foot a day in her life until now.

The drive up onto the property had been enchanting. Aptly named, the cottage itself was surrounded by a field of soft purple blossoms, the air sweetened by their relaxed waving in the breeze. The grounds around them stretched in every direction, hills of green with hints of purple now and again. For a moment, she had been full of hope. Could this be the most charming cottage in all of England?

But then she'd approached the actual house. Since living out of doors was out of the question, the broken-down mess of a reality had drained the sudden hope. She stood in the doorway and placed a handkerchief to her nose. Lavender blasted-heap-of-a-mess Cottage. Mother forgive her for her thoughts, may she rest in peace. Or perhaps Mother might torment Mr. Hunter in her rest. Did the dead speak to one another?

The few servants who had come with her stood at her side.

Lillian put her hands on her hips. "Hold off on the trunks, if you don't mind, Higgins. I don't wish to sully them by touching these floors."

"Just so." Her butler, Higgins, didn't so much as wiggle his nose, even though Lillian knew the smell wafting from inside the cottage to be rancid and sharp and quite upsetting given the fact they were to live in the space. He had the trunks placed on the marvelous front-stoop area. It was rather lovely, covered, and it ran the width of the front of the house. Certainly the home's best feature.

"Perhaps we should leave all our belongings out here under the awning and enter together to explore?" She couldn't admit that the idea of stepping foot inside not only repulsed her but in some ways sent a flutter of great unease to her center.

"I think we best." Her maid, Lucy, mimicked hands on her own hips, the stance she used to tackle something difficult. And then the three of them stepped into the front area of their new home, their cook right behind.

"You won't mind my saying that if you'd let us come early to prepare the place, you'd not have seen it in such a state," Lucy scolded Lillian.

"And you won't mind my saying that if I didn't travel with you, I'd be traveling with the insipid barrister, and neither he nor I wished such a thing."

Lucy sniffed her displeasure but said nothing further, for what could she say? They both knew Lillian had to arrive that day or not at all.

Lillian exhaled slowly. "Lavender Cottage. I suppose it is rather nice to outright own a place, is it not?" It was more a plea for hope than a ploy to make conversation, but none of her faithful servants replied. And from their silence, Lillian determined they were in as much of a speechless stupor as she. But there was nothing for it but to step into the place and make of it what they could.

Her boots left marks in the dust where she walked.

Jezebel, her cook, sniffed.

"I know, Jezzie."

"I haven't said a word, not one word."

"But you're thinking it, aren't you?" Lillian looked around. "Shall we go see the kitchen first, then? After that, the servants' quarters?"

"Don't you want to see your own chambers?" Lucy looked up towards the top balcony stair railing.

"No, I don't. Not just yet."

They made their way through the front parlor. Old yellow curtains hung in the windows. White blankets covered the furniture. The air seemed clearer—no particular smell, at least, except that itchy odor of musty furniture. "How old did they say the place was?"

"The will didn't say." Higgins pressed his lips together.

Which, to Lillian, meant that he had much more he wished to say, but propriety wouldn't allow it. They passed a charming, smaller sitting room, and Lillian felt a feather of hope light her situation. "I declare that room to be for creating. My writing, painting, needlepoint, even the weak attempts at music I might dare to inflict upon the house. It shall be my personal sitting room, to which you are all invited."

It didn't escape her notice that still no one responded. But why would they? They were as much silently aghast as she.

Jezebel came and placed an arm around her waist. "Now, I'm sure Mr. Hunter cared a great deal for you, love. It was obvious from the day you entered the estate. I cannot account for what he left you; but sure as I'm standing here, that man cared."

Hmm. Surely he had cared when he spent every last pence of her dowry at the gambling tables. He had cared greatly when he wasted away their living on the estate. And his caring was especially apparent when he left the majority of his holdings and what was left of his wealth to a distant cousin by mistake. She could only assume it was a mistake, as the will hadn't been updated in years, since before she became Mrs. Hunter. Lillian tried to think kindly of him. For a moment, tender memories of their times reading by the fire warmed her, his white hair catching the firelight, his warm smile encouraging her as she read aloud to him. "Well, be that as it may. You can be sure I shan't be marrying again, to save myself from all that caring."

No one responded to that rather bold statement either. Her servants were remarkably silent this afternoon. She was but five and twenty and many would say in a good marriageable state. With a passable inheritance, she could make as fine a match as any in all of the *ton*, but no, no. She'd come out lucky the first time, in her mind. A good enough sort of man—not cruel, at least—kind in his own way. She'd seen plenty worse.

"Shall we look around to see more evidence of this tender caring?" She hugged herself against a sudden chill. "Though I am grateful for the addendum. Without such a blessed thing as an addendum, we should have been left with nothing." During his dying days, he'd thought to write a quick addendum. She'd received the cottage, the land, and a sufficient allowance that paid for her small staff of servants and her living. She would be quite content, eventually. And independent. No amount of money could ever be worth as much as that one glorious gift. Independence. "I do apologize for my sarcasm. Sometimes it does feel a bit delicious on the tongue."

The kitchen was in a better state than apparently Jezzie had feared, and she began straightaway humming and wiping things down. "This is nothing that a bit of scrubbing can't solve. I'll have our food coming out of here as usual in no time. You three leave me be."

Lillian left Jezzie humming away in her space, feeling somewhat more hopeful. The servants' quarters were in a state of disarray and quite possibly the home of many a creature. Lillian left Higgins and Lucy to tend to that mess of a situation, with orders to throw away anything they could.

With a broom in hand, she moved back to the front room. She would have a friendly place in which to entertain the visitors if she must do it herself, and she must if she wanted it finished anytime soon. There was simply too much work to do for the servants to finish quickly without help. Who else would do it now but her? When she pulled the curtains open, a stream of sunlight shone through a break in the clouds. "Ah, the rain has stopped, at last."

She stepped back out onto the porch just as a fancy team of eight went barreling by on their small road. "Hiya! On! On thunder!" a deep voice called out to the horses as they careened past the cottage.

After a moment more of fresh air, she moved back into the front parlor. As she removed the furniture's coverings, she was pleased to see that for the most part the chairs, table, and settee were all intact; if not precisely the colors she would have hoped, the orange and green did make a lovely contrast, and upon closer inspection, she was delighted with the yellow shade of the window coverings. After a good washing, the room would be as cheerful as any she'd stepped foot in.

She started attacking the floors with a well-thought-out vengeance. Every well-beaten thought she sent out with that broom, another one came back until she dealt with her demons and the years of dust all at the same time. Certain her deepest concerns would return in the dark of night, at least for the moment, she was content with her lot. In fact, her current situation was far better than any she'd found herself in thus far. She whacked at the chairs, clouds of dust rising into the air until her sneezes became a musical background to the motion.

Lucy came in with wood for a fire and soon had one lit in the grate. "And I suppose you think you're a professional servant now, do you?" The twinkle in her eye belied the frown on her face.

"I'm not sure what else is to be done. Don't be getting any fancy thoughts that I'll be doing your work forever, mind." She winked, and Lucy laughed.

"I wouldn't dream of assuming you to start being industrious."

"Oh, no."

"I'm kidding. I'll mind my tongue. But I do wish you weren't doing the work of a servant, not raised the way you were."

"I'm finding satisfaction in it." Lillian moved the swept piles of dust together into one large mountainous mass and then pushed that one to the front door. It seemed odd to her, to sweep dirt out the front door. But where else was she to put such a pile? She was certainly anxious to see it gone from the house. It would blow away on the wind, and she'd never see it again.

The hour grew later, and her hands acquired two watery blisters before she quit. Satisfied at last with the state of one room in the run-down mess of a place, she reveled in her accomplishment for a moment, then approached her pile of dust ready to be discarded to the wind. With a flourish, she opened the door and swept the dust pile out in a great cloud. With some satisfaction, she watched as it billowed up, caught in a swirling wind, and into the face of a man.

She gasped. "Oh, I'm sorry!"

He took a handkerchief out of his pocket to wipe his face, which was a decidedly brown color. If his cravat was any indication, the man was altogether a different hue than when he had arrived.

"I'm truly sorry."

"Yes, so you said. If I might, could I please speak with a Mr. Hunter?"

She stiffened. "You've just missed him."

"Might I come in to wait for his arrival?"

"You might be waiting a long time, sir."

"Oh? And when do you expect him?" He pulled out a magnificent timepiece—gold, by the looks of it.

She decided to have pity on him and just said it as frankly as possible. "He's passed away. He no longer owns this cottage."

The man stood silent for a minute. "And might I ask who does?"

"Certainly."

He waited.

She waited, slightly amused at his discomfiture. He was a handsome man; not that she noticed such things, but he was pleasant to look upon, and so she looked, her gaze lingering for a moment on his broad shoulders. What would it have been like to marry a young man? He stood tall, nearly filling the doorway with hair the color of the sand on the beaches at Brighton, that hard, rocky sand that was such a chore to walk on. She determined he might be much like those rocks, nice to look at but unsettling, and a devil to the ankles. She wished him to be gone from her house, handsome or no.

"Well?" One eyebrow rose.

"Well what?"

"Who does? Who owns Lavender Cottage?"

"Why I do, of course. Why else do you think I'd be living in it?"

His gaze traveled up her person, and then he tilted his head to the side. "I thought you were a servant. Forgive me." He bowed. "Mr. Wentworth, at your service." He waited. But she didn't wish to give him her name, not just yet. Not caring how one was thought of was quite freeing, she decided.

"I've just arrived, and I can't think of any reason why I'd be here, were this not to be my new abode. I am the owner, as I said."

"Well, now, I couldn't say. There's plenty of reason for a woman to want to live here." His gaze flit around in apparent distaste at her surroundings. "Can't say as how I've got many reasons coming to mind at the moment. It is a bit run-down, isn't it?"

"Precisely. Now, if that is all, I have a newly discovered broken-down home to mend . . ."

"That is most definitely not all . . . did you say newly discovered? So have you just arrived?" His gaze took in their trunks and things. "Would you care for some assistance? Have you a servant or someone . . ."

She shook her head. "We are well. Thank you for your offer."

He took off his hat, and his mass of curls adjusted themselves on his head. "If you are the owner, as you say, then I've come to discuss an urgent matter with you."

She waited.

"Well?"

"Well, what?"

"Might I come in?"

"For what purpose?"

"To discuss it."

"But you haven't stated the details of this urgent matter. What do you wish to discuss with me?" She didn't really wish to invite a man into her home. She was alone except for her servants. In fact, handsome or no, the more she thought on it, the more she wanted him gone.

"It is merely a matter of your fence."

Nothing he could have said would have surprised her more—and it shouldn't have, but she was well without words.

At that precise moment, the sky opened and rain fell anew. She gasped as she became immediately wet through. "Oh, for goodness sake. Come in, then."

The pools of water that rained down off of them both soon became muddy pools on the floor, and what might have been an easy sweep was turning into a mighty scrub. Muddy rivulets and streams were soon joined by thicker sludge as the centuries of dust wettened. "Oh, great bother." She looked down past her skirts, shaking them off. "Now look what you've done."

"What I've done? I beg your pardon." His eyes sparkled in amusement, but his mouth frowned.

And it was the frown that made her whip around and lead him into the newly swept parlor. As she lifted a covering off the floor to drape across the sofa, she sneezed three times from dust that filled the air around her. "Oh, never mind." The white covering billowed out to the floor again as she dismissed its use. Then she sat gingerly on the edge of the furniture, indicating he should do the same.

"I would offer you tea, but . . ."

The door opened, and Lucy arrived with a tea tray.

"It looks as though the cook has worked another miracle. Thank you, Lucy."

She curtseyed and placed the tray between them.

As Lillian lifted her eyes to this newcomer, she found him openly staring in amazement. "You do live here."

"As I said."

"And you are the new owner of Lavender Cottage?"

"I am."

"And Mr. Hunter?"

"My late husband."

"Singular." He opened his mouth and then closed it again. Then, as though he couldn't resist, he opened it anew. "My sympathies."

"Thank you. They are not required."

"You know, I thought you were a servant." He indicated the broom she had set beside herself.

"As you said." He really was quite repetitive. "Well, I am not. There is work to be done, and I don't wish to wait around while others complete the many tasks." Lillian waited. When nothing more was said, she asked, "How do you like your tea?"

"Oh, cream, please, with two sugars."

Her mouth twitched. She made his, handed it to him, and then stirred her own, the same. She began to feel chilled, her clothes wet through. "And why have you stopped by again? My fence?"

"Oh, yes. It is in great disrepair." He replaced his tea. "And in the wrong place."

Her eyebrows rose, slowly, while she waited for there to be more to his statement.

He shifted in his seat. "And I find that the best neighbors are the ones who are carefully fenced apart." His dark eyes lit with a brilliant luminance she found herself staring into. If only she could make him out. What sort of person was her new neighbor?

He cleared his throat and then tipped his head, studying her in return.

"Oh, I do apologize. Woolgathering. My fence is in the wrong place, you say?"

"Yes. And in great disrepair. I have brought the plans, the boundary lines." He reached back in his sling bag and pulled out a folded paper. "You see here, on these plans." He tried to show her, but as she sat opposite, there was no allowance for her to make anything out on the smallest inscription and drawings. "Look, I'll show you." He stood and knelt at her side, holding what looked to be a map between them.

His wet hair smelled of something nice, spices. His jawline, so close, seemed even stronger, his shoulders broader. In fact, everything about his person magnified to an almost overwhelming awareness inside her. She immediately wished for her fan, and for some air and for him to be firmly planted on the other side of the table once again.

"Do you see here?" He ran his finger along a dotted line. "That is the fence. But this here . . ." He ran his finger along a darker line. "This is my property line. The fence encroaches on my property." He turned to her, and when their eyes met, Lillian nodded slowly, feeling a bit dazed at the close attention. It had been years since a man besides her elderly husband had looked into her face in such a way. She tried to wet her dry lips, which of course he noticed. This would not do.

She cleared her throat and sat up straighter in her seat. "I don't . . . know you. What I mean to say is, we aren't acquainted."

He paused, opened his mouth, and then closed it again. "You are correct. Please accept my apologies. Shall I introduce myself again? I am Mr. Oliver Wentworth. Delighted. Though we don't know each other well yet, I do hope we can carry on as neighbors might."

"Perhaps. I am Mrs. Lillian Hunter, once Boxwood. Widowed these past eighteen months."

"I am pleased to make your acquaintance." He nodded. "And these plans, this work, need not disturb you in any way. I can begin work on the fence straightaway if you like; I just need your permission for an adjustment of its location." In his close proximity, the words felt intimate. She fought any sense of closeness to this stranger.

"Well, you don't have it. If you must work on the fence, mend it only. I'd be much obliged. And leave it where it lies. Until I ask around a bit, we aren't going to be altering a boundary that's been keeping people happy for over a century."

"But surely you saw..."

She held up her hand and nearly laughed at his affronted expression. "I saw your map. I am sufficiently intrigued. Let's do some more exploring, shall we? Ask some questions? Certainly there is a reason that previous owners have not addressed the boundary line?" She stood. "If that will be all..."

"You're..."

She waited, watching a fascinating array of emotions flit across his face. From shock to indignation, to affront, to ... perhaps admiration, then fatigue.

But instead of finishing whatever he was going to say, he merely bowed and headed to the door to let himself out. But on the way, his boot caught on something. He slipped up into the air and fell down on his back. A water drop landed in his eye.

"Ah." He brought a hand to his eye. "Confound it! You have a leak."

"I don't know that such a thing could be avoided. I certainly anticipate we will have many." She peered over him. "I'm terribly sorry, again. It seems we are having an unlucky time of it as neighbors already, aren't we?"

"It seems. And your roof. Such a thing can be mended." He stood, somewhat stiffly. "And not allowed to collect on the floor."

"I'll take care of it. It's on the list." She gestured around her.

"Given the weather, I suggest you move it up in priority."

"Thank you for your suggestion. But you must know, I feel quite capable of figuring this all out. Without suggestions."

"I'm sure you do."

"Good day, Mr. Wentworth."

He didn't respond, but she saw the struggle on his features.

As soon as she heard the door close, she fell back against her sofa. "Our first visitor to Lavender Cottage."

Lucy entered to take away the tray. "I'll have to ask around town about him."

"And about the boundary dispute, if there is one."

She nodded and cleared the room, leaving Lillian to herself and her broom, thoughts on a retreating figure of a man who intrigued her. She hadn't been intrigued by a man since one had married her, spent all her money, and left her this lovely cottage.

She didn't like feeling intrigued.

2

OLIVER STRODE DOWN the lane, pushing his boots faster and farther from the aggravating woman. What could she mean by all that nonsense about doing more research? He had the map right in front of him. There was no question that the fence obviously encroached on his property.

And now he couldn't move forward with the mending of the fence, because they weren't sure where to place it.

He could just let the woman have her footage of property. He didn't need it, and he told himself that would be the gentlemanly thing to do. The woman had quite the task ahead already, fixing that house. And living alone as she did. Was she daft? He'd have to inquire after her manservants. Had she no family to care for her? No relative to watch over her? Offer protection?

He kicked a rock, and a splash of mud sprayed back and splattered the hems of his trousers.

He was about to sign on the purchase of his new estate, this very afternoon. And here he was inheriting a needy widow as a neighbor. He ran a hand through his hair. A stubborn, fiery, beautiful widow.

What would happen when the local gentry discovered

her? Who was protecting her against unwanted visits? The impropriety alone was enough to keep him up at night.

He stopped. "I sound like my own grandmother. *Impropriety.* Am I the governess now?"

She could care for herself. After she decided on the fence issue. He'd then leave her well enough alone to do whatever she wished with her cottage. He squinted up into the darkening clouds. And her leaky roof. And the peeling paint he'd noticed as he walked up the steps. And the million other things that likely needed fixing. His heart rebelled against the notion that he should help her.

The pause in the storm seemed ready to end its merciful hiatus and once again pour its water down upon Oliver's head. He picked up his pace. But to no avail. As if a lever had been pulled, water fell from the sky in sheets and doused Oliver from head to toe. Again.

"Isn't that just the way." Why hadn't he ridden his horse? Because he had thought it a pleasant thought to walk the property lines, to enjoy his new estate, to determine if he really would enjoy its purchase. So far, enjoyment had been fleeting.

The inn was still several miles into town. He trudged along, cursing everything he could think of. The sounds of horses and wheels in mud interrupted his internal dialogue. He turned to gratefully wave someone down and climb into a dryer accommodation into town, and he was slammed by a wall full of water.

The coachman slapped the reins against the horses, urging them faster. The crest of a lion and tiger fighting passed by him in a blur as Oliver wiped mud from his face. And then he laughed. For what else could a person do in such a situation? He laughed until his belly hurt, and then he determined that on the morrow he would make arrangements for his own carriage. Could he not afford such a thing? He grinned to himself. And much more besides.

Oddly enough, drenched and muddy, he thought his steps felt lighter as he moved along the road toward the inn. The rain thinned, and he could almost have thought himself cheerful by the time he arrived at the inn, except that the carriage that'd flown past him had also stopped there. Oliver's irritation festered anew. Who ignored another human walking in the rain?

He wasn't sure he was going to like associating with the swells. Buying property placed him in the same class as the landed gentry and, in some cases, the nobility. The same people who had snubbed him and his family for years were now his peers. He stood taller. They couldn't afford to ignore him now. But perhaps he wished to be ignored. By the time he stood at the entrance to the inn, he was no longer dripping, at least.

The woman of the inn came rushing to him as soon as he stepped inside. "Would you be caring for a bath?"

"Yes, please. Could you let me know when it's drawn?"

"Yes, sir." She rushed away while Oliver made his way to the bar, searching the room for an overly wealthy and pompous ignoramus.

His eyes scanned a room full of decent folk. They wore working clothes. They laughed with each other. Then his eyes fell on the corner table. Cravats. Shiny boots. Coifed hair and pale, deathly skin. "The swells."

Oliver was certain he looked a sight, but a cravat hung at his throat, limp though it was. His boots, though covered in mud, had once been shiny. He wanted to go laugh with the country folk at the other side of the room, but a part of him wished to meet the man who would leave another on the road, such as he had been. When he saw him at a dinner party, he'd recognize his ilk.

All eyes lifted to him when he approached their table. The nearest looked aghast. "What has happened to you?"

Oliver shrugged. "I had a bit of an encounter with the rain." His gaze studied the faces of the men. "And the splash from a carriage wheel."

No one changed their expression. All equally blank or slightly curious. So maybe the passenger inside didn't know what had happened.

He nodded to the group. "I'm Oliver Wentworth. Here in town to enquire after the old Honeywell estate."

"Are you now?" A thin man with a ready smile nodded. "Join us." He waved at the seat beside himself. After Oliver took his seat, the man smiled. "Filling the Honeywell estate is good news for all involved. Who else will you be bringing into the neighborhood?"

"Ah, unfortunately, just myself and the servants."

A man across the table picked his cards back up. "Hornsby. Finish the game of cards."

"Oh yes, of course." Hornsby placed one in the center. "Even if it's just you, I'm sure the local mamas will rejoice."

The other men ignored Hornsby.

Oliver was astounded at how terribly these men played cards. "I look forward to getting to know the families, my tenants, everyone."

They dealt him in the next hand.

Hornsby arranged his hand in a most obvious fashion. "So, we have all lived here in Somerset our whole lives. I spend most of my time in London. As do Ainsworth and Soursby. But Haddock, he's here all year, can't get him to leave."

Haddock flicked a gaze in their direction and returned to his hand.

Oliver placed his card. "I may go to London eventually. But for now, I'm looking forward to getting settled, setting up my estate, checking in with the tenants, who from what I understand have been long neglected."

Oliver won that hand and took control of the remaining sets. Ainsworth nodded at him, appraising. "My mother is having a dinner. I'll seek an invitation for you. Will you be staying at the inn?"

"Yes, until the legalities are settled." He dipped his head. "Thank you for the invitation. I should love a good meal, at any rate, and would enjoy meeting my new neighborhood."

Soursby shook his head. "If you're smart, you'll stay only as long as you have to and then hightail it to London. Get a room there."

Oliver studied him. Despite his name, he seemed a jolly enough man. Oliver found his warning curious. "Does Somerset not agree with you?"

Ainsworth smirked. "All depends what you're looking for. Soursby here had a run-in with the local nobility."

Most of their table laughed, but Soursby placed his cards down, his face a mask. "It was more than a run-in, quite frankly. She's a nuisance."

"She?" Oliver was even more intrigued.

"Oh yes. If you plan to stick around, you may as well get in her good graces—"

"As if that's possible." Hornsby shook his head. "Best to leave well enough alone, if you ask me."

"You may as well attempt to get in her good graces, though I don't know how much good it will do," Haddock grunted. "Meddling woman."

Completely intrigued now, Oliver leaned forward. "And who is this paragon of a woman?"

"Lady Joanna Kingswood, dowager marchioness, the veritable queen of Somerset and the only way you can expect to get close to a single widow in this town." Soursby lifted the corner of his mouth, frowning at his cards.

The word *widow* reminded him again of his eccentric neighbor. "Are there many? Widows?"

"Young widows." Soursby leaned back in his chair. "And yes. Normally not something I would complain about, a mite easier and less complicated than a debutante. But in Somerset? You go through Lady Joanna."

Singular. The second time he'd thought that in the course of a day. Did the new Mrs. Hunter know about this Lady Joanna? Perhaps he should stop by to let her know, with another attempt to discuss the fence. He closed his eyes, fighting his next thought but knowing it was inevitable. And looking at her roof to see what could be done for repairs.

3

Lillian awoke after the sun was already further up on the horizon than she'd planned. Every part of her body ached. The servants' chores were no easy task, but after five days of them, most of the house was livable. Someone, most likely Lucy, had placed a vase of lavender on the table in her room. She breathed in its sweetness. Lillian was ready to head out of doors.

She rang for Lucy.

"I can clean out a fire grate, but I'm still incapable of dressing myself."

"These dresses are made for help. I'm happy you're at last acting in your station again."

"Thank you for the flowers. Let's place them all through the house. This cottage is almost charming now, isn't it?"

"Indeed it is, ma'am. I think you'll be happy here."

Lillian nodded to herself. As soon as she was dressed, she made her way to the kitchen. She'd told Cook that unless they had some visitors, the food could be left there for all to consume when they were ready. Lillian would just as soon eat with the servants than by herself. Delicious smells wafted their way up to her, and she smiled. A good cook made every house a home.

"Good morning!" She smiled and scooped up eggs, bread, and a bit of ham on her plate. "This looks and smells heavenly."

"I'm happy you're resting today."

"I think I shall walk the fence line and see for myself what the issue could be." Thoughts of Mr. Wentworth's visit had not often left her mind. After she'd eaten a few bits, Higgins stepped into the kitchen and cleared his throat. "A Lady Joanna to see you, ma'am."

"What! Who?"

Jezzie wiped her hands on her apron. "Oh, she's a dowager marchioness, that one. I've heard some call her the queen of Somerset. Very well respected."

Immediately relieved she'd dressed properly today and asked Lucy to do a fashionable hairstyle, Lillian made her way out of the kitchen, stopping to turn one last time. "Could you bring tea?"

"Certainly. I'll send in Lucy." Jezzie busied herself, and Lillian walked to the front of the house.

Higgins had her sitting in their front parlor. He announced her. "Mrs. Hunter."

Lillian stepped through the door and curtseyed while Lady Joanna rose and nodded her head. Then she held out her hands. "Come here, child."

The warm tone from her stern face gave Lillian pause, but as she studied the woman's kindly eyes she decided she would like her. Her beauty was striking: rich auburn hair, her features fresh and lovely. Anyone paler would seem lifeless and dull beside her. "I'm so glad you have come."

"Thank you. Now, I'm Lady Joanna, and I've come with an invitation."

"Oh, well, please sit. Would you like some tea?"

"I never touch the stuff. But I'll take a coffee if you have it, dark and strong."

"I knew I'd like you."

Lucy turned in the doorway with the tray, heading back to the kitchen.

Lady Joanna looked about the room. "This is a lovely place. Aged, yes, but lovely."

"I enjoy it. The lighting is always wonderful. And we are working on updates, slowly."

Lady Joanna's eyes turned appraising. "So you're an industrious sort of person, like to manage your own affairs?"

"Of necessity, but since the passing of my husband, I welcome the independence, yes, if that's what you mean."

She nodded. "Excellent. You will fit right in with our ladies. Now pay attention. This is important. I have soirées, teas, and socials at my home, invitation only. And I would like it if you were to come Thursday." She reached out a card. "Here are the details."

"Thank you. I've been hoping to meet the families here in Somerset. You do me a great honor."

"I hope to protect you from the families in Somerset. My invitation is something else entirely. You'll do much of that other kind of visiting, I'd imagine, as soon as the mothers in our area take a look at you." She sniffed. "But be that as it may, you will find our group to be much more beneficial, and enjoyable besides."

The woman spoke in riddles, but Lillian couldn't dim her smile, pleased as anything to have a social engagement on the calendar. "Thank you."

The coffee arrived just as someone knocked on the front door.

Higgins answered it. Lillian heard a male voice, and then Higgins stood in the doorway. "A Mr. Wentworth to see you, ma'am."

And then he stood in the doorway, almost filling the

frame. Only this time, dressed as a working-class tenant or something. He had a utility belt around his waist. His shirt was unbuttoned and open at his neck where he had worn a cravat last week, and his pants were the thick trouser kind.

"Sensible of you, Mrs. Hunter, to hire help." Lady Joanna nodded in approval.

Mr. Wentworth tipped his head but to Lillian's surprise did not correct the woman. "I'm here to work on the roof."

Lillian wanted to send him home. She didn't want to be beholden to anyone. If he was a worker, that would be one thing. She could pay him. But this neighbor—interfering and trying to tell her where to place her fence, showing up unannounced to fix her roof—none of it sat comfortably.

"Best be about it then, man. No need to dawdle in the doorway." Lady Joanna waved her hand for him to be off.

Lillian sucked in her breath, but to her great relief, Mr. Wentworth just winked. "Yes, my lady." He dipped his head and then made his way back out the front door.

Lady Joanna stood at that point. "I will be off. Thank you for the visit. I'll expect you right on time Thursday." She air-kissed each of Lillian's cheeks and then made her way to the carriage outside.

"Thank you for stopping by." Lillian waved until the carriage was out of sight.

And then she turned on her heels to find Mr. Wentworth. He was standing right behind her. She ran into his solid chest before she saw him. "Oh. My goodness. You're right here."

He held his hands out to steady her. "Yes, I am. Are you well?"

"I am, thank you." She stepped back, her body humming from his attention. "So, I came to find you. Sir. You mustn't be fixing our roof."

"I've already begun. I came down to let you know that it

isn't as bad as you might have thought. With a few patches, I can be done in no time." He dipped his head.

"But sir. I don't want you fixing our roof. Allow me to hire someone or to fix it myself."

"What would be the point of that when I can do it?"

His eyes were so jovial, the corner of his mouth lifted in a half grin so friendly that she had to laugh.

"And then I wonder if I might trouble you for a stroll?"

"A . . . a stroll?"

"Yes, perhaps we can walk the property line together?"

"Hmm. Yes I see. I think a stroll would be in order."

"Excellent. I'll alert your servants when I am finished." He dipped his head to her as though tipping a hat and then made his way back out the front door and around the side of the house.

What was he doing? Would he climb up? She ran out the front door after him and watched as he climbed a ladder she didn't know she had and crawled out onto the roof. Then he pulled on a rope, and a pulley system brought up a box with his tools. Ingenious.

"Do you mean to make me nervous?" He did not look in her direction but just began his work. His arms were strong. His hands sure.

Lillian had never seen a man work with his hands. Not one who also wore a cravat. And she found she could not look away. He had a rougher quality to him, almost more . . . manly. She ran her hands down the front of her skirts.

"I can feel you watching me."

"I don't think I have the ability to make you nervous, sir."

He seemed to consider her statement but did not answer.

She watched him for a long time. He seemed cheerful. Every now and then she could hear him humming. After a time, she left him to get a shawl. The wind had picked up, and if they were to stroll she might need her boots. When she returned down the stairs, he was waiting for her, conversing with Lucy.

As soon as he saw her, he stepped closer to the stairs. "Are you ready?"

She nodded. "I am." Unaccountably excited to go walking with this stranger, she had to force her steps to slow and her smile to dim to an acceptable reaction to the idea.

The door closed behind them. He held his arm for her to take and led her down the front steps. Even dressed as he was, he emanated an aura that commanded respect, and she still felt like she was once again in the presence of the gentry. He carried himself well. In all things, he seemed a gentleman. She could not make him out, and the most puzzling bit of it all was that suddenly she most intently wanted to.

4

OLIVER NOTICED EVERY shift of Mrs. Hunter's fingers on his arm. He led her along the path, her skirts swishing against his legs, her feet tripping along as though they barely touched the ground.

"Tell me about Mr. Hunter."

She almost stumbled. "Oh, um. He was my father's choice in marriage for me. We never had any children, even though we were married for three years. He was much older than I." She looked down or away, anywhere but at him. "And I learned I never want to be married again."

The news hammered through him. He needn't care at all about her marriage plans. But the thought of her never marrying, never considering another . . . it just didn't sit well. She was young, and she likely deserved every happiness.

He placed a hand on hers, the air stilling between them. Perhaps he could impress upon her the thought that hope was not lost. "What if you met the right person? You could find love, find happiness?" He looked down into her face, hoping he was helping her in some way, hoping she felt the possibilities, the potential, but her eyes widened and she shook her head.

"No. I'm sorry." She removed her hand and stopped

walking. "I hope I haven't given you the wrong idea. But I'm not looking for . . . I'm not . . . I sincerely, most adamantly do not wish to be married ever again. To you or . . . or anyone."

Then he began to laugh.

The discomfort on her face turned to anger. "What is so funny?"

"You, me, I don't know. Here I am trying to help you find a bit of happiness. I was sad, thinking of you so young and planning to be alone for the rest of your life, and you thought I was offering to be the one to . . . marry you." He wiped his eyes. "Nothing could be further from my mind at the moment."

She folded her arms across her chest. "And still, I'm not understanding what is so humorous."

"Just that you, me. . ." He searched her face and then sighed. "It doesn't matter. But the point is, we can walk, as friends, along the property line without either of us assuming the other is trying to offer or reject a marriage proposal."

Her face was full of suspicion, but after a moment, she rested a hand on his arm again, and he had to admit, he felt much better walking along with her at his side.

They moved in silence until she said, "Why does the property line matter so much to you?"

He took a minute to gather his thoughts. "You know, it doesn't. Not really. But I'm a practical man. And I'm about to put in some work on the fencing. If I'm going to work on it, I want to get it right."

She nodded.

He watched her lips purse and then open again. "But what if it is set up like this for a reason?"

"Have you been doing your research?"

"I have, but not enough."

He nodded. "And if you find that it has all simply been a

mistake? Are you comfortable with moving the fence to the actual property line?"

"Certainly. I don't care as much myself; there is just this . . . *feeling* that perhaps we should not be so hasty."

He could respect that, somewhat. And he could be patient with the fencing and move to other projects, perhaps. "I signed the deed. The house and property are mine."

"Congratulations. When will you move in?"

"I have. Though I don't have a staff yet. So I don't wish my being in the house to be noised about. Visitors at the moment would only be an inconvenience, and I have nothing to offer them."

"I love visitors."

"Do you?"

"Are you surprised at this?"

"I am." He rubbed his chin. "Although I cannot account for it."

She smiled. As he watched her lips curl in a delicious, happy ribbon, he decided he wanted to see such an expression on her face often.

"Perhaps it was your less than warm reception in my home?" She turned to him, pausing in their walk to look up into his face. "I do apologize for that. We had arrived that very day, and I had spent the morning sweeping out the front room. We were wholly unprepared, and you were a lone gentleman, asking for my late husband . . ." Her voice trailed off, and her hopeful expression warmed him further.

"Say no more. We shall be the best of neighbors." Before he began walking again, he wanted to broach an uncomfortable topic. "You bring up something I've been meaning to say, although I recognize it is not my place—but you are the closest person to me and my estate, and I feel a sense of . . . not obligation necessarily. . ."

She stiffened.

"No, not obligation, but care. I feel a sense of care for you and your well-being. Have you no relatives who could come live with you? No one to offer protection from male visitors and situations that might arise?" There, he'd said it. He held her gaze, though inwardly he was wincing, waiting for the reaction.

But she lifted her chin, dropped her shoulders, stood taller, and said, "I have Higgins. My servants are the most loyal kind. And I don't plan to entertain men in my home."

He nodded, slowly. "And if they show up unannounced?"

"As you have? On two occasions?"

"Yes." He looked away—*Confound her.* "But I am the good sort of fellow. Mending your roof is hardly a risk to your person..."

"Higgins knows what to do. And perhaps, if it will make you feel better, I can send someone to your home if the situation becomes truly dire."

And this was what he found aggravating, but he didn't say so. He already felt responsible for the woman. He felt he needed to be aware, or prepared to come at a moment's notice should something befall her. He said nothing more but tucked her arm closer to him and continued their walk.

Then she surprised him. "Tell me of your home, your family."

"My father was a tradesman, a blacksmith." He waited for her to react, but she didn't. Her expression remained interested, curious. So he continued. "I have two sisters. They are all living in Manchester area. But as we grew, Father wanted me to attend university. He worked hard, doing extra jobs, becoming a personal blacksmith to a number of nobles, and saved enough to send me to Eton and then to Cambridge."

"That's remarkable really." How had he risen from being

the son of a blacksmith to having enough income to purchase an estate?

He nodded. "I agree. I am greatly indebted to him and my mother. I never know why I am so blessed." He cleared his throat.

"And your sisters?"

"They're almost of age. I've hired a governess for them and will sponsor a season if they so desire. They both have remarkable dowries at this point, but I'm not concerned about marrying them off for class or station, just happiness and love. I'd like them to be secure, cared for, and in comfortable situations."

She didn't say anything for so long that he wondered if she'd speak at all. Finally, with a quiet voice, she began to answer. He had to lean closer to hear.

She smelled of violets. It was a signature smell that he didn't often find anywhere but his mother's gardens. He breathed deeply and tried to hear her quiet words.

"I wish my father had been so considerate in choosing my suitor. He sought station, money, and a rise in my position before my happiness." She turned to him, a new fire in her eyes. "Women have no choice but to marry well. What modes of income are left them if unmarried?" She smiled. "Married the *first* time." The victorious expression on her face almost made him laugh. "But as a widow? I'm at my leisure."

He bit his tongue, all his original concerns for her safety and things at the ready, but instead of voicing them again, he said, "I've not often considered the plight of women. But as I have come upon the means to be of assistance to my family, concern for my sisters has opened my eyes."

She nodded. "You will do good by them. I can tell."

They walked along, the green of the rolling hills spreading out for miles in most directions. "So, how much of this is your property? Where is mine?"

"Don't you know?"

"No yet, not really. I've been so busy with the inside of the house . . ."

"I find that admirable, by the way, a woman working with her own hands."

Her cheeks colored prettily, and he so enjoyed the sight, he wondered for a brief moment if something more could exist between them.

"It has been exhausting and exhilarating all at the same time. I best become accustomed. As I plan to make my own way in the world from here on."

Ah yes, and the reminder that she was firmly not interested in any overture from him. He pointed out to their front. "Lavender Cottage is quite well situated as far as your land. If you were to want to obtain more tenants, you could even consider growing your own estate here. See that far hill?"

She stood higher on her toes, leaning into him. "Oh yes, with the treetop?"

"The very one. That is the border of your land."

"All of that?" Her eyes widened in wonder, and her nose lifted. "That's incredible." She spun in a circle. "And does it go as far all around us?"

"Not quite. See this fence to our left?"

Her mouth turned down. "Ah yes, the infamous fence."

"This is the line dividing our two properties. So if you look as far as you can see in that direction, that is the land on my estate. My home sits just beyond the crest that way." He pointed out the direction. They continued walking for a bit more. Then she paused.

"Oh, how charming." She pointed to a tree up ahead. It must have been the oldest tree he'd yet seen. Its trunk was large, its branches the size of other trees, and from its lowest branch, a swing swayed in the breeze.

She ran to it. "How lovely. I've been gifted a swing." She sat upon the wood board and kicked her legs to begin. But she didn't move very far or fast.

He laughed. "Do you not know how to manage?"

"I guess not." Her legs pumped back and forth but too quickly to do much good.

"Allow me." He moved around behind her, grabbed the ropes that held up her wooden slat, and gave her a push.

She jerked and gasped in surprise.

"Hold on now."

She clung to the ropes and laughed. "This is lovely."

So he pushed her again, getting her a good height in the air to begin. Then he placed his hands on her back to keep her going. Everything about it felt intimate. He wasn't sure if he should curse the moment or welcome it. As he was pulled closer to this widow next door, his sense of responsibility for her increased—a feeling she did not welcome. And his interest in her increased as well—another sensation he guessed she did not welcome.

They stayed thus, his hands lingering as long as he dared as he pushed her high into the air, her laughing and trying to kick her way higher, for many a minute—and during all of them, his heart and mind battled one another, but neither won out, and the moments on the swing continued.

5

LILLIAN GOT READY with care as she prepared to go to Lady Joanna's home. Her hair was done up in the most modern style she and Lucy remembered from her own season. She chose a morning dress she'd worn only a handful of times. Lady Joanna had kindly offered to send a carriage, for which Lillian was grateful. The weather had been peppered with rain on and off for days. Although the walk was not long, Lillian knew that if she were to attempt it, surely the sky would notice and send down a pillage just out of irony.

As Lillian stepped out of her home, another carriage drove by, far too quickly. And a man's eyes studied her. He was handsome. Dark. But his eyes left gooseflesh—not the pleasant kind—up and down her skin. He stared at her until his carriage moved around the corner. She was relieved he'd passed on by until she heard what must have been his coachman calling for the equipage to halt, so she hurried into Lady Joanna's waiting carriage, calling out to her coachman, "Please hurry. I don't wish to be detained by that other carriage."

The coachman called out for the horses to move, and she gratefully fell back against the bench as she felt the forward motion.

Who was he? For the first time, she wondered about Mr. Wentworth's concern that she lived with servants only. Perhaps he was right. Perhaps she should employ another footman, at least.

The journey to Lady Joanna's was short and pleasant. Lillian had seen little of Somerset, and she enjoyed the pretty shop fronts, the homes, the lovely people promenading. It was time she joined them with a parasol, or a full umbrella were the rain to keep up. Perhaps she would meet friends at this soirée of Lady Joanna's. She hoped so. For she'd dearly love callers, someone to fill her front room with conversation. And she wanted someone to talk to. Mr. Wentworth came to mind. He'd been a surprisingly good listener this afternoon. But he wasn't the same as a girlfriend. She longed to confide in another, someone other than her servants.

When she arrived, a footman in lovely purple livery helped her down, and she smiled up at a most pleasing home. Pillars lined the front. Gables ran along the roofline. The front door opened, and Lady Joanna herself held out a hand. "Welcome. I see you are a bit early, which in my book is right on time. Come in."

Lillian took the dear woman's hands in her own, and she air-kissed Lady Joanna's cheeks as she'd seen her do earlier in the week. What a gift to have friends. She hoped the room would be full of them, or at least contain one.

The footman announced her, and the five ladies in the room stood. They all curtsied, and Lady Joanna led her to sit at her side.

"We must all introduce ourselves to our newest member."

The ladies in the room seemed to be of all ages, Lady Joanna being the eldest by a few years. One woman with dark-brown hair and cheery dark eyes smiled at her in a way that seemed to say she wanted to be her friend. In fact, all of them seemed friendly enough. She wondered what had brought them all together. For another interesting quirk about the party, they all seemed unaccompanied by any sort of chaperone. Could it be they were opposed to such rules of society? Or were they in fact all widows? Her eyes searched their faces, and in truth, there was no way of knowing. They didn't wear the caps of married women. Lillian had lost hers the moment she could.

Lady Joanna went through the room. "That is Charlotte, Anna, Penny, Georgia, and Lucinda. They're all widows like you, and I am as well. There, now that we've got that out of the way—"

Lillian laughed. "Why, that's wonderful." She smiled at each one. "How did such a gathering come to be?"

Lady Joanna waved for a servant to bring forward a large book with quill and ink. It looked somewhat like a ledger.

"Might we call you Lillian? Or are you attached to the name of your late husband?"

"Lillian is fine, thank you."

"Just so. This, Lillian, is a unique group—I believe the only one like it. We call ourselves the Secret Society of Young Widows." She opened the pages and turned to one and then beckoned for Lillian to sit closer. "Every one of us has signed this book and, by so doing, has agreed to do all in our power to learn to care for ourselves. Independence is the way of things with us."

Some of the women sat taller; others cowered a half inch or so.

"Everyone else thinks we gather to drink tea." The group laughed at her comment, and Lillian wondered, if not to drink tea, just what were they there to do. "And we'd love for you to join us."

Lillian nodded and reached for the quill. "Happy to do so."

But Lady Joanna set the book on the table. "Before you do, perhaps you should participate in our first meeting."

Disappointed, she sat back again in her seat. "Certainly." She folded hands in her lap and sat up straight, with her ankles crossed, just like Mother had taught her to do when she was disappointed. *Hide behind propriety,* she'd always say. *Let no one see what's really going on inside.*

"Today we are going to talk about rule three."

One of the women—the one called Penny—pulled out a handkerchief and dabbed her eyes.

"Now Penny, it is perfectly normal for you to mourn your husband. We aren't going to be talking about him. This is for all future arrangements."

Penny nodded.

"And rule three is, we must never ever fall in love again."

Lillian was perfectly amenable to this rule. Or rather, the never-ever-marry-again rule. She'd never been in love even one time but had no use for it, as it related closely to marrying again. But she was curious as to why such a rule would be in place.

"We have reasons for each one of our rules. Georgia, perhaps you could share your story?"

"Absolutely. So, I was about halfway through my first season in London when I met my late husband. He was dashing, and so charming. And everything you would expect a man to be. Most women set their caps at him, but he pursued me. After only two weeks, he had already spoken with Father, and within another month, we were engaged. Everyone was so happy—his parents, my parents. And I thought all my dreams had come true." She sniffed, and Penny handed her another clean handkerchief. "Until after we were married." She shook her head. "He stayed only long enough in my bed and left immediately after, went out. He did whatever he pleased with anyone. He never smiled around me. After a while, weeks would go by and I wouldn't see him at home at all. I was lonely, unhappy. My mother came to visit, and she told me that this is the way of things, to get my own life and not to be overly concerned. My pin money shrunk, my wardrobe suffered. The household lost many of its servants. My husband started selling off furniture. And then one day I received notice that he'd been killed in a duel, over the honor of a local actress, his mistress." She wiped her eyes.

Lady Joanna's eyes held sympathy, but not much. "What do you know now that you didn't then?"

"My starry eyes then clouded my judgement. Marriage is a business arrangement. And falling in love changes the whole nature of the conversation. If you can approach it as a business, everything will be discussed in a fair and rational manner."

Lillian couldn't contain her frustration at the unfairness of Georgia's treatment. "But why would anyone want to remarry after that experience?"

Georgia Givens considered her and then shrugged. "I'm not sure I do, honestly, but we never had children. I might become lonely for companionship."

Lady Joanna clucked. "If she ever does marry again—if any of you marry again—you will be prepared to answer for yourselves, to negotiate a contract that is beneficial for you and that preserves your independence in whatever manner you can. And until then, even without a man speaking for you, you will know how to make do in this world."

Penny sniffed. "Just don't fall in love, and you should be fine." She looked as though her red eyes might overflow with tears. And Lillian hoped someone would change the subject.

"Lucinda, would you like to share your story?"

Lillian listened as each of the ladies talked about how they'd been so lost when their husbands died. They talked of how their brothers, uncles, and fathers had assumed control over their finances again—even though in many cases, the money was left straight to the women from their husbands—and how Lady Joanna had helped them start to make those decisions on their own.

And then the talk turned to the men in Somerset. No one seemed overly enamored with any of them. More than anything, they all seemed to provide amusement. Georgia turned to Lillian. "We have the greatest fun at a ball. When is the next one? We must secure an invitation for Lillian."

Lady Joanna nodded. "It is Monday next. And I think more of our society will be back in town to attend."

"We have a large group of widows. They come here to live, seeking us out. Word has spread." Georgia smiled with such a large amount of pride and love for Lady Joanna that even Lillian was touched, and she hardly knew any of them. Sitting back and listening to them talk, she could only feel hope. Friendship, support. Mr. Hunter likely hadn't the faintest idea what he was doing, but gifting her the cottage in Somerset had been the most important thing he'd ever done for her.

Her thoughts turned to Mr. Oliver Wentworth. "Have any of you met my new neighbor?"

Conversation stopped, and everyone in the room turned to her. "Who?" Georgia took a bite of her cookie.

Lucinda nodded. "I've heard of him, but I don't think anyone has met him yet."

Georgia piped up. "What have you heard?"

"Just that he's the wealthiest person we've ever heard of. And he's buying a property here to become a gentleman."

Lillian was astounded at their news and that they could know such a thing about Mr. Wentworth. "Perhaps we could invite him to the ball as well?"

Lady Joanna's eyebrow rose at that suggestion. "Are you enamored with the man?"

"No, not at all." She felt her face heat, and she wished to throw water on it. Because she absolutely was not attracted to Mr. Wentworth. But he did live close. And she thought it only fair that, as a fellow newcomer to the town, he be invited.

"I think he should be invited." Georgia nodded decisively. "I shall pay him a visit and invite him myself."

"I can invite him just as well as anyone else," Lucinda jumped in.

"And I'm not sure why the two of you think you should at all, since neither of you has any sort of reason to show up at his door, and it sounds like Lillian here is his neighbor." Anna sipped her tea.

"And I don't need to be inviting him, really. I don't have the information, nor do I have my own invitation as of yet. It just seems neighborly to think of him."

"We will get you one. As for this new Mr. Wentworth, he might be invited already and none of us knows."

The ladies were obviously not pacified by that suggestion, but at least they stopped talking about it. And Lillian was left trying to quietly recover from the conversation. Why had the mere mention of the man brought her heart up into her throat? Why did she want to bar the other women from his presence yet trembled in fear of the thought of inviting him herself? Whatever was wrong with her? She wished she'd brought a fan. As she sat back, trying to quietly listen while she found her footing again, she felt Lady Joanna's gaze, and somehow she knew she'd be talking it all through with the woman.

6

OLIVER'S NEW VALET, Richard, finished the last touches on the cravat. It felt tight. He would one day be more accustomed to the gentleman's attire, but today wasn't the day. Nevertheless, he smiled at himself in the mirror. "But I make this look good." He strained his neck against the knot. "Even though I feel like I can't swallow."

Richard smiled. "You do make this look good." He brushed the jacket down. "Will there be anything else?"

"No. Thank you." He was ready for the ball. His first ball in Somerset, his first ball as a true landed gentleman. He'd been to many—the guest of an earl, or viscount, even a duke one time. But he'd never been invited in his own right. He stood proudly, alone in his room, staring at his reflection. Gentry. And not one bit different than he was a month past. Wealthy. He grinned. So wealthy these other gents had to pay attention. He was proud of his success. His father would be. He'd hoped their meager beginnings in the shipping business would grow. If only he'd lived long enough to see what it had all become. And tonight, he'd go as an equal, to mingle with all the other landowners, people of title. He'd stand just as tall as the rest of them. He grinned. Tonight was his night.

His newly purchased carriage waited in front of his

house. As yet, no seal adorned the side, but he was working on that. His family had Scottish roots. They had a history in shipping and as blacksmiths. He was working on a design that incorporated all those elements. He settled into the comfort of the plush interior of his carriage. History. He was creating history and a legacy for the Wentworth family.

He pulled up to the front of the Willows' home—an older family who had lived here in Somerset almost as long as the trees. The men from the tavern when he'd first arrived were gathered together in a group. Perhaps some had returned from London? Or they'd never left. At any rate, he was happy to see someone he knew. "Ho there." He waved to Ainsworth and Soursby, Haddock and Hornsby.

"Got yourself a carriage now, have you?" Hornsby shook his hand and grinned. "Pretty soon we won't be able to tell you apart from the nobility."

"I did. And a valet. All is almost right in the world." He greeted the others. "And I see you've returned from London. Perhaps we could hunt this week. I'm looking for more diversion here in Somerset."

"Promenades down the center of town, tea shops, milliners, and ices not holding your attention?" Soursby laughed. "We have a group that meets for cards at that inn, The Foxtail. Join us for that at least."

He nodded. "I'd enjoy that."

They entered together. He handed a servant his top hat and coat. The other gentlemen did the same, and then they stood at the entrance to the room together. Oliver noticed many eyes turned in their direction. And he enjoyed the attention. Perhaps he would spend most of the evening filling dance cards and attempting to get to know the neighborhood thoroughly. But, he admitted to himself, his eyes sought for one person more than any other.

And Mrs. Hunter was nowhere to be seen. His group moved to greet their hosts.

Mrs. Willows held out her hand. "I'm so happy you could come, and we are all thrilled you have joined the neighborhood. Every one of us is relieved that house is finally let. And Lavender Cottage as well. How fortunate."

He nodded. "I'm pleased to have brought so much happiness to my new home. I look forward to meeting everyone and becoming fully entrenched in life here."

She smiled in approval. "Perhaps you can share your enthusiasm with your friends, who seem to think their time is better spent flitting off to London."

"I shall endeavor to convince them." He bowed.

Mr. Willows was equally amiable and waved two families forward to make introductions. "There, now you've begun a night full of dancing and merrymaking, I hope."

"Yes, I have. And I thank you."

Ainsworth stood at his side, and the others soon joined, so all became acquainted with two families of lovely daughters—the Pillings and the Fenways.

He secured sets with two of them, a daughter from each family. They moved off in a feminine, giggling, energetic bunch. He and the other gents stood just off the dance floor, awaiting the first set.

Ainsworth lifted a glass of wine to his lips. "I think you'll find the society here diverting. I do enjoy London, but the ladies are less watched here in Somerset, and there is opportunity for a moment alone now and then." He smirked. "And not all the widows are as studious as Soursby might lead you to believe. Loneliness is a loud siren call that I am pleased to answer." He stood taller and winked at someone across the room.

"I look forward to getting to know all the families here."

Oliver cupped his hands around his tea, still feeling chilled from the rain.

"Oh, don't ask Ainsworth to show you around to the matrons. He's someone they stay as far away from as possible." Hornsby sidled up beside them.

"True. I'm the rake in the room. Hornsby here is the celebrated desirable for all their daughters. Yet our actions are the same."

Hornsby laughed. "Not so. Not so."

Ainsworth raised an eyebrow but said nothing. Then his eyes focused on something across the room. "And that is who I've been waiting to see."

Oliver followed his gaze and stiffened. Mrs. Hunter.

Soursby snickered. "She went to a meeting at Lady Joanna's home the other evening."

"But there's an innocence about her I find appealing." Ainsworth downed the rest of his wine. "She's . . . someone I'd like to know." Ainsworth left them, Oliver wanting to be quick on his heels. He was teeming with some emotion he could not yet identify, but it left his hands shaking—so much that he clasped them behind his back—and his heart pounding in his chest. "What can he mean? Does he not need an introduction?"

Hornsby looked at him curiously. "I'm sure he will manage one. This isn't Almack's, you know. We pretty much do as we please with this crowd."

Oliver became all the more alarmed. Especially when Ainsworth bowed before his neighbor and she smiled one of her fuller smiles in his direction.

But it was time to go make his own bows, so he led a lovely woman out onto the floor. She was all smiles and batted her eyelashes so much he wondered if she had something in her eye.

"So, Miss Millicent, how long have you lived here in Somerset? I imagine your whole life?"

They danced in their squares, circling round and linking arms.

"I have. I've never left, except once to tour Brighton. I do *so* long to go to Bath, but I have to wait until Father is feeling up to travel."

"Oh, an expert on Somerset. Then I must know where I should go so that I'm no longer new here." His gaze flitted back to Mrs. Hunter, who was still laughing as she danced with Ainsworth. The man's whole demeanor had changed in her presence. If Oliver himself didn't know better, he'd say the man was a perfect gentleman, amiable, with excellent manners.

He ground his teeth. Then he forced himself to return his attention to Miss Millicent.

She had begun telling him all the places to visit or promenade or picnic. And he did want to hear them. He told himself that he would go exploring, but deep down he knew he was hoping to choose an appropriate place to visit with Mrs. Hunter.

"But of all things, I enjoy the ruins the most."

"The ruins? That sounds interesting, a bit intriguing."

"Oh yes, there is a rumored ghost that wanders just before sunset. And during the day, it is a lovely walk, and there is much to explore."

"Well then, I too will find the ruins to be one of my most favorite spots. Thank you for sharing it with me."

"We are planning a picnic. I shall see if Mother can secure an invitation for you."

"Oh, I would be much obliged, thank you. And perhaps my new neighbor. I worry for her, all alone and new—Mrs. Hunter?"

She pressed her lips together for a moment. "I don't believe I know her."

He nodded. "I shall introduce you."

She didn't answer, and he was under the impression that she did not seek acquaintances with other female neighbors of his, but no matter; he planned to introduce them. For it was his dearest wish that she find a community, a source of help and support that made her less reliant on him. She needed womanly advice on things as well.

At last the dance was over, and he placed Miss Millicent's hand on his arm and marched her over to Ainsworth and Mrs. Hunter.

Miss Millicent started dragging her feet and slowing their progress. "Oh no, I don't think I'd better. Mama doesn't want me knowing Mr. Ainsworth."

He paused and looked from one to the other. Ainsworth was currently engaged in what looked to be a fascinating conversation with Mrs. Hunter, and Miss Millicent's concerned expression told him everything he needed to know about the man. "I see. Then certainly we will avoid him." He led her back in the other direction, to her mother.

Ainsworth was making his way along the back wall of the room with Mrs. Hunter's hand on his arm. Oliver stood taller so that he could watch their progress.

Mrs. Millicent was saying something to him, to which he nodded politely. "Certainly, ma'am."

And then she clapped her hands. "Oh, I'm delighted. I knew we could find someone to assist us. You are a good, good man to do that. To think, when so few others have agreed to such a task."

He smiled. And when her mother wasn't looking, he whispered to Miss Millicent. "To what have I just agreed?"

She giggled. "No wonder you said yes. Mother has

asked—and you have agreed—that you promenade with us and the other ladies tomorrow noon."

"That sounds pleasant; why would others not agree?"

"Oh, that is just simply my mother being concerned that she spends too much money on bonnets, and some have learned that she spends more time than usual at each store in town."

He nodded. This outing sounded harmless enough. "Then certainly I would enjoy going."

Ainsworth and Mrs. Hunter slipped out a back door.

Alarm cascaded through him, and he bowed suddenly and rather abruptly to Miss Millicent. "Do forgive me. I must attend to something immediately. Might I come calling on the day we are to go to town?"

"Yes, thank you. We will see you tomorrow then."

He nodded again and then hurried as quickly as he could around the perimeter of the room. What would he do if he caught up with them?

It didn't matter. His very presence would shield Mrs. Hunter from any unwanted advances.

He may have pushed past a few people he would need to return to and meet properly, but none of that mattered when he thought of Mrs. Hunter in the hands of that self-proclaimed rogue. He pushed through the door he'd seen them pass through. And then he saw just the hem of her skirts as another door closed at the back of another room, what looked to be a music room. The Willows had a lovely home. He'd hoped to explore at a more leisurely pace. Perhaps with Mrs. Hunter on his arm.

He ran to the door that had just closed and stepped inside.

The room was full of ladies in various degrees of undress. Some had skirts up to their knees, rubbing their feet. Some had women sewing pieces onto their décolleté. Others had lace and material added to the bottom of their skirts. The quick glance that he flitted around the room gave him more insight than he ever wanted to know about this mysterious room for women at a ball. More than one woman screamed. Everyone hastily tried to cover themselves. He turned his back and slipped out the door, out of the room, and into another, breathing heavily. How could he ever show his face in this town again?

Mrs. Hunter came charging into his hiding place. "Just what were you doing?"

"Do you think they will recognize me again when they see me next?"

"Certainly." She crossed her arms.

He moved to sit. They'd found a quaint library, and if the circumstances were different, he might have quite enjoyed a perusal of it. But as things were, he buried his head in his hands.

A soft indent in the sofa beside him and cool hands on his arm informed him that Mrs. Hunter was still nearby. "I don't feel it is too terrible of a thing to happen."

"You don't?" He lifted his head enough to see her out of one eye. "Naturally it's terrible. It's the equivalent of being socially ruined."

"It absolutely is not." She patted his arm. "I do not think it's possible for a man to be ruined. All those women, now, they could argue their own varying degrees of ruination by you, but that is unlikely, as the room was full of women." She snorted. And then he felt the sofa shaking.

When he turned to her and she was red in the face from trying hard not to laugh, he couldn't help but join her. "It was rather alarming for me as well as them, you know."

She snorted again. "Oh, I do apologize and feel terrible

for your own emotional well-being. But really, have you ever heard of such a thing before? Who walks into the ladies' room at a ball? What were you thinking?"

He paused long enough that she could see he was serious. "I was in search of you."

Her eyes widened, and then she closed them. "And so you followed me into the women's retiring room?"

"Well, how was I to know?"

She thought about it for a moment and then shrugged. "I don't know." She leaned back on the sofa. "But let us give this some thought. I do believe you should return to the ballroom as though nothing has happened. You must be extra charming, dance immediately, and continue wooing the ladies through the night."

"But I know no one but a few families."

"You know me. And I know a whole group of young widows. They are lovely."

He nodded. "Would you care to dance with me?"

"I would love to." She stood. "Now, let's get you out there before word spreads and you aren't there. Now, listen, this is very important. You must act as though nothing out of the ordinary has happened. You must deny the scandalous nature of things; if it is brought up in polite company, you can suggest the subject be changed to spare polite ears, and that certainly accidently opening the wrong door is not such big news as so and so is making it."

He studied her. "You are quite proficient at overcoming an embarrassing situation."

She smiled. "You wonder if I have experience?"

"Well, frankly, yes."

"Let's get out there, and we can talk about it. In short, no, I do not have experience overcoming embarrassing situations. And yours is by far the worst I have heard of, let alone experienced."

"You are not making me feel any better."

"I know. I apologize. Come." She stood in the doorway, insisting that he join her.

He held out his arm, and she placed her hand on it.

"Now, I shall assist and act as though nothing has happened, and between the two of us and the other widows, we just might be able to get you out of this scrape."

"Thank you. Would you believe this is my first ball as landed gentry?"

She eyed him in silence for so long that he turned to her. Her brow rose. "I would believe."

They continued walking through the rooms he'd crossed to hide where he was, and then they walked out onto the dance floor as if nothing were wrong. The chords were beginning for the next set. And if anyone in the room was aware of his faux pas, they did not show it. The next set was to be a country dance.

"This is excellent. These are usually long. Pay attention to the lead." Lillian motioned to the front of the line.

"I know how to dance a country dance."

Her raised eyebrows told him his tone could use some adjustment. "Apologies."

"Mm."

They joined a group of three other couples.

Mrs. Hunter took care of things immediately. "Georgia, Penny, you are not going to believe who I found."

Their eyes sparkled with interest as they looked from her to him and back.

"This is Mr. Wentworth."

Then the women shocked him with exclamations of delight: "We have come to this ball looking for you." And, "Just the man we were hoping to meet."

The chatter and volume rose as their group talked together. The attention they drew from others was a boon, as it was positive and might drown out any negative repercussions of his earlier actions.

Mrs. Hunter danced like she was walking on clouds. The very ground seemed to rise to meet her feet as she glided from place to place. Her hair shone, and her eyes matched. Before he meant to or knew what was happening, he found himself enchanted with her and wished to call on her the very next afternoon.

But as soon as the dance ended, she was whisked away by a man he'd never seen before, and he was surrounded by the women she'd just introduced to him. He asked them all to dance and filled his evening as actively as he possibly could in hopes to drown out what possible rumors might be spreading.

And he did enjoy himself. The women were independent, smart, confident. And he preferred their attention to most others.

At another point in the evening, he found himself in line next to Mrs. Hunter again with several of the other widows he'd seen but not been introduced to and, if he were to guess, a few more from their group besides.

One of them, with rich auburn hair, said, "Now, take Mr. Wentworth for example. He's in the lovely position to go where he pleases, do what he pleases, with a servant or without, and in fact, he can one day marry whomever he pleases."

He nodded, at once curious and uneasy at the direction of the conversation.

The auburn-haired older beauty gestured to him while speaking to a wide-eyed younger woman. "You are not much different than he."

"Surely you are mistaken." His words came out before he could recall them. "I apologize. I speak out of turn. We have not yet even been introduced."

"That is quite all right. I am Lady Joanna. And you are

Mr. Wentworth. There—introductions have been made. You will excuse my bold statements. I feel to instruct some of our new members."

He watched curiously as she kept a running dialogue throughout the dance.

Mrs. Hunter stood closer than was necessary one time. "She would never talk this frankly and openly were others from the ball in our group."

"Am I to feel flattered or irrelevant?"

She laughed. "I'm unsure."

"Flattered." Lady Joanna winked. "Always choose to feel flattered when the other choice is to feel irrelevant."

"Good advice, that."

"She has been a large help for me as I've just started out in my new home."

Oliver felt a small sense of relief that Mrs. Hunter had found a group that could counsel her and help her as she made her way, like a family might behave. "I'm relieved to hear it. She sounds like she might have a good amount of wisdom for any who choose to listen."

Their cozy group on the line rotated as all lines did, and they were joined by Mr. Soursby, Hornsby, Haddock, and Ainsworth.

"So I heard you have at last seen the inside of a woman's receiving room?" Haddock winked good-naturedly at Oliver.

Oliver bit back a groan. Perhaps he wouldn't be spared at least some chatter about his experience.

7

"What?" Miss Penny Fletcher put a hand over her mouth while she danced, trying to look back over her shoulder at Mr. Wentworth to hear his response.

"Oh, believe me, it was as horrifying for me as it was for the young ladies." He loosened his cravat.

Mrs. Hunter cleared her throat and widened her eyes. And Mr. Wentworth nodded in her direction.

"But it wasn't as newsworthy a moment as you might suspect. Open door, close door. That's it. And now I have survived to tell the tale."

Before the men could jump in with more questions, Lillian laughed. "And where have you four been?"

Ainsworth had the audacity to wink. "We have been seeking out just such a group of beautiful women."

"Yes, you are the most sought-after at the ball." Hornsby grinned. "We heard, even just right before we joined you, that group of men in the corner—"

Every female eye within hearing distance turned to look. The men standing there, though handsome, were not surprisingly so, and they stood taller, noticing the sudden interest in their direction. "They said that this group right here is the most sought-after in all of Somerset."

Lady Joanna sniffed. "Is that right?"

"Yes. They are seeking introductions."

"Perhaps we shall avoid them, then." Lady Joanna took a long look in their direction, narrowed her eyes, and turned to the four who had joined them. "And you are?"

Lucinda laughed. "They are just looking to practice their roguish ways."

Lillian gasped and then laughed. How refreshing to be with such women.

Hornsby stood taller. "We don't know to what you are referring."

"Then I'm sure I don't know either." Lucinda batted her eyelashes in total mockery.

"Is there a particular way of the rogues you want to know more about?" Ainsworth took a turn around the middle with Lillian. His eyes gleamed with a little too much interest.

"Actually, I have no interest at all in roguish ways." Lillian smiled and then moved on to the next person to circle. Their country dance ended. Everyone bowed or curtseyed.

The music for a waltz started up. Ainsworth took a step toward Mrs. Hunter and dipped forward as if to take a bow, but Mr. Wentworth slid right in front of him, took her hand, and led her out onto the dance floor.

"What are you doing?" She half laughed and looked over her shoulder at a very shocked-looking Ainsworth.

"I heard the chords to our song."

"Our song?" She placed a hand on Mr. Wentworth's shoulder.

As he looked down into her face, she realized just how intimate a waltz could be. His face was close enough that she could study the strength of his jawline, the length of his lashes, his austere eyebrows. She almost laughed at the direction of her thoughts.

"What is so amusing? Have I not got the steps right?"

Shocked at his question, she looked closer and saw what she'd never noticed before. The hint of his insecurity flickered across his face.

"No, you are a magnificent dancer."

He guided her across the floor, her feet skipping along after as if they were floating.

"I am merely laughing at Ainsworth. You do know that is very bad ton to cut in front of him like that?"

"Is it?" One eyebrow lifted and wiggled before lowering. "Then perhaps it is good I am not really ton at all, isn't it?"

Her smile grew. "Are you not? You look as ton as the rest of us, whether for good or ill."

Something about her words made him stand taller, and with that apparent burst of confidence, he stepped closer. "Ainsworth doesn't deserve you." His eyes darkened, and the glint of warning surprised her.

She remembered her own feeling of foreboding when he drove by in the carriage outside her house. Perhaps there was more to know about Ainsworth than his jovial dancing let on. Either way, she could not let Mr. Wentworth get away with his overbearing ways.

"Whether or not he deserves me is up for me to decide."

He opened his mouth. She saw the challenge, but then he closed it and nodded, once, with the slightest dip of his head. Movement in his jaw seemed to battle his choice of silence. But he said nothing.

"So, how is your house? Are you settled?"

His features softened, lines smoothed, and he nodded. "Yes. I find everything about my new home pleasing—the rooms, my new servants." He eyed her. "The fence line is still in need of repair . . ."

"Oh yes, I know. I have asked my steward to look into it for us."

"You have a steward?"

"I do. Lady Joanna suggested we all employ one."

"Ah, the imitable queen of Somerset."

"Is she?" Lillian laughed. She could see that people might call her that, especially if she and the women who attended her teas made a mark for themselves in the county, which she guessed they likely had. Women who had identities of themselves, not bound by good will or legal ties to their husbands, were making a mark because dear Lady Joanna had taught them how.

"And what is this secretive smile I see playing on your lips? Are you plotting my slow demise by fence post?"

She tipped her head back to see into his eyes. "No, but now that you mention it . . ."

He dipped his head, his eyes searching hers, seeing deep into her thoughts, the interest heady. "What were you thinking just now, really?"

Because of his humility, she decided to open up to him. "I was just comparing my experience now to that of my one season as a debutante."

"And what are the differences now? An old run-down cottage, less pin money?"

How odd that he would think along those lines. "Oh no, I was thinking something entirely different. My thoughts were more directed toward my experience, and I find this time, as a widow, far more enjoyable than the last."

"Do you?"

"Yes. That is not to say that I rejoice in the loss of my husband but that I find the newly found independence . . ." She searched for the correct word. "Thrilling."

"Thrilling?"

"Yes, thrilling. That is the word. I am the manager of my estate, however small and in desperate need of repair; I am its master. And that is thrilling."

His eyes lit, and he nodded, slowly. "This I understand." He spun them. "For this is precisely how I feel."

"Do you?" She grinned, feeling a new appreciation for her stubborn and intrusive neighbor.

His eyes sparkled with the same energy she felt. "And I agree with you. It's thrilling."

The time for their set was coming to a close. The ending measures were sounding. And she found she wished to linger more in his company. "Come to dinner. We are so close. Let us share meals from time to time."

"Would such a thing be proper?"

"And that, my dear neighbor, is one of the many reasons I so enjoy my new status. Because no, it would not be improper for you to pay a call. Dear Higgins will be there besides. But you will find I am completely without the usual team of guardians bent on protecting me before I can be properly married off."

He frowned, and she knew he had more to say on that topic as well, but he didn't say more. "Then I would be most pleased to come and dine with you."

Her smile grew. "Thank you. Come tomorrow. And by then, I should have some answers from my steward."

"Excellent." He led her off the dance floor, to the very opposite corner from where Ainsworth stood waiting.

"You did that on purpose."

"What? I have no idea to what you are referring."

"Hmmm. Well, here he comes."

Ainsworth stormed in their direction, but Haddock stepped forward and bowed over Lillian's hand. As she was led away, a mother and daughter approached Mr. Wentworth, and in short work, he was joining them on the dance floor for the set, which left Ainsworth standing again on the edge with a frown.

"Ah, we've confounded the infamous Ainsworth."

"Yes, it appears we have."

"Thank you for our set." Haddock was light haired, handsome, and friendly.

"I'm pleased to know you better."

The couples bowed and curtseyed to one another and then to their corners, which brought her face to face again with Mr. Wentworth. His grin, a bit impish, made her wonder if he'd designed just such a thing.

8

OLIVER CLIMBED UP on his horse, and Cinnamon pawed the ground. The low-lying fog hovered and swirled around his legs. "What a singular morning."

The land all around him was clothed in small white swirls lifting up in soft curls; but the heavy thickness blanketed the ground. He tore out in the middle of it, enjoying the rippling disturbance made as he cut through the fog. It rose up all around him. It would soon burn off in the rising sun.

He told himself he wasn't going to visit Mrs. Hunter. He deliberately directed Cinnamon to head to the opposite side of his property, to the one point on his land where he couldn't see hers. But as soon as the horse reached that back corner and Oliver turned to survey his property, seeking a bit of peace, Cinnamon impatiently pawed the ground again.

"What is it, little lady?"

The dancing hooves continued, and he let her have her head.

She took off back across the fields, the land tearing by as she ran. He laughed out loud at the exhilaration, the speed smooth and glorious as they ran together across the land where everywhere he looked belonged to him.

Almost everywhere.

They approached the fence line, and he didn't even stop her as she leapt over it, tearing out across Mrs. Hunter's land, turning to head up toward her house. And before he could stop her, they were careening out through the immediate property around her house and just missed a bucket of water tossed out into the side yard.

"Whoa, girl, whoa."

The horse skidded to a stop. He looked back over his shoulder at Mrs. Hunter laughing at him. Her hair was tied back in a scarf. She looked like a servant, honestly, or one of the girls from his town back home growing up. She was dressed to work. And, judging by the water, she was involved in something of the sort right now. He turned and walked the horse back over to her. "Good morning, Mrs. Hunter."

"Good morning." She wiped a hair out of her face and leaned against the doorframe. The color in her cheeks made her that much more attractive. For a moment, he enjoyed the appealing imaginings of just such a vision each morning of his life. And he stunned himself at how much happiness the thought brought him.

But he knew she was far from desiring any such thing. She'd told him often enough how much she enjoyed her independence.

But here she stood, and she looked happy to see him.

He grinned back. "And just what are you planning on doing today?"

She wiped her hands on the front of her skirts. "Today I am going to clean out the attic."

"Oh, ambitious indeed."

"More than you know. For you haven't seen this attic. It is filled with all manner of things. I'm not sure how long it has sat in such a state, but I'm certain most of it can go."

"Why not just gather it for the burning?"

"Because there might be useful items. Someone could benefit."

"Not you."

"No, I find I have little use for things. I'd like fewer of them." She shrugged. "But perhaps the tenants."

"Have you tenants?"

She stood taller, the pride in her situation obvious. "I do. And we are acquiring more this year."

"Why, that's excellent. Well done, Mrs. Hunter."

Cinnamon sat remarkably still now that they were at Lavender Cottage.

"Well, it's good to see you at your leisure, Mr. Wentworth. But . . ." She looked inside. "I have some things to finish up here if we're to be ready for guests." She stepped closer. "And of course we are expecting you for dinner."

He bowed his head. "Thank you."

"You're welcome." Her smile was large and genuine. He wondered if he could ever convince her that she might enjoy marriage? Had he just thought that word? Had it come out so easily in his mind when thinking of Mrs. Hunter?

She waved one more time and then closed the door slowly. He missed her presence immediately. The door opened again. "I did have a question for you. If you have a moment." She rocked back and forth on her feet, and he found he enjoyed this Mrs. Hunter more than all other versions of her he'd seen.

"Certainly." His grin grew. "At your service always."

"It's just the roof."

"Has my fix not stuck?" He lowered himself off the horse and rested her reins on the fence, near some grass for Cinnamon to eat and occupy herself.

"It has stuck, I believe, but a new one sprung last night during the rain."

"Ah, where is that ladder?"

She opened the door wider. "I've asked for them to move it right here, inside the door."

He slipped past her, but there was not nearly enough room for her and him in the same doorway. Halfway through, he stopped, enjoying their closeness. "So, is the independent Mrs. Hunter asking for my help?"

She puffed out her air. "Yes."

"What was that? I didn't quite hear your response."

With hands on hips, she laughed. "Yes, I do need your help, but what I was hoping was . . . if you could just show me what you do up there so I can do it next time?"

"You?"

"Certainly."

"You're going to go scrambling around on a rooftop?"

"Why not? If you do the same, why can't I?"

He didn't have much to say in response to that question. Why not, indeed? Except that rooftops and skirts didn't work well together, except that her shoes would be a nightmare up there, that she would likely fall, that she didn't seem strong enough to wield the tools—so many reasons. But then again, if she knew how, she would be able to care for herself, and as that seemed to be her goal, all he said in response was, "Excellent point. If you can find your sturdiest boots, I shall do a rooftop-mend demonstration."

The excitement that lit her face warmed his toes, a sensation he found odd but enjoyable as it burned up inside him and filled him with a desire to bring that same excited hope to her expression often.

She stepped into the house at a run, presumably to change her shoes. And he reached down to grab the ladder. Heaven help them both. He leaned the ladder up against the eaves and adjusted it, digging it into the soft earth, hoping it was as sturdy as it could be.

Then she came out, her hair still tied back, her long skirts flowing around her.

"You need to go up first. I'll keep it steady."

"Excellent." She moved to the bottom rung, and he put his hands on either side of the ladder so that he stood directly behind her and she was almost in his embrace. "Like this?" Her words came softly.

"Yes." His breath puffed against the scarf on her head. "Climb up slowly, watch your skirts."

She stepped up one rung, holding her skirts in a fist in front of her. "They do seem to be in the way, don't they?"

As she climbed up higher, he diverted his eyes, but he had to look back when she reached closer to the top.

"Be careful up there. Climb out onto the lower part of the roof and stay there until I climb up beside you."

She reached the top. "This is a bit scary," she called down to him, but she moved forward anyway, reaching out onto the roof and pulling herself onto its surface. She fell forward, then rolled and tucked her legs beneath her and sat near the edge of the roof.

"Well done. Okay, I'm coming. Don't move."

He scrambled up quickly and moved to sit beside her.

"Goodness." She breathed deeply. "I did it." Her hands shook as she adjusted her skirts.

"Are you well?"

She nodded and then paused and shook her head. "Actually, I'm quite terrified."

"Are you?" He dipped his head in concern to see her face. Her shaking increased. "No, don't do that. Look at me."

She lifted her eyes. "I'm—I'm trying."

"I know you are. Keep looking at me." He smiled. "You're remarkable. Look what you've done."

Her nod was short, and her shoulders shook. "I don't think I could ever do this again."

He chuckled. "Well, then it's a good thing you have a neighbor who loves to get up on rooftops."

"I thought I could do it."

"Well, you don't have to, for even if I become repulsive to you, you can certainly pay for someone to fix your roof. A tenant would be an excellent choice."

"Oh, true." She hugged her knees. "You are so correct. A tenant would be an excellent choice." She put a hand on his arm. "Not that you're not an even more excellent choice—a gentleman—and you would probably hire your own roof person before you did it yourself."

He nodded. "I would indeed. But that doesn't mean I don't enjoy helping here. I knew when I met you and heard of your situation that if I was buying Honeywell, I was also buying the opportunity to help out the widow next door."

She stiffened. And he belatedly realized the error of his comment, but he couldn't regret saying it, not if it was true.

"Well, I won't be a burden to anyone. If you must, go home and I shall summon Higgins or Lucy."

He leaned back and laughed. "What kind of gentleman would I be if I left you here on the roof? I'm the reason you're up here in the first place."

She pressed her lips together.

"Now, since we are here, I think we should take a moment to look around."

"I don't think I can move."

"You don't have to, that's the beauty of it. Look up." He looked out across their land. "Everything you see from here is either owned by you or me."

Her soft intake of breath made him smile. She lifted her chin and then sat up taller so that she could see more. "All of that."

"Yes." He smiled. "It's remarkable."

She studied their surroundings for a minute or two and then said, "It's even more beautiful from up here. I never knew one could take such pride in their estate."

"I've longed for moments like this my whole life."

"It's incredible, really, what you've accomplished."

"Thank you. I'm quite pleased." He leaned back on his elbow. "And happy with the legacy I can leave my children. More than anything, I'm pleased about that."

"I don't have any children. I guess Lavender Cottage could be left to the next widow." She laughed, somewhat humorlessly, if he were to really analyze the sound.

"You could still have children . . ."

"That would require me to be married." Her back was to him. But her quiet response felt like a lid over the hopeful fire in his heart.

"Would it be so distasteful to you?"

The eyes she turned to him flashed with fire. "It would be a lot. Now that I know, now that I have seen what life can be, I don't think I could give all this up." She rested her head on her knees. "Except for this part about climbing on a roof, I've found great joy and satisfaction in my life such as it is."

"Well now, let's see what needs to be fixed."

"No!"

He held his hands out. "Just me. I'll climb to where the leak might be, and you stay put."

Her sigh told him that even that part seemed difficult to her at the moment, but she pointed him in a direction. "It was leaking right next to the original leak in the front room."

"Ah, that will be simple enough, I'm certain." He left her, climbed over to the spot he'd patched, and saw the problem—and that it would be an easy fix. "I can do this, no problem. How about I come earlier than we'd determined for dinner, and I'll fix it then?"

"I'd be much obliged." Her voice hardly carried.

"Oh, come. You sound so deflated about all this."

"Would you not be? I'm sitting here trembling in fear on my own roof. I know I am perfectly safe, yet I am stiff with great anxiety."

"We are going to get you down so you feel yourself again. Watch closely what I do." He scooted over to the ladder and turned his back to the great vista they had shared together. "Then you simply place your foot down on the second rung." He put his boots on the rung. "I will wait here to help you place your feet and to navigate your way to the ground."

"Thank you." She looked down. "I feel so foolish."

"You must not. For finally I have found a way to truly be of service to you."

"And I don't enjoy that thought."

"Why should you not? Just as you wish for independence, I have a great need to be needed. Surely you can think of this as a service to me."

"And there you see why we would never suit. For you'd forever be trying to be of assistance, and I would forever fight you."

"Have you given much thought to whether we would suit?" The idea pleased him so much, he was able to ignore her opinion that in fact they wouldn't suit.

But her face colored in such a charming shade of red, he knew he mustn't tease her.

She didn't answer him but moved so that she could mimic his actions. He backed down the ladder to give her space. "There now, you can do this. You must simply pretend that we are low to the ground and that I am here to help simply because I long for the feel of you in my arms." He winked, thinking to make her laugh, but the truth of his words hung in the air around them, and she didn't laugh.

"Must I go backwards?"

"I'm afraid so."

She sucked in her breath but then seemed to find her inner courage, for she turned from him, scooting backwards on the roof. She sent her one booted foot out over the edge. "Do you see it?"

"I do." He placed his hand on her ankle. "I've got you. Crawl backwards toward me. I need your other foot too."

"I'm coming." Her other boot stuck out over the edge as he guided the first boot to a rung. The other one soon followed beside it.

"Now keep moving back, lowering your boot to the rung beneath the first. I'll be right here behind you."

She did as he said. He knew she must be petrified, but her incredible courage impressed him.

"You're doing wonderfully."

She backed into him, standing fully on her boots.

He clung to the ladder with one hand and reached out to grab the house with the other so that the ladder would not separate out from the wall. "Now hold onto the sides of the ladder, and we'll descend together."

She paused, standing within the embrace of his arms, her back pressed against him. "This part isn't so bad."

He spoke in her ear. "No, it's not bad at all."

They descended together, and if he hadn't known she was scared, he would have longed for the moments to linger. But the trembling in her hands was obvious, and he knew her legs shook beneath her skirts.

As soon as they both stood on solid ground, she turned to him and clung to his chest, her arms around him. "Thank you. I'm sorry I behaved so."

"No apology is necessary. You are quite brave. I'm astounded at all you accomplish over here in your cottage."

"I'm not sure I can move quite yet, but I'd like to go into the house for tea."

"Shall we sit here and wait?"

She hesitated and pressed her teeth into her lower lip.

His eyes could not look away from that soft indentation. Her full mouth invited his attention like nothing ever had. But he averted his eyes when her lashes lifted, and she looked up at him. "Perhaps I shall try to walk." She shifted her weight but her legs buckled beneath her.

While supporting her weight, he breathed, "I could carry you." His words came out far more hopeful than he meant them.

Her eyes lit with hope even though her expression showed a good amount of hesitation.

"Come, I'll get you in there as quickly as possible. No one shall see, and you shall only have to endure my arms about you for the briefest of moments."

"It's not that at all—oh bother. Yes, please, could you carry me? My knees are trembling so. I'm not certain I shall ever be the same."

"You will. A cup of tea by the fire will be just the thing."

"Let us get this over with, then." She lifted her arms up around his neck with a grimace.

He scooped her up in his arms, cradling her close to his chest. Then pushed open the door.

Lucy turned the corner. "My heavens! Are you well, Mrs. Hunter?"

"Yes, I'm fine. I'm so embarrassed, just took a fright really."

"I think she could use some tea, a warm fire, and perhaps a blanket?"

Lucy nodded and ran back in the direction of the kitchen.

"Now, where am I to place you?"

"My private sitting room. It's on the other side of the front room, where you've been, briefly."

He chuckled in memory. "Ah yes, when I met the paragon of a woman, Lady Joanna."

"Oh, what she would think of me were she to see such a display of weakness."

"Well now, just a moment. I see nothing of weakness here."

"Oh really, Mr. Wentworth? I require carrying into the house. What is weakness if not this?"

He led her through the front room and past two doors.

"In here, please." She pointed.

The room was the loveliest he'd seen in her home. He carried her to a fire and set her in one of two chairs that were situated at its front. The walls could use some fresh paint, but the windows let in a great amount of light. The seating was charming. Her easel was set up in the corner, and a small harp as well, on a tabletop. The story of who Mrs. Hunter was grew larger and more pleasing.

Lucy entered with a tray for tea and left it on the table between them. Higgins followed shortly after with a blanket. "Here you are." He stood at her side. "Will there be anything else you require?"

"No, this is just what I wanted, thank you."

He bowed his head and left the room with the door open.

"Please sit, join me for tea."

"Thank you."

She pulled the blanket open and draped it across her lap. But she still shivered.

"Here, use my jacket." He slipped it off and draped it on her shoulders.

She smiled and seemed to sink into his jacket.

He reached for the teakettle. "I might fumble a bit, but I am happy to pour your tea as well. How do you like it?"

"Same as you. Two sugars and cream."

"You remember something as simple as how I take my tea?"

"Of course."

He stirred the tea, clanking the sides enough that she at last said, "Thank you, that's plenty."

He laughed, made his own, and then sat back in his chair while they both sipped.

"In answer to your question."

"Which?"

"The one where you said, 'What is weakness, if not this?'"

She groaned. "We needn't answer that one."

"I wish to. For, Mrs. Hunter, nothing at all in today's reactions speaks of weakness. I see nothing but courage and strength."

"Hmm."

"Truly. For despite your fear, you climbed on top of a roof. Think for a moment. You, Mrs. Hunter, were up on a roof moments ago."

Her smile started small and grew. "I see what you mean."

"How many of your contemporaries can say the same? I would wager that even the venerable Lady Joanna has never set foot on a roof."

She took a longer sip. "You know, you have a point there. I'm certain she hasn't." She replaced her cup. "And none of the other widows either." She sat back and stared off across the room. "They're all so accomplished. They read their own ledgers, know how to talk to their stewards, make their way in the world, but sometimes, I feel like I'm just barely surviving over here. When all I want is to successfully run this place, have guests to come calling, take tea, have dinners, and live a happy and full life."

"Those seem like excellent goals. And here we are taking

tea; I will come for dinner too, I believe. I am in your debt. So you shall have to come as a guest to Honeywell."

"I would enjoy that."

"Perhaps you could also assist me in hosting such a thing. I haven't the faintest notion."

"Yes, certainly. I could be of assistance there."

"So, in my efforts to help you, you could pay me back by assisting in those things that a lady of my house might?"

Her eyes widened, but she said only, "Yes, and you could do the same for me, for the things a man might."

"Certainly."

She shifted the blanket from her lap. "I'm warm now." But she didn't remove his jacket, and he chose not to mention its presence on her shoulders. "You know, I need to paint this room. Next time you see it, it shall be lavender."

He looked about him. "That will be pleasing."

"I think so too."

They talked for many minutes of anything and everything, of life and the normal everyday happenings in the cottage or on his estate, and he settled into such a lovely feeling of companionship that he quite forgot the time.

So much so that when Lucy entered to take the tray, the tea had long been cold. And when Higgins stood in the doorway and announced the arrival of Mr. Ainsworth, he was jarred so completely from his comfortable state that he stood. "What the devil does he want?"

9

LUCY, HIGGINS, AND Lillian all stared at Mr. Wentworth with open mouths. Higgins immediately closed his, but Lillian and Lucy exchanged looks before Lillian cleared her throat. "I beg your pardon?"

"Oh, I am sorry. I don't know what came over me." He sat back down but then stood again. "Shall I leave? I've trespassed on your company long enough, I believe." He took four steps toward the door but then stopped and turned back. "On second thought. Perhaps I should go greet Mr. Ainsworth? Seems the better thing to do." He paced back towards his chair. Then turned towards the door. "Where have you placed him? The front room?" His question was asked of Higgins, but the man turned to Lillian to respond.

"He is in the front room."

"Thank you, Higgins—" Lillian made a move like she might leave the room, but Mr. Wentworth held up his hand.

"I just don't like this situation. You here alone in the house with your servants. Any man could descend upon you at any time, just simply show up . . ." He paced back toward the door. "And we have the very example of the problem sitting in your front room right now." He continued walking back and forth. "And here you are, not fit to be seeing anyone at all."

"Pardon me?" She was part amused and part annoyed.

"You are of course fit to be receiving whoever you like . . ." He returned to his seat. "But Ainsworth. He is the worst sort . . ." He looked away. "Forgive me. Until this moment I could never have found myself classed with the gossips."

Lillian turned from him. "Higgins, would you please tell Mr. Ainsworth that I am not receiving callers at the moment?"

"Very good, ma'am."

Mr. Wentworth leaned back, breathing out in relief.

"And would you please show Mr. Wentworth to the door?"

"Very good, ma'am."

Mr. Wentworth stood again. "Right. Excellent. I shall go by way of the side door?"

"However you like."

He nodded again.

"And Mr. Wentworth?"

He paused and turned.

She stood, and the servants left the room.

"Thank you." She reached for his hands. "Thank you for everything today. I think you are correct. I could use the help of a neighbor, and I find our arrangement very agreeable. Also, we expect you for dinner early, at six."

He nodded and then left the room. Lucy waited to show him to the side entrance.

As soon as both men had left Lillian's house, all three of her servants joined her in the sitting room.

Jezzie ran to her. "Are you well? What happened?"

"I don't know. I wanted him to show me how to fix the roof so we wouldn't have to call on him for every leak, but as soon as I got up there, I panicked. I literally froze, and I was shaking." She swallowed. "How mortifying. He had to help me down, and then my legs shook so badly I couldn't walk."

"Oh no." Jezzie rested hands on her cheeks, but she looked suspiciously devoid of sympathy.

"So Mr. Wentworth carried you in and cared for you by the fire." Lucy looked like she was about to swoon.

"And what of Mr. Ainsworth?" Higgins seemed disgruntled, which for the perpetually emotionless butler said a lot.

"I don't know. He's given me some attention. He asked to call on me. I guess today was the day . . ."

None of her servants seemed overly pleased with the idea.

"Have you heard much about him from the other servants? What's the word?"

Lucy looked uncomfortable. Higgins looked as staid as he always did, and Jezzie was watching Lucy.

"Do you have something to tell me? What is it?"

Lucy shuffled her feet. "I don't like to say. But he does have an undesirable reputation."

"How undesirable?"

"Of the worst kind."

Lillian thought that over a moment more. "Well, we shall have to watch ourselves, then, shan't we?" She stood. "And now, remember we have included Mr. Wentworth in our dinner plans for this evening. Higgins, would you join us so that we are chaperoned?"

"I would be happy to serve as footman as well."

"Oh, thank you." She turned to them all one at a time. "I thank each one of you. We make a merry team, do we not?"

"That we do, ma'am. Now I'll be getting myself back to the kitchen." Jezzie smiled and squeezed her hand.

"And I'll be checking the place settings."

"And I the silver."

"And I shall go transform myself into something resembling a woman of leisure." Lillian laughed.

"I'll join you to help you dress."

"Thank you." How was she so blessed to have hired these three?

Lucy had been with her from the beginning. She had been Lillian's lady's maid and now did that and more. Higgins was the friend of their old family butler. A more loyal servant she didn't think she would ever find. And Jezz—Lillian smiled. Jezzie made everything better. Who didn't love their cook? Jezzie had been a part of her family estate when Lillian was growing up. She was the assistant cook at the time, but in Lillian's opinion the better cook. When Lillian married, her father had let her take some familiar servants with her.

Her throat tightened at the memory. Her parents had assured her they were sending her into the best possible situation. Her mother had kissed her goodbye after the wedding with only a slight mist to her eyes. Her father had congratulated them both and waved to her as she drove away in her new carriage.

And her husband had nodded off almost immediately on their journey to her new home. He was old. And—she hated to think ill of the dead—a wastrel. Every day when he'd come home swaying in drunkenness and shouting of his losses, sometimes sobbing out his agony over losses, she cringed inside, knowing that each and every visit to the tables stole from her children.

But she'd never had children.

And she told herself the dowry was never hers anyway.

He'd never been the mean sort of husband, or the violent type. She had read all the books in his library and taught herself to paint with the many hours she had to herself. Lucy and Jezzie even then had become friends. If one had friendships with servants. Higgins had stuck by her in almost a protective role, for which she was grateful. Perhaps her father had known what he was doing when he sent her with familiar servants.

Her parents were too old to travel, and she couldn't abide living once again in their household, in their control. Last time she'd been offered up without her choice. That would never happen again. They hadn't even been able to travel to the funeral. So she'd sent them letters assuring them of her happy state as a widow in Somerset.

And she was happy. The longer she lived her new life, the more hope she had that happiness would be hers. As the household prepared for their first dinner guest, she walked through the front rooms and into the dining area. The papers on the wall were peeling. She'd not paid much attention until now, but with an eye tuned to see what a guest might notice, she saw that the tiny edge that curled down near the ceiling was a glaring flaw she might notice the whole evening through. It would itch and pester her.

Unless.

She grinned and moved a chair right below the offending piece of paper. "I can take care of this . . ."

10

OLIVER SHOWED UP at the front door to Lavender Cottage in his best jacket. Perhaps such a thing was unnecessary, but he got the impression Mrs. Hunter was excited to entertain and that she might take this dinner engagement as something of a trial run for more guests at a later date. He admitted to liking the idea that he was something special, just as much as he liked the idea that he might become someone to casually drop by, as his horse had led him to do earlier this afternoon.

He shook his head. Before today he hadn't thought he would ever in his life see Mrs. Hunter trembling in fear. She had seemed, up to that point, nothing but indomitable. But something about the fact that he had been able to assist her broadened his shoulders and kept his head held high.

Higgins answered the door. "She's in the dining room." He bowed and indicated which direction he should go.

Oliver found that odd, but he followed in that direction until he stood in the doorway. And words would not form as his brain tried to find something to say in greeting.

Mrs. Hunter stood on the tips of her toes, reaching up to pick at a bit of paper that was stuck to the wall. Her hair looked as though it had once been styled in a more formal way, but now it was covered in strips of paper. The floor was strewn with paper, both large sheets and small pieces. Chairs were pulled up close to the wall all around the room where, he assumed, she'd stood on them.

She had not yet seen him. Her hands were grasping for one more bit of paper at the very top, and she could not reach. Then she bent her knees, ready to jump up off her chair to try and reach the ceiling—or at least that was what it looked like to him.

Oliver ran forward. "Gah! No." He reached her and placed a hand on her arm. Then he bowed. "Allow me?"

She opened her mouth, then closed it, then checked the room around them, then patted her head. "Um. Is it that time already?"

Her face had speckles of white; a strand of hair hung, free from her style, just outside her line of vision.

He bit back a laugh, cleared his throat, and said, "I think it's the perfect time to peel paper from the wall." He held her hand and gestured that she could get down. Then he stood on the chair and reached for the paper. It was old, but some of it was stubbornly stuck.

"See, it's that piece right there." She pointed and stood right below him. A lovely scent of lemon drifted up. And he smiled.

Then he caught hold of a corner, and the whole thing started peeling. "Look, I've got a big piece."

"Careful. If you're slow, you'll get the whole thing." She clasped her hands together.

And he was immediately caught up in the removal of this one strip of paper. Slowly, gently, he pulled at it. And it fell away from the wall, little by little, responding to his pressure. He held his breath as the last bit of it came unstuck.

Mrs. Hunter exhaled loudly. "Oh, well done!" She clapped her hands together.

He grinned down at her, enjoying the happiness that beamed up in his direction. "Is that the last of it?"

"I believe so." She turned about, lifting her eyes to the upper sections of the walls.

"Oh. Would you look at that?" Oliver pointed to the opposite corner. "We can't have that piece up in the corner."

She eyed him, hands on her hips. "You like this."

"I do. It was oddly satisfying. Now, let's go get that last piece, shall we?"

She laughed. "If we don't it will bother me until I've managed a way to pull at it myself."

He nodded. "Just so."

The second piece came off as easily as the first. When he climbed down, he rubbed his hands together. "Now, if I can get my hands on the broom, we will be finished."

"You'd sweep?"

"Certainly. I do expect that we will be having dinner?" He waited, eyeing her with amusement.

"Of course." She shook her head and left the room.

He was left marveling at this woman. Who in the upper classes behaved this way? Before today, he'd have ventured to guess that no one did.

When she returned, she started attacking the bits of paper and mess around the floor herself. So he moved chairs and helped as she went along. Before a few more minutes passed, they'd scooted a large pile of paper rubbish into the corner.

Mrs. Hunter brushed a hair away from her eyes. Then she stood taller. "Mr. Wentworth. Thank you for coming." She lowered herself into a deep curtsey.

He grinned in response. "I'm delighted. And this lonely bachelor appreciates some company and food to fill his stomach."

"Shall we be seated?" She indicated a place at her right. She sat herself at the head of the table.

And then Higgins and Lucy brought in their meal.

After a moment of eating the lovely ragout of beef, Oliver put down his fork. "This is the best meal I've had in a long time. I am now envious of your cook."

"As you should be. She was the best in my household growing up and the best amongst my parents' friends."

"You really are well taken care of. You're managing your house in an expert manner, all by yourself."

She laughed and then sipped her wine. "Do you think so?" She indicated the mess of the walls around them. "I completely lost track of time. Really, my mother would have been appalled."

"Well, I was not. It added to your charm."

"So I should entice all my guests into menial house chores upon their first arrival?"

He toyed with his own wine for a moment. "Not all, just me."

Her eyes shot to his, and for a moment, he was spellbound by their intensity. Then she looked away. "I do thank you for talking me down off the roof."

"That was a pleasure. Though I hope to never see you quite so petrified again."

"I can assure you that it is my greatest wish to keep such a sight from you."

"And what will you do with these walls?"

"I haven't decided." She shrugged.

"What? Yet you still pulled all the paper?"

"It started with the tiniest little lift up there." She pointed to the far corner. "And once you begin, well . . ." She took another bite.

"You are caught up in the completion of it. I know. I could not have left it unfinished."

Higgins stepped in and stood against the wall.

"So I think I shall paint it? But I am completely unaware..."

"I will assist."

She lifted her chin, and he saw the refusal cross her face.

He preempted her voice by lifting his glass. "But let's talk more of your attics."

She half lifted her glass, then lowered it. "My attics. Really, Mr. Wentworth. I can manage my own affairs. I will not be the bothersome, needy widow next door you seem so bent on seeing as tiresome."

"I do not see you as tiresome."

She lifted an eyebrow. "But you do see me as a chore, as something to consider when purchasing your property."

He had to concede, she was correct. He'd admitted as much. But now he longed only to help her, and somehow she and Lavender Cottage had gotten under his skin. "I admit to feeling responsible for you, for the house."

Her frown deepened.

"But. It is a pleasurable responsibility. This is a charming home and deserves to reach its best potential."

She narrowed her eyes. "Perhaps you can assist me in finding workers who could come and complete some of it?"

He nodded. "I hired local servants. I will ask them to find someone for us."

Her fork stopped on the way to her mouth. "Us?"

His face heated. But he covered himself. "Oh, you are a stubborn one. I too would like to do some work on my home."

"Excellent. As long as we know whose home is whose and who is doing the work, independently."

"Believe me. I could never forget such a thing."

"Do you know I haven't seen your estate yet?"

"I am painfully aware that my nearest neighbor has not

so much as crossed my threshold. And since the fence still has not been mended, it is easy enough to cut across to reach my home."

"I'm ignoring the fence comment, and I will tell you that as far as paying a neighborly visit, remedies are in the works as we speak. Cook has a gift."

"Then you will be all the more welcome."

She nodded. "Thank you."

They finished their meal and would have normally retired for port or whatever the ladies did when separated, but she stood. "Would you like a tour?"

Pleased he'd be offered such a thing, he held out his arm for her to take. "I'd like nothing more."

She led him through her home, and he enjoyed watching her more than seeing the walls about him.

"And this room you've seen, though I don't know if you looked at it properly. It's my favorite."

They entered her sitting room.

"I don't usually allow anyone but my servants here, but perhaps since you've already been inside, you'd like to come sit for a moment?"

"I'd love it even more if you would delight me with music on your harp?"

She colored prettily, and for a moment, he thought he was talking to a young debutante. "If you would like. I haven't played for others in a long time."

"I would very much like." He made himself comfortable near the table with the harp. "Growing up, we were more of a working-class family, and I wasn't favored with music. At Oxford, I attended as many musical events as I could. I found it spoke to me in ways nothing else could."

He seemed to have pleased her, if her smile was any

indication. "You and I share that same affinity, then. I only wish I could play as well as others so that we could be even more entertained. But I shall do my best."

She sat to play, and he was immediately charmed. For she was quite talented. Her first piece was classical. Then she moved to something more country. And he nearly laughed aloud when she played a song he'd sung as a kid.

"Sing." She laughed. And began to sing the words. With an accent and everything. He enjoyed it so much that he joined her.

"I, Darbyshire who're born an' bred,
Are strong i' th' arm, bu' weak i' th' head.
So th' lying proverb says.
Strength o' th' arm, who doubts shall feel
Strength o' th' head, its power can seal
The lips that scoff, always.
The rich vein'd Mind, the Mountain hoar,
We sink, an' blast, an' pierce, an' bore
By th' might o' Darby brawn.
An' Darby brain con think an' plon,
As well as that o' ony mon;
An' clearly as the morn.
Strong i' th' arm, an' strong i' th' head,"
The fou' fause Proverb should ha' said,
If th' truth she meant to tell.
Bu' th' union, so wise an' rare
O brawn an' brain, she didna care
To see or speak of well."

When they finished, he eyed her. "I don't know if I should be amused or insulted."

"And why would you be insulted?" She narrowed her

eyes with a crooked smile, realization crossing her face. "You're from Derbyshire." She turned away a hand at her mouth. Then she wiped her eyes. "That is perfect."

"I quite agree." He stood, wanting suddenly to be much, much closer. "May I?" He indicated a seat next to her.

"Certainly. Is there ... another song you wish me to play?"

"I would love for you to play the rest of the evening, were you to never tire." He reached his hand over and placed it on the arm of her chair. "I find this whole evening to be one I would care to repeat over and over again, were you willing." He stared into her face, studying her expression, trying to see deeper into her eyes.

She opened her mouth and then closed it. Then she pressed her lips together.

"Say no more." Oliver held up his hands.

"But I've said nothing at all."

"You don't need to. Everything you think crosses your face."

"Oh? And what was I thinking?"

Did he dare? The lift of one feminine eyebrow challenged him.

"Well, let's see if I can have a go at this, shall I? You liked the idea. No, you adored the idea, then you thought you shouldn't, and then you felt as though I was disturbing your independence, and before you could continue that train of thought to outright resistance, I interrupted you."

She looked away.

"Am I correct?"

Higgins stepped into the doorway. "A Lady Joanna and others are here to see you and Mr. Wentworth."

"Oh my." Mrs. Hunter stood.

"What is it?"

"Nothing."

"Something is wrong?"

"Why should anything be wrong?"

"As I said"—he motioned around on his face—"everything crosses here."

"You are not as correct as you think about your surmises. And nothing at all is wrong with the lovely widows paying me a visit. I was merely remembering our paper and hoping that they would be spared the sight."

Oliver did not believe her, not for a second, but he nodded. "Should we receive them?"

"We?"

"Higgins did say they were paying a call on me as well as you."

"He did, didn't he?"

"Now why would they do that?"

"I'm not sure."

He stood. "Well, I find my curiosity is quite the strongest of all emotions at the moment. Shall we go find out?"

"Just like that? Together, as though we are receiving them?"

"Is that not how things are done?"

"It would be if we were in actuality together."

"Hmm." The more he thought of her in that way, the more pleased about it he became.

"We are most definitely not together, so whatever is bringing that smile needs to stop, this instant. And we can't give that impression to our, I mean, my guests. And maybe you should just leave. Out the side door."

"You want me to sneak away as though you are hiding my visit?" His eyebrows rose up as high as they would go.

And she turned crimson red. "Certainly not. Quite right. We shall walk in as though nothing is happening but two neighbors at dinner."

"Which is precisely what is happening."

"Exactly."

"That's what I said."

"No, you said precisely... oh, stop. I'm nervous."

"Yes, and I cannot account for it."

She breathed in once, twice, then stood taller, lifted her chin, and placed her hand on his arm. "Let us go greet our guests."

"Excellent."

"And you can stop grinning so broadly. You look just like a rooster. Next thing you'll be preening."

He immediately frowned.

"You needn't look displeased. Just look... bored."

"I don't think I've been bored a day in my life."

"Pretend."

They approached the front sitting room. The door to the dining room had been closed. Higgins announced them.

"A Mrs. Hunter and Mr. Wentworth."

The drawing room was full of eight women, who stood, and Lady Joanna, who nodded her head and reached out a hand.

The room sizzled with confidence. Oliver's heart skipped a beat as they entered, and he almost forgot to bow.

It was going to be a long visit.

11

ADMITTEDLY, LILLIAN WAS happy to see her widow friends. But she also knew there was no coincidence in the fact that Mr. Wentworth was here when they chose to pay a social visit, during the dinner hour and in such masse.

She relied on her social training and hurried in with hands outstretched. "Lady Joanna." She curtseyed. Then greeted the others. "I'm so delighted you have come. Some of you know Mr. Wentworth."

He bowed, as gallant as anyone, "I must be the most fortunate of all men in Somerset."

"Oh?" Lady Joanna eyed him. "And why is that?"

"To be surrounded by such company, of course."

"Yes, well, you are correct. The company you share here is the most elevated in Somerset on many counts." She lifted a finger to her pearls.

"I'm so pleased you would come pay a visit. Won't you be seated, Mr. Wentworth, and all of you, what can I offer? Would you like tea? Coffee?"

"Coffee would be lovely, yes, thank you." Lady Joanna sat on the edge of her seat, the perfect lady. And Lillian was less uncomfortable and more impressed.

Lillian sat beside her. "And to what do I owe this pleasure?"

"I wish to know Mr. Wentworth better. He is of growing interest to us, I believe."

"Am I?"

Lucy entered with a tray. Higgins followed with another.

"It all depends. What are your intentions with our new friend, Lillian?"

Mr. Wentworth looked as surprised as Lillian felt. She waved her hand with a half-embarrassed laugh. "I'm sure he doesn't yet know his intentions. We are neighborly. That is what we've discussed. In fact, he's saved me a time or two, on the roof, in my front room. We're in the middle of a fence dispute, really." She'd said too much. She knew it. But she felt some incomprehensible need to explain in no uncertain terms just exactly what Mr. Wentworth was to her.

"I see." Lady Joanna lifted her chin. "And what say you, Mr. Wentworth? From whence do you come?"

"Manchester. My family earned their living in trade—in shipping, where we established ourselves."

"And your mother?"

"My mother?"

"Yes, was she well cared for? Provided for?"

"She was the choicest member of our family to Father, if that's what you'd like to know."

Lady Joanna seemed pleased to hear that. She readjusted herself in her chair. "And now? You've established yourself? Bought land?"

"Yes, I have."

"And so I wish to know, what are your intentions? You've come calling more than once, you've assisted her, been alone in the house with her, and as she has no one else to speak for her, we'd all like to know what your intentions are."

Mr. Wentworth's smile grew. "Yes. You are the people here to look after her."

Lillian felt the strength of sisterhood. She searched the faces of the women who had come. Charlotte, Penny, Anna. And the others. Some looked to her. Charlotte smiled. But Lillian needed to help them understand. "You see, Mr. Wentworth. I am not alone in the world."

"I'm happy to hear it."

"And Lady Joanna, Mr. Wentworth and I have talked about this. He knows of my desires to remain independent."

"Talked about it? Has he proposed to you?"

"What! No. He has not." She glanced at Mr. Wentworth, who did not seem as unnerved as she. In fact, the more she studied him, the more pleased he looked.

He adjusted his seating so that he sat as tall and straight as she'd ever seen him. "I have not. But I am not opposed to the idea."

"What are you saying?" She wanted to laugh at the ridiculous conversation, but upon hearing his words, her heart hammered inside, and an unexpected sort of hope filled her. No. She did not wish for any such thing from Mr. Wentworth or any man. Never again. She shook her head. "I don't want to know what you're saying."

"Wise words." Lady Joanna nodded. "These things are only entered into with full knowledge and understanding."

"Naturally. It's more of a business arrangement, and should be mutually beneficial." Mr. Wentworth nodded. But when he turned to her, his eyes were filled with humor, and she relaxed somewhat.

"You're not in earnest."

"Of course not. A man can propose to a woman without the help of a room full of her friends."

Her hands shook, so she clasped them behind her back.

"Sensible." Was he considering proposing? Even after all her talk of not wanting such a thing? She wished to pull him back into the hallway so that she would talk to him properly. He was in jest. He'd said so.

"Now that we've established where we stand... or at least caused us all to consider where we stand, we may as well have a meeting of our Secret Society of Young Widows right here as anywhere. Mr. Wentworth, you may be a part."

"I'd be honored to do so."

"It's provident you are here. You shall play the role my steward usually plays."

His eyebrows rose, but he said nothing more.

Lillian was having a hard time recovering from her previous realization that she might want Mr. Wentworth to propose. What kind of nonsense was that? No matter what her romantic sensibilities might crave, she simply could not submit herself to such a loss of independence, not when it had so recently been granted her, not when she had goals and a house to finish and, frankly, a life to lead. She sighed quietly. A somewhat lonely life, she had to admit. And a part of her longed for the companionship she'd never had. Yet not only did she most decidedly not want to marry, but he had been in jest. He hadn't really wanted to propose. She was twice silly to hope for such a thing, even in a brief moment of addled brain.

"Now, Mr. Wentworth, perhaps this exercise will also be beneficial to you. I feel it an opportune time to discuss with these new widows how to respond to a marriage proposal."

Lillian gasped.

Mr. Wentworth choked. "Pardon?"

"Yes, so we need you to act as the man in love proposing. And each of the girls will come up with a response."

"Don't you feel that is a bit... much?" Lillian tried to be polite. In no way did she want to insult her only friends.

Lady Joanna waved away her concern. "It is the very thing that must be practiced, understood, dissected, until it holds no more romance. And why is that? Penny?"

"Because it is the very act of being lost in love that can lead us to make unwise marriage decisions."

"Precisely. Now, I shall show you what I mean. Mr. Wentworth, if you would?"

He stood and came forward.

"Kneel before me as if your dying wish would be to have me for a bride."

His fist opened and closed twice before he got down on one knee.

Lillian wasn't sure he'd ever want to return to her home again. She was equal parts mortified and fascinated by what would be said. And she was fairly certain he was not enjoying himself.

But he cleared his throat, and with a flourish, one arm out, one hand on his heart, he said, "My dear Lady Joanna. It would give me the greatest happiness if you were to agree to be my wife."

She lifted her chin. "As proposals go, that one was fair, but we shall pretend I am in great love with you. What would I normally do right now?"

Penny giggled. "Fall at his feet and agree to marry him."

"Exactly. And that is what we can never do."

"But what if we wish to marry him?" Penny's eyes sparkled.

Her *him* sounded a bit too personal to Lillian. She wanted to add, *Hypothetically speaking.*

"Yes, he's a fantastic catch," Anna pointed out. "Any woman would be pleased to get such a proposal."

"Isn't he just what you explained would be a man worth marrying?" Charlotte shrugged.

"He's wealthy, established, of good character." Penny leaned forward to be closer to him.

Lillian clenched folds of her gown in her fists without noticing. What were they saying? Did every woman in the room hope to marry Mr. Wentworth? Her neighbor?

Lady Joanna clucked. "You may rise."

Oliver got to his feet.

"But you see, now is not the time to answer this question. You may wish to, but instead, you ask him to stand and you say, 'Thank you for the honor of your proposal. Shall we talk about it for a minute?'"

The ladies nodded.

"Can you do that?" When everyone in the room nodded, she added, "And then you work out your contract. What kind of pin money are you expecting? Who is working out the household finances? What happens to the money you have inherited? The money that is yours? Your estate? What will your children inherit?"

Lillian nodded. And she felt Mr. Wentworth's eyes on her. They lit with a strange hope. And she groaned. He couldn't be thinking anything about this conversation would lead to their becoming more than simply neighborly. No, he had made a joke of it just moments before. The thought was oddly disappointing even if he was incredibly handsome all of a sudden, and the most sought-after man of every woman present.

Penny fluttered her eyelashes. And Lillian wanted to stand in her way to block whatever enticements she was throwing at Mr. Wentworth. What a ridiculous way to feel, yet she could barely maintain her composure.

"Now, let's you all try it. Anna, you go first. Mr. Wentworth, if you will?" Lady Joanna pointed to Anna, who immediately turned bright red.

"Oh, oh my." She held her palms to her cheeks. "I shall try."

Lady Joanna waved a hand in Mr. Wentworth's direction. "If you will."

He glanced at Lillian and when she shrugged, he moved to kneel in front of Anna. "Will you marry me?"

"Oh, come now, you must try to woo her, try to make her want to lose all sense and say yes to you." Lady Joanna's face was as stern as ever. Lillian suspected something about this gave her great enjoyment, because for a moment, her lip twitched.

"Acting was never my strongest talent." He dipped his head.

"Perhaps with someone you know better it would be easier?"

Lillian's stomach twisted.

"Why don't we give Lillian a try?"

He rose slowly, avoiding eye contact.

She watched his back straighten, and then he turned. She expected to see restraint, a mask. This was awkward enough. But his eyes were full of emotion. They sparkled and held hers with an intensity she had never felt. He stepped closer, and the room grew quiet. Everyone all but disappeared. Here was a man she might have liked to propose to her the first time she'd received an offer. Here was someone she would have been happy to be set up with by her parents. This man could have brought her joy and satisfaction all her days. Why, oh why hadn't he been the one? He reached for her hand. The rough calluses on his caught at her gloves. He knelt in front of her. "Lillian."

His voice was soft.

She stepped closer to hear.

"I would be most honored if you would agree to become my wife."

Her heart leapt to her throat. Words fled from her mind—all but one. One word that could make her the happiest of people. The word she could never say. "No." All the breath left her body, and she turned. "No."

No one said a word for several heartbeats. Then Lady Joanna said, "If that's your answer, ladies, that is the precise manner in which to deliver it. No explanation or long, drawn-out excuse is necessary. Your choice is yours, and you may speak it thus. Now, if you do want to marry this man, if he is a good choice for your happiness, and for your financial security, then you would need to say something more. Lillian, why don't you practice your other statement while your amour is right there, before we give someone else a chance."

Lillian turned back, and she couldn't look into Mr. Wentworth's eyes. She said, "Thank you for the honor of your proposal. Could we sit and discuss the particulars for a moment before I make my decision?"

"Excellent!" Lady Joanna clapped. "You see, ladies! That is the way it is done. Come now, Mr. Wentworth. Let the other ladies have a go."

"Lillian." His voice was quiet, insistent.

She lifted her lashes.

When their eyes met, she knew his intentions. He had been sincere. He was going to ask again, this time for real.

12

OLIVER SAT AT his desk in the study. The thick, dark wood shone with the new polish the servants had been working to rub into all the wood throughout the home. Double doors let out onto a verandah. The walls of his study were lined with books, most of which he'd brought to the home. But some were excellent older copies he had been pleased to discover when he arrived. A fire crackled in the fireplace. His eyes lifted, as they often had, to a large portrait of his father that hung over the fire. His words, before he passed away: "I've given you much to ease your way in the world. But what matters most I cannot give. You must find someone to complete you, someone you can love and rely on and confide in, and the two of you must create together what matters most."

Oliver had taken that to heart. But in no way had he expected to find a woman so soon who he could imagine making such a life with. He smiled. They were so incredibly suited for one another. She didn't even know how well.

He shifted attention to his ledger. Usually he derived great pleasure from the numbers, from his financial situation. Everything was going well. By all projections, he would be considerably wealthier at year's end. He'd set aside dowries for future daughters, and their worth grew along with his income. He shuffled through the paperwork. He'd asked his steward to collect opportunities to buy land in the area, and also to seek out properties in London. He wanted a townhome, right off Grosvenor Square. His mind wandered and immediately went to Mrs. Hunter—Lillian. In his imagination, she stood at his side in London, welcoming guests to his home. She sat by his fire on a sofa he'd put there just for his wife. She helped their daughters prepare for their first season. How had it become all Lillian in his mind?

His awareness of her had crept up on him like the dew in the early hours of morning. Suddenly it was there. And he couldn't shake it, nor did he want to. Early interest had become something much stronger, and when he'd been asked to propose to her, something had passed between them, something real. And he knew she wanted it too.

But she also wanted nothing to do with marriage.

What a complicated situation to be in.

So he bided his time. He'd prepared an offer, a financial offer for her. When the time was right, he planned to let her see it.

His butler, Severs, stood in the doorway. "A Mrs. Hunter to see you."

He shot to his feet, scattering papers to the floor. "Show her in to the front parlor. I'll be in directly."

"Very good, sir. She's brought something from her kitchen. Shall I ask for tea?"

"Yes, please, and whatever she requires."

He paced the floor of his study. She'd come to call. Of course she'd come. Had she not said she'd come? But so soon after their mock proposal. Had he expected her to stay away? His pacing continued. Yes, he had. He had fully expected her to hide. What did it mean that she'd come so soon?

Then he stopped. "Of all the ridiculous . . ." He straightened his jacket, stood tall, and exited his study. "Behave normally."

He waved off Severs, who would have announced him and instead watched Lillian from the doorway. She was situating her gift from Jezzie onto plates and pouring his tea. He smiled. Such a pleasant domestic view warmed him to his toes and nudged him into the room.

She stood with a large, natural smile. "Mr. Wentworth."

"Hello, Mrs. Hunter. You've come—and, I hear, with promised gifts from your cook."

"That I have. She made these especially for you. I'm not sure how she knows of your fondness for tarts, but she is convinced of it."

"And she is correct. I am unduly fond of tarts." He joined her at her side on a low sitting sofa. "It is rumored among our tenants that Jezz's tarts are the best in the area by far."

Lillian laughed, and it was such a musically merry sound he wished to hear it again as soon as possible. "And how have the tenants all tasted of her tarts?"

"She sends baskets round to them all."

"Yours and mine?"

"Apparently, there is not much difference between the two groups. Many share families. They say they consider our land to be their home."

She nodded, looking thoughtful. "I've learned a few stories about those who lived on our land long ago."

"Oh? And what are those?"

"Just that . . ." She looked away, suddenly pink in the face. She sipped her tea. "Forgive me. They say that the first two owners were lovers. That is to say, they fell in love and married."

He watched her face, uncertain as to why she would inform him of this particular history.

"And that is part of the reason for the fence line remaining untouched all these years. Even with the passing down of the property and the inheritance going from one family to another, all have honored the original intent."

He nodded. "I'd like to hear more of their story."

"I don't know much of it myself. But I'll pass along anything I do learn."

He lifted his teacup and eyed her. "So our two houses were owned by a pair in love." His wiggle of both eyebrows made her laugh.

"Oh stop. And this reminds me. I do have to apologize for the widows society. What could they have been thinking, dropping in when they did and inflicting such an exercise on you?"

"I found it rather enjoyable, and enlightening."

"Oh?" The concern on her face gave him pause.

"Yes, the ladies all consider me quite a catch."

She looked away. "Interested in pursuing the widows, are you?"

"No—well, I don't know. I don't have anything against a widow. She would be perhaps more enjoyable than a very young debutant who knows nothing of the ways of things." He counted to five before continuing, unsure how bold he wished to be. "I think the right widow might be preferable above all others."

She stood and moved to the window, her skirts shifting about her. "Penny Fletcher is lovely. And seems completely enamored—if that's what you mean."

"Mrs. Fletcher? Did she?" He thought back to her blush and how she would not meet his gaze. "I don't know. I thought her rather embarrassed."

"Hmm."

"But that wasn't the enlightening part. I was pleased to

see that none seemed bothered by my background, by my history in trade."

Her eyes widened in surprise. "And why would they? You've made a remarkable living for yourself. You're landed gentry now, well respected by all in the neighborhood, by Lady Joanna herself."

"Oh? Does the queen of Somerset respect me?"

"Well ... yes, actually. She had very complimentary things to say about you." Lillian reached for another tart. "So you can move forward knowing that you are highly sought-after, respected, and fully considered a gentleman." She snorted. "Even though you climb roofs and help peel paper off walls."

"And you? Are you still gently bred, if you do the same?"

She returned and sat closer to him, unless he imagined it. "I am a widow. And therefore it doesn't matter what people consider me." Her eyes sparkled. "And that brings me all the satisfaction in the world. You cannot imagine being sold off to a man who could be your grandfather, being told when and what to spend, being gifted food and clothes. Being always beholden to another."

"You're right. I cannot imagine." Watching her fire and light, watching her great satisfaction in her own independence, his hopes dampened somewhat. "But perhaps it could be forged in such a way as to be palatable, to make you happy?" The hesitation on her face gave him a little more courage. She didn't outright deny his suggestion. "Come to my study. Your meeting with the widows got me thinking. I couldn't sleep last night, pondering the typical plight of a widow. I'll admit to never once having given any of this a moment's thought. But perhaps you would have some insight into what I've come up with?"

He held his arm out, and she placed her hand upon it. "I could take a look. Are you planning to propose to someone?"

"Perhaps I might. But either way, your meeting inspired me to be prepared and to be mindful of the widows."

She nodded, her face blank.

When they entered his study, her soft intake of breath and small smile gratified him to no end.

"This is my favorite room in the house."

She stopped in front of his father. "You resemble this man. Is it your father?"

"It is, but no one but you would say the same. I inherited all my mother's looks."

She shook her head. "No. I see that the hair color is different and the set of your jaw, but look at those eyes, look at his brow. Look at the expression. And the set of his mouth. You are the same. I would know him simply because I know you."

Oliver felt himself choke up and his eyes grow misty. He looked away. But then he decided to be honest with her, to be open, so he turned to her and stepped closer. "Your words speak balm to the heart of a son who misses his father every day." He brought the back of her hand to his lips. "Thank you."

"Oh. You're welcome. I didn't mean to make you miss him."

"I love missing him. I fear every day, when minutes go by and I haven't thought of him, that I will stop remembering my father."

She nodded and reached for his hand to offer comfort. "I'm sorry."

He drew her over to his desk. "I wasn't going to show this to you, not yet. But it seems a good enough time to get your reaction. I wonder if it would sit well for a woman in your situation, if you could take a look and see if I have thought of everything."

She sat in the chair behind his desk, her soft neck turned

down to look at his papers. He stood behind and reached forward over her; his finger gently brushed the skin of her neck, just ever so slightly. He was gratified to see her skin rise following the trail of his finger. He shifted things and uncovered the first page. "So, see here. I thought the first thing to be addressed was that of the family budget. After listening to Lady Joanna, I don't want to have such a thing as pin money or my money. I think we should sit together and discuss what money is to be spent in a month and then move forward with that."

"We?" She didn't turn around but sat very still.

"Oh, no. I mean. This is just a possibility for when I do get married."

"You seem to have thought this through."

"I have. So, keep looking. This line shows the monies we could set aside for you were I to die before you. And the delineation of the entire estate left in your hands."

She said nothing, so he kept going. "And this line would be the suggestions for the children, the dowries, the heir." He moved down. "I also continued thinking along these lines about our daughters, their future. What if one became a widow? Is there a way to draw up marriage settlements, or my own will, so that they are taken care of? I know there are provisions, but I would like to explore that deeper. I want to take these thoughts to Lady Joanna, but I most especially wanted your thoughts."

She didn't say anything for some time. Her finger ran down the numbers, but then at once, she turned to him, fire in her eyes. "And this is supposed to make me want to marry you? You've decided everything, you've planned it all out. Do you think your wealth will entrap me again? All these numbers look good on paper, but you could change this whenever you want. I know what it means to not truly own anything. I'm never doing that again. This is no guarantee, and I've already seen how I wish to . . . to manage things. What if I don't want to fit inside those boxes? What if I don't want to be controlled in any way at all? Had you thought along those lines, you'd not have even created any of this." She fluttered her hands about. He'd never seen her this emotional. "There's something about those neat little numbers, lined up on a page, final and binding . . . my heart clenches, and I feel afraid, and . . . you're trying to trap me in or something."

"No, no. I said nothing of you at all. I wanted your input because you are a widow and would know. You could speak for all widows."

She sucked in her breath. "Were you truly thinking of asking another?" Her face lost its color, and she clenched her hands together. "I need to go."

"What? No, we've been having such a nice time of it, until now."

She stood. "I wish you every happiness. Please don't address this topic with me again."

"Let me walk you out?"

"I know my way!" She waved him away as she turned down the hall in the wrong direction.

He watched until she passed by his door again without a word. With his shoulder leaning up against the doorjamb, he sighed. That had gone even worse than he had worried it might. And what was her biggest concern? Was it that he had been planning out his offer to her or that he'd been planning his offer to someone else? Would he ever understand women? He thought not, or perhaps not Lillian at least.

But he couldn't wish her away. The whole interchange had only convinced him to try harder to set her mind at ease and to win her heart.

13

Lillian loved Mr. Wentworth.

She wrung her hands and paced in front of her harp.

How could she have let something like that happen?

She ran out into the hall. "I must go see Lady Joanna."

Lucy hurried to her, handing her a pelisse and calling for Higgins. "I shall be walking with Mrs. Hunter into town."

"Very good." He dipped his head.

"You don't need to come with me," Lillian said to Lucy.

"But I do. I know you're a widow, but it just isn't safe. Widow or not, it's better with two."

"True. We might encounter any number of people we wish to avoid."

As they hurried down the lane, Lucy did not say much, and she didn't ask Lillian what had caused this sudden rush to see Lady Joanna. Lillian loved her servant all the more for it.

They did have a long way to go. Perhaps Lillian should have used the cart. It wasn't exactly high-class, but it was useful for shopping and would have been useful to visit town as well.

"Whoa, ho there." The sounds of a carriage slowing down made her move off the side of the road. Then Mr.

Wentworth leaned his head out the window. "Can I offer you a lift?"

Of all the people in all the world to appear just now, the last she wanted to see was Oliver Wentworth—yet her face smiled, her heart lit, and her rebellious feet tripped over happily to the door. "Thank you. We are off to Lady Joanna's home."

"That's quite a distance to walk."

She lowered her head in acknowledgment of the obvious.

He hopped out and held the door for her and Lucy to climb in.

Once they were settled and he'd told the coachman where to go, he sat across from Lillian and Lucy. "I'm pleased to run into you." His gaze flitted to Lucy, and Lillian was even more grateful for her maid's presence. She did not wish to discuss any of the earlier subjects.

"You left rather abruptly, and I wished to be assured of your well-being."

"As you can see, I am well."

"I'm happy to hear it." He tapped his thumbs on his breeches. "And perhaps Lady Joanna can assist you also?"

"Perhaps." She looked away. Then she felt guilty for trying to say as little as possible when she was in fact benefitting from his generous offer to drive them into town. "And how have you been?"

"Well. I've been well. I've given a lot of thought to what you said." His gaze flitted to Lucy again, who was attempting to appear as though she wasn't listening. "And I am well."

Lillian hid a smile. "I'm pleased to hear it."

"And your servants are well?"

"Yes. We are all well." She would laugh later, she hoped, at this most awkward of all meetings. But what could she say to the man she loved, whom she had told not to ever address the topic of marriage again? And did he love her? Or did he plan to propose to someone else? Was he simply neighborly? Had she ruined everything? And did she want to be in love? She certainly had been convinced she never wanted to marry. Would she lose everything if she were to do so?

She was in desperate need of some advice. And she needed to be as far from Mr. Wentworth as possible. For even in the past few moments in the carriage, she'd noticed the breadth of his shoulders, the light in his eyes when he smiled, and the lovely manner in which he spoke. His deep voice sent tremors through her. Pleasant tremors. And her ability to think clearly had flown away—literally left out the carriage window. What were the widow's rules? Never fall in love. Never fall in love, and here she was, desperately in love with Oliver Wentworth.

Lady Joanna would know what to do.

The carriage pulled in front of her home. Mr. Wentworth climbed down and reached a hand back. When Lillian placed her hand in his palm, he closed his fingers around hers. The moment lingered, gooseflesh raced up her arm, and she had an irrational desire to lean further in, closer to him. But she kept walking, and he had to release her as he held a hand out to her maid. What a gentleman. Far more than any man she'd known, he was caring and aware of those around him, and he was attentive to her needs—and he had even helped her maid down from a carriage.

"Perhaps I'll be by to check your attic?"

"Perhaps," she called over her shoulder and hurried up to the front door.

"Be home. Be home," she muttered to herself as they waited.

The butler opened the door. She couldn't remember his name.

"I'm here to see Lady Joanna. Is she home and receiving callers?"

"She left word that if you arrive, you are to be admitted any time, day or night."

"I don't know what to say. Thank you."

He held open the door wider and showed her into a small sitting room. Lucy followed him away to converse with the servants. She heard the most interesting things when they made calls together.

Lillian only waited one minute before Lady Joanna swept into the room. "I knew you would come calling. You've come sooner than I expected."

"I'm in desperate need of your advice."

She patted the chair next to her. "Sit, tell me everything."

When she told Lady Joanna that Mr. Wentworth had taken upon himself to figure out his finances without consulting her, that she wasn't sure if he was talking about her and his finances or just his and another widow's, and that she had realized she was in love with him, the woman nodded. "And?"

"And what?"

"And did you discuss whether or not you agreed with his proposals?"

"No. I couldn't be sure he meant me."

"But wasn't he coming to you for your opinion?"

"Yes. He was." She thought about it for a moment. "I was so disturbed that he'd taken the time to work out a whole budget for me as if we were married that I didn't really stop to think if I liked his budget. But Lady Joanna, it was lovely. Very generous."

"Yes, yes, but is your money protected? Your inheritance? Are you cared for if he too should pass away? Are your children cared for?"

"I think so, yes. But I was wondering if I could have your

steward look at it and help us come to terms . . ." She stopped speaking, her eyes growing wider. "But Lady Joanna. I do not want to be married."

"Why not?"

"Because of all that I would lose. Lavender Cottage, my money, everything."

"I thought we just established that you wouldn't lose any of it."

"I know, I know. But really, would it really and truly be as he says? You know I have no recourse if it's not."

"He seems a trustworthy fellow, if I were to venture a guess, but more than that, you can get it set up in writing, in a contract as part of your marriage agreement."

"Can I?"

"Yes, most definitely. We haven't had that lesson for you yet. But it's most certainly recommended."

A great relief filled her. She trusted Mr. Wentworth. She thought she did. But she was also unsure about a great many things regarding him. And, more than that, she had something to confess to Lady Joanna. "I've broken a rule. I love him."

She clucked. "Falling in love is only a problem if it makes you lose your head. That is precisely why we showed up at your home and practiced that activity with the two of you. See where it has taken us? From acting simply out of love to making certain you decide wisely."

"So do I have your blessing?"

"My child. You do not need my blessing. But if you want my educated opinion about whether or not he would be respectful of you, whether or not your own assets would still be intact, then yes. I offer my full support of the union, should you choose to accept him, if he offers again."

"Again, that first time didn't count."

"It looked like it counted to him."

"He did have a particular intensity in his eyes, didn't he?"

"Mark my words. That man loves you. What else would motivate him to write up all his finances for you?"

Lillian had no way of knowing, and she didn't know how to get him to bring up the subject again. Suddenly shy, she looked away, troubled. "Thank you for your assistance. What you do for the ladies, for me, is so important. I wish everyone could hear it."

"It wouldn't benefit the debutantes, though possibly a father or two would give heed."

Lillian frowned. "I wish mine had." She waved her hand as if to brush thoughts of her first marriage away. "But how do I get Mr. Wentworth to ask me? Again."

Lady Joanna stood. "I will not advise in the ways of capturing a man. You will have to figure that out between you."

Lillian followed her out to the door. "Thank you again. Perhaps this will come to something, perhaps not, but now I at least know what to do."

Lucy was waiting for her, and the two of them made their way down the steps and across the street, Lillian feeling less worried than when she arrived but still not entirely certain of her next step. Did she wish to be married? And if so, how would she go about securing a proposal from the one man she had ever loved? Whom she'd pushed away and in fact already declined once? Even though that was just playacting, she'd been pretty serious.

The walk home was long. And her heart and mind were full. With every step, she hoped he would approach in his carriage again. Where had he been off to? When at last they arrived home, Lucy went indoors, but Lillian wanted to stay outside. She was too restless to wander about the house, too distracted to dig into the work that must be done in the attic. So she made her way down the property line. Walking helped clear her mind. Before long she found herself at the swing. As she sat and pushed herself off the ground with her toes, she asked herself what was so bad about being married.

She didn't know. Being married to Mr. Hunter had been lonely, sometimes unbearably so. And she wasn't free to visit her family or friends. She hadn't much pin money. She was at his mercy in all things. And that had been a miserable existence. But perhaps not all marriages were the same? If Mr. Wentworth was willing to be so giving with his money, he might be the same with his time and lenient with where she might go and with whom.

She kicked off again and again, her mind cluttered and busy with racing thoughts.

And then she saw a figure, alone, walking in her direction. The field grass seemed to open and close around him. His shoulders were broad, his stance tall. His hat sat askew on his head, which made her laugh. "Oliver."

She'd never dared say his given name, or think it, but it slipped out now as though she'd said it her whole life. *Oliver.*

Her swing slowed and stilled while she watched him approach. He didn't hurry, and his measured steps reached her in a rhythmic expectation her heart called out with each beat, until at last he stood in front of her.

"Oliver."

The corner of his mouth tugged up. "I've learned the story of this swing."

"More of it?"

"The owner of my land was a man, desperate in love."

She sucked in a breath.

"And the woman who lived in your cottage was strong, independent, and . . . beautiful." His eyes searched hers. "He knew that between the two of them, they could find happiness, joy, a true union of love."

"Did she agree?" She could barely breathe, her concerns melting in front of her in the form of this dear man. The sun broke through a cloud and caught his hair. She longed to run her fingers through it.

"Yes, on one condition."

"And what was that?"

"That they keep the cottage and the swing so that others might benefit from its magic."

Her lips turned up in a smile. "Is it magic?"

"They believed it was."

"And do you?"

"It must be, for I've been enchanted. From the day I pushed you higher into the air on this swing, I knew my life would only be complete with you in it. I've tried to respect your wishes, tried to keep my distance, but . . ." He moved forward and knelt in front of her. "But might we find some way, any way to be together that would give you all that you desire?" He lifted her hand in his own. "For all that I desire sits in front of me now on this most magical of swings."

She studied him and knew she could no longer resist such a man. "So what are you saying? Have you something to ask of me?"

His smile started small and then grew into something so stunning that she held her breath.

"Lillian Boxwood Hunter."

"How did you know my full name?"

"I made inquiries; now hush, you are interrupting." He cleared his throat with some amount of theatrics. "Lillian Boxwood Hunter. Would you do me the great honor of being my partner, my confidante, my fellow decision maker, with all the independence and freedom you so desire, from this day forward as my wife?"

She laughed and then knelt in front of him, put her hands on either side of his face, and pressed her lips to his.

He responded immediately with his arms around her back. She kissed him again and again, until she was filled with such happiness, so much joy that she could no longer kiss him, for her mouth refused to do anything but smile.

He scooped her up into his arms and spun her around. "I am the happiest of men."

As he pressed his forehead to hers, she rested her hand at the side of his face. "I haven't given my answer."

"You're absolutely right. Shall we sit and discuss finances, then?" He headed in the direction of his house, not setting her down to walk on her own two feet.

"No, please no more talk of finances. If I never see another ledger it shall be too soon."

"But I thought . . . Am I to be the happiest of men?"

"As long as I can keep the cottage."

He tipped his head. "But you will live with me?"

Her laugh rang out around them. "Certainly, but I cannot bear to part with it. Perhaps we shall let it out to another widow?" She held up her finger and stared him down. "And the fence stays where it is."

"Understood. And I quite agree with you. I owe a great debt to that fence, and this swing." He spun her around again and then set her down on her feet.

"Then, yes. I will marry you, and we two shall be the happiest of people in all of Somerset."

He linked her fingers with his, then stopped. "This will never do." He took off her glove and let it fly away in the wind, brought her naked hand to his mouth, and kissed the back. "I shall be the most boorish and domineering type of husband and forbid gloves of all kinds on your hands."

"You shall? And what else will you forbid?"

As they walked off along the property line together, she waited and watched him, and then he shrugged. "I cannot think of a single thing."

"I have something to forbid."

"Oh? And what's that?"

"I forbid us to be sad. There is only happiness permitted on the Wentworth Estate."

"The Wentworth Estate. I like that."

She turned to face him again, her chin lifted as she studied his face. "I love it too."

"Mrs. Wentworth, what say you of kisses? Are they allowed?"

"Oh required, certainly. With great frequency."

"Then come a little closer." His grin made her laugh, but he covered the sound with his lips, and she soon found herself lost to his kisses.

Epilogue

LILLIAN SAT AT her desk in a beautiful morning room Oliver had commissioned just for her. Her harp was joined by a pianoforte. The light was perfect for all of her endeavors. They had just had breakfast together, and he planned to ride out to visit the tenants of their joint estates. But he stepped back in the doorway, his grin contagious. "Have I told you that you look beautiful right there?"

"Right here? In this spot?" She considered him. "Not yet. You've told me over there by the piano, in the kitchen, the attic." She felt her face heat. "That time in the nursery." She coughed, and he laughed, obviously delighted. "And in our bedroom every morning."

She reached for him. He stepped across the room in two strides, pressing his lips to hers. "Well, you are. You astound me. Your heart, your mind, your hair, you. You are beautiful."

She kissed him back, loving him more than ever.

Then he handed over a stack of letters. "The mail came."

"Oh, thank you!" She began sifting through her correspondence. The widows kept in touch often, the ones who had married and those still in Somerset. Their words were some of her most entertaining.

The top letter was not from one of them, though, but from a dear friend she'd known as a child—Phoebe Atwater.

Dear Lilly,

I came home, and your parents told me that you have recently become widowed and then remarried since I have talked to you last. I sorrow that we have not been in touch during what must have been challenging times. And that is entirely my fault, but if you hear my past circumstance you might understand somewhat. I've been living in the farthest north location you can imagine, on my late husband's tiny holdings. I was sequestered away. And the details I may share some day, but suffice it to say, I was unable to contact anyone to let them know my situation. But he has passed away, a carriage accident on the cliffs. And I will not speak ill of the dead, much, just to say I am finally free. I am writing to seek out a place of lodging. I am a good tenant. I don't need much, just a bit of independence. If you could write back with any news of some situation available, I would most appreciate your assistance.

Yours, etc.,
Phoebe Atwater

Lillian began her response immediately.

My dearest Phoebe,

How thrilled I was to receive your letter. In truth any news of you would have made me smile, but to hear your situation so greatly improved has filled me with immense happiness. And I have a solution to your dilemma: Lavender Cottage, the home I lived in when I was newly widowed. It resides on my estate, and I would be only too happy to let it to you. Please come at your earliest convenience. I am anxious to introduce you to a group of women here who I think will be of utmost help in your situation.

My friendship,
Lillian

An award winning author, including the GOLD in Foreword INDIES Book of the Year Awards, **Jen Geigle Johnson** discovered her passion for England while kayaking on the Thames near London as a young teenager. She still finds the great old manors and castles in England fascinating and loves to share bits of history that might otherwise be forgotten. Whether set in Regency England, the French Revolution, or Colonial America, her romance novels are much like life is supposed to be: full of brave heroes, strong heroines, and stirring adventures.

A Promise Forgotten

Heather B. Moore

1

Mrs. Charlotte Ashford adjusted her black bonnet and black shawl, but there was no help for keeping the drizzling rain off. Even baby Emily was getting wet, despite Charlotte's attempts to cover up her nearly one-year-old daughter.

But who'd ever been successful at keeping a one-year-old contained? And today's dreary day and drearier circumstances were no help.

For today, Charlotte was saying a final goodbye to her husband, and to his extended family and all that she'd known for the past two years.

"I don't know when we'll be able to pay our respects again, Daniel," Charlotte said. "But I thought I should update you on Emily's progress. She doesn't walk yet, but she is pulling herself up on furniture quite successfully."

As if to punctuate Charlotte's narrative, her child babbled, "Mama, mama."

"Yes, I'm your mama." Charlotte looked at her brown-eyed Emily. Brown eyes like Charlotte and Charlotte's father. Emily also had dark-as-night hair and a perpetually pouty mouth. Also like Charlotte. In fact, Emily looked nothing like her father, Daniel. "But we're here to talk to your father. Can you say, *Papa*?"

"Mama," Emily promptly said, then used her dimpled hands to grab ahold of Charlotte's bonnet strings.

"No, dear," Charlotte said. "We'll get wetter if you do that."

As if the universe agreed, rivulets of rain cascaded from her bonnet and splashed against Emily's cheek.

Emily clapped her hand over her cheek. "Ow."

Charlotte really shouldn't smile, especially at a time like this, but the rain couldn't have hurt in the least. Yet Emily's reaction was darling.

"It didn't hurt," Charlotte said. "It's only water. See?" She held out her gloved hand, which was mostly wet, and Emily patted it.

"Mama!"

"I'm here," Charlotte said. "We need to say a proper goodbye to Papa. Can you help me?" She took a step closer to the grave marker of the Ashford family cemetery, the spiky grass slippery beneath her shoes. None of the other family members had come out with her, and it was just as well. Charlotte wanted to do this final farewell on her own.

"Goodbye, Daniel. We will always remember you, and we hope to return someday."

"Bye-bye," Emily echoed. She tried to grab Charlotte's bonnet ribbons again.

"Yes, bye-bye," Charlotte whispered. If anything, the rain seemed to drive even harder, and the temperature seemed to sink even lower.

There was really nothing else to say, nothing that hadn't already been said to the silent grave marker displaying the name *Daniel Hugh Ashford*. Her late husband had been the vicar of a small hamlet a day's ride from Charlotte's childhood home in Somerset.

Charlotte turned from the lonely cemetery and made the

trek to the manor where her next part of the day would begin. The part she dreaded even more than saying a final farewell to her late husband. For, today, she'd be traveling back to Somerset—a place she'd thought she'd never return to, unless it was to preside over her mother's deathbed. Even now, a shiver traveled Charlotte's spine at the thought of living under her mother's thumb.

But there was no alternative.

Daniel had left her no legacy, his inheritance had already passed to his younger brother, and the vicarage had been taken on by another man. Thus, Charlotte had been living on charity for all this time, and it was either the Ashfords' charity or her mother's.

Her mother had won out, and Charlotte hoped to high heaven she would not regret it. There had been little communication between the two women, primarily because Charlotte's marriage to Daniel Ashford had been a last resort to save her from becoming a spinster.

The only person Charlotte regularly communicated with from Somerset was her oldest and dearest friend, Thea, whose full name was Lady Dorothea Gravesend, Baroness of Blackdene.

Charlotte, you must return to Somerset. My days are so long and uneventful. We will fill them together. And I have yet to meet your darling Emily. Please consider returning. I'll come up with something to bribe you with if necessary.

Much love, Thea.

Oh, how Charlotte missed Thea.

They'd played together as girls, and they'd gone to the same finishing school. They'd planned out their futures together. Thea would marry a duke, and Charlotte would marry a baron.

None of that happened. No, Thea had married a baron, Lord Reginald Gravesend, who was twenty years her senior. And Charlotte? She'd married a vicar. Not exactly by choice, though.

"There you are," a sharp voice rang out as the front door to the manor swung open. Daniel's sister-in-law, Mary, motioned for Charlotte to hurry inside.

"Don't dally," Mary said. "We've supper on, and then the carriage will be here soon after." Her narrowed gaze landed on Emily. "You're going to make your own child ill by taking her out into the rain. Shameful, just shameful."

Mary disappeared into the dark hall of the manor. No one in the Ashford family would ever consider lighting a candle on a rainy day, so Charlotte stepped into the dim interior of the place she'd called home since her marriage.

She'd only been married to Daniel for a few months before he died. It wasn't until several weeks following his untimely death from lung disease that Charlotte had discovered she was with child. It was a miracle, really, that Charlotte had conceived at all. Her husband had only visited her bedroom twice during their marriage. But that was her secret.

"Are you hungry, Emily?" Charlotte asked her daughter.

"Mama!"

Emily knew more words than just *Mama*, but perhaps she was tired—a foreboding thing since it wasn't even midday yet. And they still had a long journey ahead of them.

The dining table hadn't been set, which meant they were to eat in the kitchen. Another testament to Charlotte of why it was time to leave. She was in the way, she was a burden, she was only there on the good graces of Daniel's brother and sister-in-law.

His brother was nowhere in sight, not that Charlotte expected any sort of friendly goodbye. No.

"Well, sit down," Mary said. "You can mash up whatever Emily likes."

"All right, thank you." Charlotte kept her daughter close and made sure she got a few bites into her.

The meal was silent since Mary kept her two children upstairs in the nursery. She certainly didn't approve of Charlotte doing everything for Emily, but Charlotte had no funds to pay a nurse, so there was little choice. Her dowry had gone to improving the vicarage, and with her father now passed away and her mother keeping a tight fist on all financial matters, Charlotte merely existed day to day.

That would all change soon. Charlotte didn't know how, but she was determined to make it so. She'd find a way to gain her independence. Perhaps she'd work in a shop or take on embroidery commissions. Her mother would certainly cry foul, but how else was Charlotte to provide for her daughter?

The carriage couldn't come soon enough, and when it did, the driver hefted Charlotte's single trunk—the one that contained Charlotte's only possessions in all the world. Now it sat strapped to the back of the carriage, getting soaked by the rain.

Mary watched the goings-on but said nothing, while she folded her hands in front of her and kept her mouth set into a prim line. Her dark clothing was indicative of mourning for Daniel, which Charlotte had worn as well. But the year had been up for some time now, and she planned to don lighter colors once she reached Somerset.

Charlotte looked from the waiting carriage to her sister-in-law. Should they not embrace in farewell?

But Mary made no move nor gave any sign of accepting affection.

Well then.

"I will write and keep you updated on Emily," Charlotte

said. "If there is anything that you need from me, do let me know."

Mary gave the briefest of nods, and Charlotte could almost feel the admonition of *Please go now* rolling off the woman's shoulders.

Charlotte carried her child into the carriage and settled in after drawing the rug about her lap.

She should be happy about leaving relatives such as Mary and her husband. Leaving the sorrow that seemed to never take a break from their lives. Leaving the unspoken accusations of Daniel's death somehow being due to Charlotte's negligence of her husband's health.

All of it had weighed her down.

But the guilt only twisted in her belly, morphing into a new worry—that of returning to Somerset. True, living with her mother didn't help with Charlotte's apprehension, but there was more. Much more. Somerset was also the town of her broken dreams and her crushed heart.

For the man she'd believed she'd someday marry, the man she'd been in love with since she was thirteen years of age, had been found alive.

2

IT WAS NO small feat to return from the dead and reclaim your property and inheritance from a cousin who thought that his entire future had been set.

But that was what Hildebrand Parry had faced upon his rescue over a year ago. The ship leaving India's coast had indeed been ravaged by a typhoon, and just as the newspapers had reported, Brand had been swept into the sea.

Yet in contrast to the blaring headlines, Lord Hildebrand Parry, Baron of Wilshore, had not died.

He was a strong swimmer, and the ship hadn't been more than a mile offshore since the captain had been doing everything possible to make it back to land. Although Brand had thanked his lucky stars that he'd not been drowned, he'd lost all manner of identification.

He had no way to persuade the next ship's captain that he was indeed a wealthy baron from Somerset and that he would make good on any payments once land was reached on the Crown's shore.

No, Brand had found himself working the docks like any common laborer. And after he was finally signed on as a sailor, he had deserted the crew at the first touch of English soil. Brand had never looked back.

Nine months wasn't really so long to be thought missing, was it? Apparently for his mother and sister, it had been a lifetime, and all estate matters had been transferred into the illustrious Percival Parry's meaty fingers.

"You're deep in thought," a woman said from the door of his study.

Brand turned to see his sister, Thea, standing in the doorway. Her pale-gold hair was drawn into an elaborate twist, and her blue eyes, so much like his, were alive with merriment. She'd been married in his absence to an older gentleman, Lord Reginald Gravesend, Baron of Blackdene. Their lands and holdings were on the south side of Somerset, so Brand saw his sister at least once a week. He suspected it would have been more if his mother were still alive.

But, alas, she'd passed away before he returned to England.

"You've come to interrupt my day, haven't you?" Brand said, rising from his chair to greet his sister.

"I must exercise my talents, brother," Thea said with a coy smile.

Brand chuckled as he crossed the room, then he bent to kiss her cheek.

She smelled of lavender, reminding him of their mother. Yet his sister was a softer version of the stoic Baroness Wilshore. Nothing had gone amiss when his mother was alive. Life was regimented, formal, and proper in every situation. In contrast, Thea was full of smiles and teasing, paralleled by her unfailing good humor and positive view of life.

"What brings you here so early?" Brand said. "Don't tell me you expect me to feed and entertain you all morning? You know I've business to attend."

"I know." Thea was unperturbed as she swept into the study, with its high windows letting in the morning light.

This room was perhaps Brand's favorite in the entire house. He hadn't changed a thing since his father's death some years before, and he probably never would.

Thea ran her fingers over the spines of a row of books on one of the bookcases, then paused by the windows overlooking the vast side lawns. "I've received correspondence that might interest you."

"Oh?" Brand leaned against the credenza and folded his arms. His sister was forever cajoling him to attend socials and musicals and other functions that he would rather avoid at all costs.

Thea turned and faced him, her expression a mixture of secrecy and delight.

"Don't tell me it's one of those frightful balls where I'll be expected to wear a starched cravat and ask every young miss to dance," he deadpanned. He'd gotten quite used to wearing the most casual of clothing in India, and the rough-woven clothing of a sailor on his journey home. Thus, he now avoided formal clothing whenever possible.

Thea's lips curved. "Nothing like that, dear brother. I know how you detest formal balls. My news is good, and it will interest you very much."

"Pray tell, dear sister," Brand said with mock begging. "Do not keep me in suspense any longer."

Thea drew in a deep breath and lifted her chin. "I've received word this morning that my dearest friend is returning to Somerset. She will be here by tonight."

All warmth left the conversation as Brand's stomach did a slow twist. Thea's *dearest friend* could only be one woman. And that woman had betrayed him in the worst way. No, it wasn't something he'd ever divulge, not even to his sister. So here he stood, facing his sister, waiting for her to twist a red-hot dagger straight into his heart.

Thea's smile had only broadened. "Can you believe it? Charlotte is coming home! With her baby! I will be the best godmother to ever walk the earth."

Brand heard every single word his sister had said. Each one had pounded its way into his soul. But he had absolutely no reply. And now Thea was striding toward him, her hands outstretched.

"It can be the three of us again," Thea gushed, grasping his hands, which had suddenly turned very cold. "Just like when we were young."

Thea continued to talk, but in truth, her words buzzed about like angry flies, growing louder and more insistent until Brand wanted to swat them away and lock the door to his study so that he wouldn't have to hear anymore.

But Thea didn't seem to notice, not one whit. She released his hands and fluttered past him. "I'll speak to your housekeeper about the tea."

Before Brand could complain that the very last thing he wanted to do was have tea with his sister and listen to more gushing about Mrs. Charlotte Ashford, his sister sped out of the room.

Brand closed his eyes. This could not be happening. Oh, but it seemed it was. And there was nothing he could do about it.

He scrubbed a hand through his hair, not caring if it stood up on all ends as a result. He'd have to be clever if he was to avoid all appearances of Charlotte. Perhaps he could pretend he'd contracted some horrible contagious illness only now made manifest. Or he could depart for London and ... what?

Another voyage to India might be in order. One in which he truly did not return.

But as he heard the echo of his sister's voice in the

hallway as she spoke with the housekeeper, Brand knew that he couldn't leave his beloved country again. The estate was his to run and care for. Both his parents were gone now, and it was up to him. There would be no hiding from Charlotte, so somehow, some way, he'd have to learn to coexist with the woman who'd taken his heart and never returned it.

3

CHARLOTTE DIDN'T KNOW why she was crying. She certainly hadn't meant to. But as the hired carriage pulled up the long drive to her mother's home, the tears had started. She suspected they were tears of stress and not because she was relieved to be home or relieved to be free of her in-laws. Or perhaps they were tears of self-pity. Charlotte was an expert at that.

"Emily, dear," she murmured against her baby's warm cheek. "We're almost home."

Home was a relative word.

As the carriage approached the manor house, so many memories threaded through her thoughts. The meandering stream where she'd played with Thea and *him* for hours when they were children. The wild roses that, no matter how often they were cut back, grew full-size again the very next week. The stable of horses where Charlotte used to have her pick of mares. No longer, she knew. Her mother had written last year that all the horses had been sold.

Her father's occupation as the owner of a textile mill had made them well-to-do. His will had stipulated that as long as his wife was still alive, she'd have all rights to the home and grounds. Upon her mother's death, Charlotte would receive a stipend, but the property and home would go to her father's nephew.

Even this home would be temporary for Charlotte.

The manor loomed, its appearance more shabby than Charlotte remembered. Had the windows always looked so sad? And the front gardens so neglected? Her mother had never written Charlotte for financial help, and it wasn't like she could have provided it anyway. A vicarage never had any surplus.

Still, Charlotte was surprised at the condition of the manor. And suddenly, all the stress she'd been feeling about *herself* and *her* situation morphed into worry and concern for her mother. Charlotte's fears were confirmed when the front door opened and a diminutive figure stepped out.

Charlotte's mother, Mrs. Lavina Rochester, had greatly changed.

Even as Charlotte stepped down from the carriage, she saw the gray in her mother's hair, the tired lines about her face, and a dress of outdated fashion. All the reservations and angst melted away, and Charlotte's eyes filled with tears for a different reason.

Her mother hovered on the porch, as if unsure how to greet Charlotte.

"Mother," Charlotte said, her voice only at half strength. "I'd like you to meet your granddaughter, Emily."

Her mother's eyes darted from Charlotte to Emily. "Oh. Goodness. She is so . . . small."

"She'll be one year old next month." Charlotte walked toward her mother as the carriage driver unloaded her trunk.

Emily's sleepy gaze settled on her grandmother, then back to Charlotte.

"Can you say, *Hello, Grandmother?*" Charlotte said in a sweet tone.

Emily's expression became more alert, and she looked again at her grandmother. "Mama?"

Charlotte held her breath, watching her mother's reaction. It wasn't quite the word for *grandmother*, but Emily hadn't ever discriminated between related words. Then Emily did something remarkable.

She reached a chubby hand toward her grandmother and said again, "Mama?"

Lavina Rochester's tired, worn face creased into a smile. "Is she talking to me?" she said, wonder in her voice.

"Yes, I believe so," Charlotte replied.

Her mother grasped Emily's hand. "She's so small and tender."

"Do you want to hold her?" Charlotte could see the hesitation as well as desire in her mother's eyes.

"Will she fuss?"

"I don't think so," Charlotte said, and in a moment, her mother was holding Emily.

"Mama." Emily patted her grandmother's cheek.

"Grandmama," Lavina said, her face lit up like the sun.

"Gama," Emily repeated.

Lavina laughed, and it was a laugh that Charlotte hadn't heard for a long time. A blessing to hear it now, because it was only at this very moment that Charlotte felt like she'd finally made a good decision in her life. Coming home had been right.

But the misgivings started up again the moment Charlotte stepped inside her childhood home. The place felt empty and cold. In fact, it felt like there had been no burning hearth for some time. She moved through the hall and paused at the entrance of the drawing room. The furnishings were gone, save for a settee and one wingback chair pulled close to the cold hearth.

She heard her mother thanking the carriage driver, then the front door shut.

The only sounds about the house were her mother's approaching footsteps. Where was everyone?

"Mother," Charlotte said, turning to face her. "What has happened? Where is all the furniture?"

Her mother held little Emily close, as if to ward off Charlotte's words. "I've had to sell some things," she said in a stilted voice. "There were some . . . debts that I only recently discovered. A solicitor notified me, and I've paid them down the best I could—" Her words broke off, and she looked away from Charlotte.

"How much did Father owe?" Charlotte was stunned, truthfully. Her father's mill had done well. He had talked about investing in other businesses and had been known to boast a time or two about how they'd profited.

Her mother's gaze returned to Charlotte's. "It's unseemly to speak of such things only moments after your arrival. Come into the kitchen. I have a stew on, and I daresay we could both use a little warm comfort."

Since Emily made no move to ask for her mama, Charlotte followed her mother through the house and toward the kitchen. Other things in the house were missing. The hall table that her mother used to take pride in stocking with a vase of fresh flowers. The missing great clock that used to tick away the time had left a gaping space on the wall. Also missing were the thick rugs her father had delivered one sunny day, and gone was the gilt mirror that used to hang near the staircase.

All of it was gone. Replaced by loneliness and dust.

Charlotte wondered how long this had gone on—her mother living like this. And when she stepped into the kitchen, by far the coziest room in the house, she was struck with the simplicity once again. There was a small fire in the cooking stove, and the room was much warmer.

And her mother cooking? She had cooked early in her marriage, but for most of Charlotte's childhood, they'd had a housekeeper, a cook, and a man-of-all-work.

Regardless, the stew smelled delicious, and Charlotte was suddenly ravenous. "Let me help," she told her mother, because Charlotte was pleased that Emily was so content right now.

So Charlotte ladled stew into two bowls and set them on the table. Emily chattered with her nonsensical babble but kept her audience captivated. It was always that way with her baby. Even on the hardest, most discouraging days, Emily brought in light and joy.

A knock on the front door made everyone pause.

"Who could that be?" her mother said in such a way that Charlotte wondered how often her mother received visitors.

It was true that evening was fast approaching, but her mother's face had paled considerably. So Charlotte offered, "Should I answer it?"

"Yes, that would be helpful." Her mother clutched Emily a bit closer.

Charlotte nodded and rose to her feet. Emily didn't protest Charlotte walking out of the room; nevertheless, she hurried to the front door. The hall was much cooler, and she fought off a shiver before she swung open the heavy door.

"Charlotte!" said an elegant woman, with beautiful blond hair peeking out from a lovely hat. "You're here! You're really, really here!"

In less than a second, Charlotte was swept into her best friend's arms. The fine silk of her dress and the wonderful fragrance of her hair were sore reminders of what Charlotte had missed living as a vicar's wife.

"You came," Charlotte breathed, then pulled away to survey Thea.

"Of course I came, you goose," Thea said, her beautiful smile radiant.

Behind her stood a carriage with the family crest of Wilshore.

"Are you staying at Wilshore?" Charlotte had to ask. Thea and her husband lived at the Blackdene Estate south of Somerset.

"I am," Thea gushed. "Isn't it wonderful? I told my husband I'd be gone two nights so that I can catch up with my dear Charlotte."

This amused Charlotte greatly since it was less than a half hour's ride between the two properties. Wilshore was easily walking distance from Charlotte's home as well. But Thea had always been gifted with extravagant gestures. Besides, dark would fall soon.

"Come in, come in," Charlotte said, tugging Thea by the hand. "I have someone for you to meet."

"Gracious," Thea said as she stepped inside. "It's been ages since I've been in your home."

Charlotte knew her smile was too bright. What Thea must think of the place . . . Charlotte had been shocked herself. But Thea was too much of a lady to comment on the disrepair of the home.

Footsteps sounded from the kitchen area, along with the babbling of Emily. "Mama?"

"Oh my, she's beautiful," Thea breathed, tugging off her gloves and crossing to meet Charlotte's mother in the middle of the hallway.

Without even a question, Thea took little Emily into her arms. "Aren't you the beautiful thing? Boys from all over the county will be dropping at your feet."

Charlotte laughed. "Don't give her any ideas. She's already waited on hand and foot."

"As she should be," Thea crooned, placing a kiss on the top of Emily's head.

Emily didn't fuss but looked enamored of the well-dressed woman who was paying compliments. Her brown eyes had widened, and her soft pink mouth mimicked a rosebud.

"She likes you," Charlotte said with a smile and a bit of relief. Shouldering the responsibility for Emily for so long had been overwhelming. But now, two other women were completely doting on her.

"Tomorrow," Thea began in a cheerful tone, "we must give Emily the grand tour of Somerset. And then we'll dine at Wilshore. It will all be informal, of course, because I don't want this darling child tucked away in some faraway nursery."

Charlotte didn't have the strength to turn down her friend right now. The day had been long and arduous. But tomorrow . . . Charlotte would have to find some excuse. For the last place she intended to step foot on was any part of Wilshore Estate.

4

"IT'S APPALLING AND disgraceful, I tell you," Thea said, her hands on her hips, her pretty face furrowed in determination.

Not often did Brand see his sister so upset over any matter. Of course, this one concerned her dearest friend, but he also wondered if she was exaggerating. For if Thea was to be taken at her word, the neighboring estate of the Rochester family had completely fallen apart.

"When was the last time you visited Mrs. Rochester?" Thea asked in a pointed tone.

Brand set down his fork at the dining table where he and his sister were breaking their fast. He couldn't exactly remember when he'd last been to Rochester Estate. He'd made every effort to not cross any part of their grounds.

"That long?" Thea said, her tone too high-pitched for comfort.

Brand met his sister's steely gaze. "I don't remember the *exact* day, but surely it hasn't been all that long. And I would have noticed vast amounts of crumbling, as you have claimed."

"Have you visited since you returned from India?"

His sister was direct, he'd give her that. Besides, he'd had no reason to call upon the mother of the woman he thought would be waiting for him upon his return. Even if he'd been presumed dead for a handful of months. Truly . . . no man in his right mind—

"Hildebrand," Thea cut in. "Are you even listening to me?"

"I *am* listening," he said. "Now what were you saying?"

Thea smirked. "Don't turn this into a joke. This is a serious issue. Mrs. Rochester didn't even have a fire in her hearth."

Brand lifted a shoulder. "Perhaps it was too early in the day for a fire."

"It was nearly dark," Thea said. "And you know that even though summer is just around the corner, the nights are still chilly." She folded her napkin neatly, then stood from her place.

Brand rose to his feet too, in a show of acknowledging her departure. Thea moved away from her chair, and Brand sank back onto his.

"Oh, no you don't, brother," Thea said, motioning for him to stand again. "You're coming with me."

Brand's mouth opened to protest, but his sister overrode him.

"If you think I'm batty, then you can tell me after our visit," Thea continued. "But until then, we're going over to the Rochesters' so that you can see for yourself."

"Surely I don't need to—"

Thea fixed him with a stare that could have stopped a French army in its tracks.

"All right," Brand murmured, duly chastised. He speared another bite of his ham.

"I'll be down in ten minutes," Thea said, triumph in her voice. Then her gaze perused the length of Brand. "Is that what you're going to wear?"

He looked down at his person. His breeches were a light-camel color, and he wore a waistcoat over his shirt but no type of jacket. No cravat either. "This is what I'm wearing." He met his sister's gaze, wondering if she was going to challenge him on it. She would have been appalled at the number of times he'd been shirtless on the ship while he worked as a sailor.

Instead, she merely pursed her lips and vacated the room.

At last, a little peace and quiet, yet that was no good either. Peace and quiet gave him time to think about the other occupant of the Rochester manor. *Charlotte.* She would be there this morning, no doubt. And apparently, Brand was about to rip off the bandage of their past in one fell swoop.

There was no time like the present, he supposed. It would be better than meeting by chance at one of those dreadful socials his sister was sure to drag him to eventually.

By the time Thea had come downstairs with her gloves pulled on, her hat in place, and a pelisse about her shoulders, Brand had quite steeled himself to face whatever the events of the day would bring.

After all, he was a survivor of many physical challenges—so he might as well throw his heart into the ring.

"Let's walk," Thea said, her gaze scanning him again.

"And ruin your dainty slippers?"

She lifted the hem of her skirt to reveal the toe of a fine leather boot. "I'm prepared, dear brother."

Brand smiled. "Very well, then. Let's be off." He kept his tone light, when in truth his pulse had started a slow thrum, increasing in pace the closer they grew to the border between the two lands. Rochester Estate was much smaller than Wilshore, yes, and at one point, Brand's father had attempted to buy the place.

The late-spring weather had produced an abundance of flowers about the properties, threading through the trees and bordering the paths. Another pang struck Brand as he wondered if Charlotte still collected and pressed flowers. In her youth, she'd made all manner of bookmarks and included pressed flowers in her correspondence. He'd once been the recipient. And no, he wouldn't admit he still had the letter and the intact flower tucked away. Somewhere.

The moment Brand saw the Rochester manor, he understood what his sister was speaking of. Neglected grounds were the first indicator, and the house itself had a sagging look to it, as if repairs had been in order for quite some time. Mr. Rochester had been deceased for years, yet Mrs. Rochester had continued to run a fine home. What had changed?

Thea wasted no time in knocking on the front door of the manor, and Brand's heart seemed to echo her sturdy knock. In only moments, he'd see Charlotte again. She was a married woman—well, widowed—and he wondered what sort of changes had come over her.

Surely he'd changed as well. One of those changes had been to lock his heart completely tight.

The door creaked open, and Brand released a breath.

The woman standing before them was Mrs. Rochester, much altered from his memory. She'd aged, to be sure, but she also looked diminutive. And that had never been a descriptor for the woman.

"Lord Wilshore?" Her gaze shifted. "Lady Blackdene! How nice to see you again."

Brand bowed, then lifted his head, assessing the hallway behind Mrs. Rochester while trying not to be overly obvious about it. The place was bare. Completely bare. He scarcely hid his frown while Thea spoke.

"It seems I can't stay away from visiting you and Charlotte," Thea said. "I'm already missing Emily. Is she awake yet?"

"Oh yes." Mrs. Rochester tucked some hair beneath her lady's cap. "That child has been up since dawn. Fussing, too. Charlotte has her in the back gardens now. Seems to be soothing."

Brand released a breath. Charlotte was not inside the house, then. A small reprieve. One to be relieved over?

"Well then, perhaps we'll join her in the garden?" Thea suggested.

"Oh, she would love to see you both," Mrs. Rochester said, her smile sad.

Brand wondered at the sadness in her smile. This was not the woman he remembered—the woman who was stiff and prim and unyielding. Ironically, similar in personality to his own deceased mother.

Mrs. Rochester drew the door open wider. "Come through here, if you please. The garden paths on the side of the house are quite unruly this time of year."

Brand followed the women through the hallway, and they passed a few rooms that looked to be shut off. He noticed the missing spaces on the walls. Not that he remembered the portraits or paintings that used to hang there, but the discolored wallpaper was clue enough. The rear doors of the house opened onto a terrace.

This terrace Brand remembered, although it was much altered now. The clay pots were not filled with blooming flowers but looked barren. The trellis of roses were wild and full of thorns. And just beyond, the fountain that used to burst with clear water was now silent and murky.

"Charlotte," Mrs. Rochester called. "You have visitors."

A murmured reply came, and Brand couldn't help looking in the direction of the voice.

There, rising from the bench on the far side of the fountain, was a woman with an abundance of dark hair. She was taller than he remembered. No, that couldn't be possible. It was the lift of her chin, the erect level of her shoulders, and how her hair was up, not down as he remembered it being so many times.

Charlotte wasn't taller. She'd grown up—into a woman. Just as he'd become a man.

And she was beautiful.

Brand wasn't sure if the heart could recall the past in such minute detail, but it appeared his could, because this first glimpse of Charlotte Rochester Ashford told him he had not gotten over her after all.

The knot in his stomach began to fray, making him feel out of sorts. He needed a drink, a strong drink, and perhaps another one after that. In fact, he wouldn't stop until he forgot the shape of Charlotte's face, the depth of her dark-brown eyes, the way that even though her hair was pinned up, he could vividly imagine how it would tumble about her shoulders.

Brand had survived a shipwreck, he'd spent days surviving off the land, he'd worked like a common laborer on the docks of a foreign country, he'd sailed the high seas manning rigging as a sailor ... But never had his mind been so disjointed as it was now, coming face-to-face with Charlotte.

"Thea," she said. "You've returned."

Her voice was familiar yet lower in tone than he remembered.

"Oh, Charlotte," Thea said. "I hope we haven't awakened Emily."

"No." Charlotte's smile turned up the corners of her dusty-pink lips. "She is deep asleep. She's quite worn herself out."

Charlotte walked toward them, and Brand's gaze shifted to the child in her arms.

The frayed knot in his stomach splintered completely. Charlotte had married a man who wasn't him. Charlotte had conceived and borne a child with that man. She was a mother now, first and foremost.

And he was staring, quite openly.

Charlotte was looking at him, too, although her gaze flitted away as she spoke to Thea. "I'm afraid I'm not much entertainment," Charlotte said.

"Oh, nonsense," Thea said. "The social whirl is tiring, and my husband wants to spend most evenings in. So visiting my dearest friend and her darling child is easily the best part of my day."

Charlotte smiled.

Brand should have worn his jacket, if only to provide a barrier to how that smile nudged against his heart. Here he was, unable to look away from a woman who had chosen another man over him. Brand must enjoy punishment very much.

"You are well, Lord Wilshore?"

It took him the space of a heartbeat for him to realize Charlotte had spoken to him.

"Yes." His reply was perhaps curt, but he dared not say more. He needed to get ahold of his emotions before saying anything else.

"He cleans up well," his sister teased. "You should have seen him upon his return. You'd have thought he was born a pauper."

Charlotte smiled again, but there was a depth to her eyes that told Brand that she was curious. Well, she'd have to live with that curiosity. No one knew the extent of his experiences, and no one ever would.

"Can I hold her?" Thea asked.

And once again the conversation had shifted.

"Are you sure?" Charlotte asked as she handed over the sleeping child, who had hair the same color as her mother's.

Brand swallowed past the lump in his throat.

"I'll take her and set her down in her crib," Thea offered.

"Let me show you the way," Mrs. Rochester said.

And just like that, Brand found himself standing at the edge of the terrace alone with Charlotte.

5

WHEN CHARLOTTE HAD first opened her eyes this morning and guessed at how her day was about to go, the guess hadn't included Lord Wilshore walking into her garden just as she got Emily to sleep in her arms.

She had to think of him as Lord Wilshore because the alternative—Brand, or Hildebrand—felt much too ... friendly ... intimate somehow. They'd been childhood friends, but both of their childhoods were far, far in the past. Years in the past.

And now, here he stood, looking everywhere but at her. When only moments before, he'd been staring at her quite candidly.

He'd changed. Physically. His blond hair was a darker gold now, longer than she remembered it ever being. And the blue of his eyes had taken on more gray. The angle of his jaw had sharpened, and his shoulders were broad, made even more obvious by his lack of a jacket. Yes, he seemed lean, almost too lean if she were to judge. Perhaps it was because he'd grown taller, by at least a couple inches.

Charlotte fought back the urge to rush after her mother and Thea. Emily could awaken and fuss again if not set down just so. Then the process of soothing her would begin anew.

Yet she knew that fleeing from the presence of Lord Wilshore would be rude. And that was the last thing she wanted to be, for she owed him an explanation at the very least.

She'd promised to wait for him, that last night before he left Somerset to travel to the harbor and set sail for India. One year, he'd said. One year, she'd agreed. She'd wait for him.

She'd thought he might steal a kiss, but he said he wanted something to look forward to. He'd pulled her close and whispered that at the very first ball they attended when he returned, he'd dance with her three times. Send the gossip tongues wagging. And then he'd kiss her. From that point on, there would be little doubt of their future together. As husband and wife.

But he had never returned. They had never danced, let alone three times. And that kiss had never happened.

News of his death had hit all the English newspapers, and the weeks and months passed, until Charlotte had finally agreed to marry another man. Not for love—that had never been possible after losing so much. With Brand gone, it hadn't mattered much who she married, and her dowry only attracted so many suitors. Daniel had seemed the logical choice at the time. But oh, how wrong it had been.

Charlotte had never thought she could grieve more than when she'd heard of Brand's death. She'd been wrong about that too. She'd grieved even more deeply when she heard of his return. Because of what might have been.

What he must think of her now.

"It is good to see you well, Mrs. Ashford," he said, his deep tone a matured male voice.

His words were simple, yet pain lanced through her at how he'd called her by her married name.

"Lord Wilshore," she began, hating the tremble in her voice. "I was so pleased to hear of your . . . rescue."

"Were you?" Something hard flashed in his eyes.

"Yes," she breathed. "If you only knew how much I . . ." Her voice faltered. What could she say? How much she'd missed him? How much she regretted her marriage? If she regretted it, then she would be the worst mother, because little Emily had been her salvation. The man before her didn't seem amenable to that admission.

And he'd changed more than physically.

She could see that in the blue of his eyes, in the set of his jaw, in the way he seemed to be bigger than everything in the garden.

"How much you *what* . . . Mrs. Ashford?"

"Don't call me that," she said before she could stop herself. She was so mortified by her outburst that she turned from the intensity of his gaze.

"What shall I call you, then?"

He was not going to let this rest. Why couldn't he excuse himself and go into the house? Or better yet, leave the property?

"I think we know each other well enough to skip formalities." Although she, too, had called him by his title. "And . . . I owe you an explanation for . . . the past."

She glanced at him. There was no expression on his face. Only a watchful waiting.

Her breath felt faint, and her thumping pulse heated her neck. "When I heard of the shipwreck, I—"

"Come in, you two," her mother called out from the back doors. "I've set a tea, and Thea says she has some important things she wants to discuss."

The interruption was both a blessing and added torture. Charlotte hadn't any idea what she was about to say to Brand. And now they'd have to delay the conversation, which would only create more sleepless nights for her.

"All right," Charlotte said in an even tone.

Brand motioned for her to go ahead of him. It wasn't like she expected to walk with him into the house, arm in arm. That would have been too formal. Yet feeling his gaze boring into her back as she joined her mother inside the house wasn't her first choice either.

Once inside the house, they walked to the kitchen, where tea was laid out. It was no secret now that the drawing room had been emptied of furniture. Tea in the kitchen would have never happened in any gentry folk's home.

Thea was all smiles, though, and didn't seem bothered by the reduced circumstances that Charlotte still had to figure out. What had happened to her father's stipend, and why hadn't her mother said a word?

"Emily went down like an angel," Thea reported as Lavina poured the tea. "And we won't stay long, because I'm sure you need to catch up on *your* rest."

Charlotte felt Brand's gaze land on her again. She supposed she did look tired, because she was tired. Traveling, in addition to the past months and, well, years of hardships eventually took its toll.

"Thank you," Charlotte told her mother as she accepted the tea. She took a sip and nearly winced at how watered-down the tea was. If she weren't in such mixed company she'd add extra sugar to it.

"Well, I'll get right to the point," Thea said. "Charlotte, do you remember Lady Joanna Kingswood, the dowager marchioness?"

Charlotte remembered Lady Joanna enough to know she'd been widowed twice.

"She's begun a new society recently," Thea said. "And I think you'll be perfect for it."

Charlotte blinked. Lady Joanna and the Rochesters had never moved in the same circles. Yes, if they happened to be at the same social, there might be a brief greeting. "What sort of society?"

"A secret one," Thea said, her expression smug.

"If it's so secret, how did you find out about it?" Brand asked, his tone dry.

"Because . . ." Thea's eyes sparkled. "I know everything in Somerset. So of course I'd know about this."

"Of course," Brand echoed.

Thea leaned forward and clasped Charlotte's hand in hers. "It will be just the thing for you, my dearest friend. You need association with those who are your age and in your same shoes."

Charlotte frowned. Whatever could Thea mean?

"Lady Joanna has started a Secret Society for Young Widows." Thea sat back in her chair, a satisfied smile on her face. "From what I understand, there is quite the gathering at her high tea events. Think of it, Charlotte, all those women who have been through what you have. It will be wonderful bonding."

Charlotte blinked, then blinked again. *Wonderful bonding?* That sounded so . . . so . . . cold. As if being a young widow was something to base a social life around.

She began to shake her head as she formulated a reply. "I don't think so," she said. "I can't imagine being in a roomful of other widowed women. It would all be quite maudlin."

Thea's brow pinched. "I'm sure it wouldn't be like that. Lady Joanna is a lively sort. A woman who makes the best out of any difficult situation."

Charlotte hadn't time to come up with a reply before Thea pressed on.

"The estate is beautiful. You should go just to see the place up close." Thea smiled as if she'd just solved a complicated puzzle and everyone should thank her for it.

"I think Charlotte needs some time to adjust to Somerset

again," Brand cut in. "She has recently moved and has a young child to care for."

All eyes turned toward Lord Wilshore. Charlotte was surprised at his words; they almost seemed ... considerate. *Caring* would be too much of a stretch.

"That's precisely my point, brother," Thea said. "She needs support and friendship from women who are in her same situation. Even though I'm her best friend, I've never been widowed or had a child."

Brand's eyes flashed with something that Charlotte couldn't decipher. Unless it was the reminder that Charlotte had dismissed all thoughts of her loyalty to Brand and married another man.

To say the least, just because Brand seemed averse to the notion, Charlotte found herself quite intrigued. And quite determined to learn more. "Are there really so many young widows in Somerset as to warrant a society?"

Thea tilted her head. "I can't speak to a number, but even a handful would be worth the time. Either that or a scrumptious tea at Lady Joanna's."

Charlotte smiled, although she'd feel completely out of place at the home of Lady Joanna. She'd been a marchioness at one point, for heaven's sake, and her son was a current marquess. "I will consider it," she said, not knowing if she'd even be invited to such a society. How did one go about inquiring?

She returned her focus to drinking more tea. Although she felt Brand's gaze on her—assessing, most likely—she wasn't about to give him any clues to her thoughts. It was none of his concern anyway. She felt guilty enough for her past decisions, and seeing him this morning had brought it all roaring back.

In fact, as soon as they left, she'd join her daughter in a nap.

6

"You've got to do something, Brand," Thea said as they trudged back to Wilshore.

"*Me?* Why should *I* be involved?" he muttered, perhaps a bit too articulately.

Thea stopped dead and turned to face him with a huff. "They're our neighbors. Well, *your* neighbors, more specifically. There's no reason their estate should be so ill-managed. It's like Mrs. Rochester has wool between her ears or something. I can't believe that their funds can be so low."

Brand frowned. "What do *you* know about managing an estate? It's obvious that whatever you've heard about their financial affairs was exaggerated over the years. Perhaps Mrs. Rochester has a secret fetish and spends all her money on French perfume."

Thea slapped his arm. "Oh, stop. You have eyes just like mine, and not even you could say things are right over there. We must help them."

Helping the Rochesters would involve speaking to them, among other things, such as sticking his nose in business he didn't want to be a part of. Because if there was one thing that was certain, Brand knew that no matter how tightly he'd locked his heart against Charlotte, he could still feel the pain of her betrayal when he looked at her.

He'd thought he'd been over her, completely over her, but now...

"We need a plan," his sister said as she started walking again. "But we have to be sly about it, because Mrs. Rochester certainly has her pride."

Brand hid a sigh. "Perhaps I can put in a few discreet inquiries through my solicitor, Mr. Wright."

"See?" Thea crooned, linking her arm through his. "Was that so hard?"

Despite his aversion to getting involved with anything to do with Mrs. Rochester or her daughter, Brand chuckled at his sister's determination. The morning sun had warmed considerably, and he decided it would be a good day to take out his new hunting dogs that he'd purchased last week. He had some training to do to get them into top shape for the fall hunt.

But his sister wasn't through with him yet. "Let's invite them for supper tonight," Thea said. "Mrs. Rochester looks as if she needs a little cheering up. And poor Charlotte. What an ordeal."

Brand didn't reply but instead tightened his jaw so that he wouldn't say anything too revealing to his sister. *Poor Charlotte indeed.* What about poor Hildebrand? *He* was the one who'd been shipwrecked, *he* was the one who'd worked and slaved his way back to England, *he* was the one who had to go through an extensive legal battle with their cousin to regain all rights to the property, *he* was the one who'd discovered upon his return that not only was another man occupying his house but another man had married the woman he'd pledged his heart to.

How long? he wanted to ask Charlotte. How long had she waited to marry after learning that he was missing? *Missing* was the significant word here. He'd been reported lost at sea, not dead.

"Not dead," he muttered.

"What?" Thea said, looking up at him.

He cleared his throat. "*Instead* of supper, what if you invite them to tea this afternoon, so it can be a more casual affair with the ladies? I don't want to intrude."

His sister looked at him like he'd grown a horn on his forehead.

"Sometimes I wonder what is knocking about in that head of yours, Hildebrand." She released his arm and gathered her skirts to hurry up the stairs to the front door. "I'll speak to the housekeeper about tea and send an invite to the Rochesters. And then I daresay there's a bit of housekeeping to order too. Really, Brand, the front drawing room needs to be dusted and winter drapes changed for the summer ones."

All of this was said in a flurry of words, followed by Thea disappearing inside his home.

Brand paused on the first step, his foot perched on the edge. *Blast.* It seemed his sister would not be dissuaded from her course, which meant that he'd need to come up with his own plan of action.

Mind made up, he strode into the house and composed a letter to his solicitor. Once that was delivered to his valet to post, Brand headed to the stables. The horses were all in fine form, and the day was already too warm to take a morning ride. He'd given that up to accompany his sister on her mad errand.

His dogs were another matter. No one knew this, but he credited a dog for saving his life in India. No, the dog didn't pull him out of the water, but as Brand was lying upon the beach he'd awakened to a dog licking his face. The tide was coming in, and Brand didn't know how much longer he would have stayed unconscious.

"Mabel and Racer, let's go," he said, teasing the two young hunting dogs as he walked to the back of the stable.

Both of them barked, but only once, in response to Brand's greeting. The two English setters were already handsome dogs, and they were well on their way to becoming fully trained.

Brand bent to scratch both of the dogs' heads. Caring for a dog or two was the least he could do after his experiences in India. He whistled for them to join him, and they both raced out of the barn and into the sunlight. Brand chuckled at the sight. He'd let them run, then call them back soon enough.

For the next couple of hours, Brand worked with the dogs, teaching them to follow his commands. He hadn't realized how far on his property he'd gotten until he'd crossed the meadow that bordered the Rochester lands.

Brand paused and told his dogs to rest, and while they sat in a patch of shade, Brand surveyed the place. Nothing about this meadow had changed over the years, and Brand suddenly realized it was the place of his last meeting with Charlotte all those years ago.

Evening had fallen then, and the wildflowers had spread across the grass like a rug. Similar to how they were now. Brand moved to where the two dogs lay, and he sat in the grass alongside them, stretching out his legs.

The dappled sunlight coming through the trees was the perfect temperature, not too warm and not too cool. Unlike India, which was either hot or very hot. Brand tugged at a piece of grass, then twirled the blade between his fingers. There had been a time when Brand had wondered if he'd ever see his home again. Those times had been tough, and in order to keep his thoughts logical and focused on the future, he'd thought of Charlotte.

Despite the days of heat and backbreaking labor, Brand

had stayed motivated to find a way back to England. He couldn't bear the thought of not seeing his homeland and the woman he'd loved . . . Charlotte. It had always been Charlotte, even when he was thirteen and she but a girl of eleven. He remembered telling his parents one night that he was going to marry Charlotte Rochester.

His father had chuckled and said, "A man changes his mind many times. Just you wait."

But his mother hadn't looked so amused. In fact, later that night when everyone in the household had retired to bed, his mother came to visit him. Brand would never forget what she'd said to him.

"Son, there are some women you'll become infatuated with," she said. "That is completely natural. Even though you're young, you must understand that your future title of baron means that you'll have to choose a wife carefully. And I'm afraid that the daughter of a tradesman, such as Mr. Rochester, is below our family's social status."

Brand had understood what his mother had said, but he didn't want to agree with her. He soon found out that his mother would take every opportunity to remind him of his duty to the family name. As if marrying another titled woman would be the pinnacle of his life. He'd promised Charlotte that he'd take a stand against his mother once Charlotte was old enough to marry. She'd just reached her seventeenth birthday when he'd left for India, intent on educating himself on part of his father's business and returning with experience and a solid reputation. Returning as a man. Who would marry the woman he wanted to spend the rest of his life with.

But his mother had died, so there'd been no one to defend his choice of bride to. And he'd returned to discover that no bride waited for him.

Brand closed his eyes against the rising pain that twisted

hot in his chest. Would it ever ease? Living a short walk from Charlotte was not going to help matters. Perhaps... perhaps he should seek out a wife. He didn't expect to find a woman whom he was as passionate about as he used to be about Charlotte, but surely there was a woman out there for him. And perhaps his heart would begin to heal properly. Right now, there were still plenty of cracks in it.

Snap.

Brand blinked his eyes open and turned his head. Both of his dogs were on their feet, alert. Was someone nearby in the woods?

Another snap, this one louder. Too loud for a small animal.

Mabel barked.

"Hush, girl," Brand said immediately.

And he was about to rise to his feet when a blue dress came into view at the edge of the meadow.

Charlotte.

Breathe.

She affixed her gaze on Mabel. "Well, hello there, pretty thing. Who's your master?"

It would only be a matter of seconds before she saw him, so Brand climbed to his feet and stepped out of the copse of trees.

"Oh," Charlotte said, flinching. "I didn't see you." Her gaze darted to Mabel. "Is this your dog?"

Brand didn't miss the tremor in her voice. Was she nervous? He also didn't miss the book in her hands, and he wondered if she was pressing flowers into it. "This is Mabel and Racer."

Charlotte smiled at the dogs, who were eying her curiously. "Can I touch them?"

"Of course." And of course the dogs would make a snap decision that Charlotte was their new best friend.

Charlotte laughed as Mabel licked her and Racer nestled against her hand. "They're beautiful. Did you raise them?"

"Not quite." Brand should call the dogs and leave the meadow. It wasn't technically proper to be conversing with a young, single woman, despite the fact that they were neighbors and she a widow. Yet no one was about. "I purchased them a few weeks ago. They're young and full of enthusiasm, but their manners are coming along."

Charlotte's gaze remained on the dogs as she scratched their heads and gave them plenty of attention.

Brand's heart pricked. Perhaps he'd been too formal and dismissive of her. Perhaps if they talked things through, they could at least be cordial. But the knot in his stomach had returned, and the feeling of betrayal climbed up his throat. His gaze slid over Charlotte's bent head. Her abundant dark curls peeking beneath her bonnet, the slope of her elegant neck, the lace edging of her bodice, her ungloved hands scratching the dogs, the curve of her smile . . .

She was no longer a girl or a budding young woman. She was a mother. She was a widow. Out of mourning—that was clear by the pale blue of her dress. Invariably, Brand's thoughts shifted to Charlotte's relationship with her husband. A man she'd vowed to honor, love, and cherish. A man she'd shared a bed with . . . conceived a child with . . .

The anger was back. The jealous seeds sprouted into a full-grown tree. He recognized it for what it was, yet he despised himself for these cycling thoughts that never seemed to ebb.

"I should get them back and watered," Brand said, knowing his tone was clipped. He was back to his rigid formality.

Charlotte immediately straightened, her deep-brown eyes upon him. "Lord Wilshore, might I speak to you for a moment? I believe it is fortuitous that we are alone, and if you but grant me an audience, I would be deeply grateful."

Brand should claim a busy schedule, because his sinking heart told him the conversation would not be pleasant. Not in the least.

"Of course, Mrs. Ashford." He ordered the dogs to sit and be still. "As you wish."

The dogs looked between the two of them expectantly.

Charlotte bit her lip and nodded. "Thank you." And then her eyes filled with tears.

Blast.

The very air about them seemed to stall, waiting...

"I am so sorry, Brand," Charlotte said, her voice choking. "Please let me explain, even if you don't want to hear it."

She knew him so well, even after all these years.

"When I learned of the shipwreck, I could not believe it at first," she whispered. "I knew tragedy existed in the world. I'd lost my own father, and my relationship with my mother was strained. But to lose *you*... you were still young, and you had seemed so invincible."

Brand wanted to retort, but he didn't. He would hear her out this once. Then no more.

"I read all the papers that I could find," Charlotte continued. "I pestered Thea for any scrap of news, but she was swimming in her own well of grief. Your mother had died, and Wilshore Estate was in a major transition." She wiped at the tear sliding down her cheek.

Brand was above all emotion, though. He felt as if he was watching another couple having this conversation. The words and details had nothing to do with *him*.

"Then Thea married, almost the moment your cousin moved in and took over. It seemed that my entire childhood had been altered in a blink of an eye. You were thought dead.

Thea was married. Wilshore was no more. My mother and I weren't speaking. Each day the burdens only became heavier. I was sinking. Then my mother announced that a husband had been found for me, and Daniel Ashford would be arriving the following day to make introductions."

She broke off and looked down at the book clutched in her hands. More tears trickled down her cheeks.

Brand had to do everything in his power not to pull her into his arms. Soothe away the tears. Tell her that he understood. Her pain was his pain. But his body had stiffened, and the warm sun upon the meadow, drawing out the fragrance of the wildflowers, only felt like beauty mocking what was already broken.

"Daniel was . . . kind. He listened. He sympathized." She wiped at her tears, which seemed to have no end in sight. "I suppose that's one of the qualities of a vicar."

Her tone was ironic, even bitter.

She lifted her gaze to meet his again, and Brand's heart did jolt this time. In her gaze, he didn't see the tears of a sorrowing widow, but he saw a simmering fire . . . of anger.

He took a step back, as if the emotion vibrating from her was a physical assault on his person.

"Daniel Ashford was a good vicar," Charlotte said, her tone stronger now. "But as a husband . . . I don't think there's ever been a lonelier wife than me."

7

MORE THAN A week later, Charlotte was still wondering why she'd said all of that to Brand. Why had she disparaged her own husband? Her husband was dead, cold in his grave, and would never be able to defend his honor. Yet Charlotte's callused heart had spilled over the moment she'd started talking to Brand. Perhaps it was because she wanted to prove to him that she still . . . what? Cared for him? Regretted that she didn't wait for a few more months? Been more patient?

But the words had left her mouth, and she'd seen the shock and confusion on Brand's face.

Then she'd run from the meadow.

The dogs had barked at her sudden movement and fleeing footsteps. Brand had not said a word. He hadn't called after her. He hadn't pursued.

But what had she expected?

"Nothing," she whispered to herself as she waited for the butler to open the doors to the house of Lady Joanna. "He owes me nothing."

And *nothing* was exactly what had happened. Later that day Charlotte had gone to tea at Wilshore, but only Thea had been in attendance. It wasn't like Charlotte knew what she wanted to say to Brand anyway, should she see him again so soon. But there hadn't been an opportunity in the first place.

Thea had returned to her husband's estate with a promise to write every day. Charlotte had laughed, but it had proved to be true, and she found entertainment and delight in Thea's quips through her many letters.

Entertainment and delight were new things in Charlotte's world. The time at the vicarage had been quiet, too quiet. Oppressive, really—and she hadn't comprehended the full weight of it until she'd left.

The front door opened, and a butler with streaked gray hair nodded at her. "Ma'am? Might I announce your name?"

"Mrs. Charlotte Ashford," she said, unused to this type of formality. It caused her to straighten her spine and square her shoulders. Perhaps she should have worn one of her silk dresses instead of the muslin. Over the past week, she'd begun to alter her old clothing, finding that she'd developed more curves since having her baby. She was no slender young miss any longer.

As Charlotte stepped inside the grand hallway, with its thick rugs, a chandelier, and a gold-accented end table, a sense of awe and discouragement swept through her. This would never be her life—living in a beautiful home, living financially secure, with an abundance of friends.

She was even more aware that she was a quarter of an hour late when the sounds of light laughter and feminine voices fluttered from the drawing room.

The butler motioned for her to go inside the room, and after a couple of careful breaths, Charlotte walked in.

Immediately, the voices stopped and heads turned. The first person Charlotte saw was Lady Joanna. She sat regally amongst the group of women, as if she was a queen upon her throne. Her dress was a lustrous peach silk, quite bold, but it was fitting since Lady Joanna also wore pearls at her neck and a pearl headband set against her coiffed auburn hair.

Lady Joanna didn't rise to her feet but instead extended her hand. The multiple rings on her fingers twinkled in the sunlight streaming through the stately windows of the drawing room.

"Mrs. Ashford, I presume?" Lady Joanna said, her voice a low purr. "Welcome. Come in, and let us make introductions."

Since her hand was still outstretched, Charlotte continued to approach her. Then she grasped the lady's hand and gave a half curtsey. "It's a pleasure to meet you, my lady."

"Oh, we don't stand on ceremony here," Lady Joanna said. "Call me Lady Joanna."

Charlotte blinked.

"And you must meet Mrs. Penny Fletcher and Mrs. Georgia Givens," Lady Joanna said, indicating two women on one of the settees. "And this is Lady Anna Lyndham and Mrs. Lydia Steele. Next we have Mrs. Lillian Hunter, recently moved to Lavender Cottage."

Charlotte's mind was a whirl as the introductions continued. She tried to remember names, but within seconds they all flowed right out of her head.

"Now that we are all here and happily settled, we will begin with official business," Lady Joanna said. "As a few of you know, Charlotte Ashford has recently returned to Somerset. She lost her dear husband over a year ago, and she has a little girl by him."

Smiles and looks of sympathy flashed to Charlotte. She wasn't bothered by them, because all of these women had similar fates. Her shoulders relaxed a fraction.

"First, we will review the rules of the Secret Society of Young Widows," Lady Joanna continued in a firm voice as her gaze landed on each of the women. "You may repeat after me if you so desire." She paused. "First rule: your husband must be well and truly dead."

Charlotte's eyebrows lifted.

Mrs. Fletcher brought a wrinkled handkerchief to her nose.

"Second, your reputation must be intact," Lady Joanna said.

Charlotte straightened. She understood without further explanation what Lady Joanna was requiring.

The woman looked about the room, a sternness in her gaze. "Thirdly, you must never do something as foolish as to fall in love again."

Well. Charlotte was truly shocked, but it seemed the other women had heard this before.

Lady Joanna lifted a hand. "Now, falling in love might be an added measure to your marriage, but definitely not the reason you will get married again—*if* you remarry, that is." She drew in a regal breath. "If you do remarry, your husband-to-be must sign the Continuation of Care contract. This contract will detail how you will be provided for during your marriage and if you should be a widow a second time."

Charlotte felt quite out of breath. This was no charity society or gossip society but a society that sounded like it might . . . help her navigate the next few years.

Lady Joanna's deep-green gaze landed on Charlotte. "Now, the first order of business will be presented by Mrs. Givens."

The young woman with a rather narrow face, who looked only a year or two older than Charlotte, took the floor.

"Today, we will hear a lecture from Lady Joanna's solicitor, Mr. Norton. He will explain to us what to expect when meeting with a solicitor," Mrs. Givens said. "He will give us an idea of how to prepare and what questions to ask. At the end of his presentation, we will practice speaking to him and asking our questions."

Charlotte's eyes about bugged out. This was very forward-thinking. They were to *practice*? As if Charlotte would ever have a chance to meet with a solicitor. She supposed her mother had to every so often.

"Very good," Lady Joanna said. "Please show in Mr. Norton."

Mrs. Givens swept out of the room, on an eager errand, and only a moment later, a man entered. His shoulders were slightly hunched, and Charlotte guessed him to be at least sixty years old. His hair was nearly all white, but his light-blue eyes were as sharp as a hawk's.

Mr. Norton held a large book that Charlotte guessed was a ledger. In his other hand, he carried an inkpot and a quill pen. "Good afternoon, ladies," he said, a slight scratch to his tone. He gave a distinguished bow to the general room. "Shall we begin?"

The women about Charlotte seemed to either titter or freeze. Perhaps one or two felt as astonished as she.

Mr. Norton made an elegant figure as he strode across the room. He set the ledger on an end table and pulled it out a couple of feet, then he sat in the nearby chair.

"Now, ladies, the first thing to understand is that a solicitor is focused on the numbers in the columns and not so much on your personal preferences," he began. "Therefore, if there is an item or expense that is needful to you, you must speak up."

Lady Joanna clasped her hands together, a knowing gleam in her eyes. "For instance, my first husband didn't understand why I needed a different set of gloves for each dress. But it was important to me, so I had to speak up for myself in order to have an allowance especially for gloves."

A couple of appreciative murmurs arose among the women.

"When I was widowed the first time," Lady Joanna continued, "my financial circumstances were greatly reduced. I could no longer afford a pair of gloves for each dress."

Charlotte could say she was shocked to hear such frank conversation from a lady of high stature. It was mind-bending, to say the least.

"Thankfully, Mr. Norton, who has been my solicitor these many years, was kind and patient with me. He answered all of my questions."

The tips of Mr. Norton's ears pinked.

"So it is today that I am passing that knowledge onto you," Lady Joanna said. "You must learn to ask the right questions. Don't be afraid to look through the ledgers that your husband kept. Write down your questions this week, and at our next meeting, Mr. Norton will help you navigate them."

Mr. Norton nodded. "In my experience, nearly half of my clients either keep poor ledgers or deliberately hide information. This can result in future ruination."

At those words, Charlotte's stomach pinched. Something wasn't right in her mother's household, and Charlotte wondered if the clues could be found in her father's ledgers.

"Now," Mr. Norton continued, his sharp gaze moving among the women. "Who will be first?"

Everyone seemed to hold their breath.

"Mrs. Ashford," Lady Joanna declared. "Her mother has struggled with maintaining their modest estate, and it would behoove Mrs. Ashford to become educated without delay."

Charlotte guessed that her ears were now burning, and she was trying to decide if she should be offended by the outright criticism.

Lady Joanna must have anticipated such a scenario,

because she added, "Now, Mrs. Ashford. We are all friends here, but most importantly, nothing in these meetings ever leaves this drawing room. You can trust that whatever is divulged will go no farther than this room."

Charlotte's throat felt as dry as summer dirt, but she rose and crossed to the chair opposite Mr. Norton. She sat primly and folded her hands in her lap. Despite the fact that perspiration now prickled her neck, she was completely fascinated by what would take place next.

"Good afternoon, Mrs. Ashford," Mr. Norton said. "What may I help you with?"

Charlotte swallowed, then looked at the other women.

"Go ahead," Lady Joanna whispered. "Pretend we aren't here."

"Do I tell him what I'm worried about?"

Lady Joanna gave a triumphant nod.

So Charlotte met the light-blue gaze of the solicitor. "I'd been gone from Somerset due to my marriage, and when I returned home last week, my childhood home was nearly in ruins. I don't know how to approach the subject with my mother. Whenever I try to ask, she changes the topic swiftly."

Mr. Norton's nod was grave. "Have you looked at the household ledgers?"

"I have not," Charlotte said. "Should I?"

"I'm afraid you must, especially if your mother is not divulging any information," he said. "Tell her your intentions, and if she will not let you see the ledgers, then request that you be in her next meeting with the solicitor."

Charlotte exhaled. Could she be so bold with her mother? So demanding?

Mr. Norton opened the ledger on the small table, then turned it so that Charlotte could see. He pointed at a column of numbers. "You need to review each column and compare to the year before. Note any changes. That is where your research should begin."

Charlotte leaned forward. "And how do I know whether a change is good or bad?"

"Fair question," Mr. Norton said, then he looked at the other women to make sure they were included in the conversation. "If the income is less, then some of the expenses will need to be reduced. If reductions are not made, then that is where financial woes begin."

The coifed heads bobbed, and Lady Joanna smiled. "This is true. When I found myself in dire straits after my first marriage, I had to make small and large changes. I sold a few things, and other things I went without."

Charlotte stared at Lady Joanna. Looking at the woman now, she'd have never guessed that the former marchioness had undergone such trials.

Charlotte retook her original seat, and the next woman, Mrs. Fletcher, sat across from Mr. Norton. He proceeded to explain to Mrs. Fletcher how to tally up the sums and weigh them against the household income.

"You always want to keep spare funds on hand," Mr. Norton said. "Emergencies may arise, such as an illness or weather-related disasters, that are out of your control."

All heads nodded.

Before another woman could be tutored by Mr. Norton, Lady Joanna clapped her hands together. "We'll start our tea service, then Mr. Norton will continue after. During our tea, let us hear from Mrs. Lydia Steele. She has successfully partnered with her cousin in a new business venture."

Impressed already, Charlotte turned to look at Mrs. Steele, a plump woman with a mass of blond curls.

Once the tea was brought in, Mrs. Steele began to talk of the business agreement she'd entered into, and some of the parameters.

"I invested one thousand pounds into a lace company, and we have rented space in two factories."

Charlotte soaked up every single word Mrs. Steele said, as her own ideas began to take root and shape. If only her mother would take her into her confidence. It had to happen—that was the only thing for it. And it would happen today.

8

BRAND SCOWLED AS he read the letter from his solicitor, Mr. Wright. The inquiries into Rochester Estate had proved fruitful, but now Brand was facing information that he hadn't expected to uncover. If the findings were accurate, then the man of business, a Mr. Grant, who was over the Rochester affairs, had apparently been pocketing money.

Brand read through the details again. The sum settled upon Mrs. Rochester as the widow had not been paid out in full. Only about a third of the amount could be accounted for, and the rest was labeled as *paid toward debt incurred by Mr. Rochester*. That's where the solicitor had to really dig. He'd visited financial institutions, met with creditors, and discovered there was no debt.

Thus, the conundrum.

For a moment, Brand wished his sister were a man so that he could discuss this turn of events with her. He already knew what she'd say—she'd tell him to meet with Mrs. Rochester and Charlotte and simply present the facts to them.

Two weeks had passed now, since the time he'd spoken with Charlotte in the meadow. She'd been upset, she'd cried, and then she'd run from him. He'd spent hours going over their conversation in his mind and trying to decipher the meaning behind her words. She'd gone into the marriage with the vicar with pure intentions, it seemed.

How did Brand feel about that? Hurt, to be honest. She hadn't been forced, though she'd been pressured by her mother. Which meant Charlotte had *wanted* to marry the man. Had she grown to feel something for him? Had it become love? Was that why she'd been so upset about her apparent loneliness? Marriage hadn't been what she'd thought it would be?

"Sir," a voice said from the doorway of his study. "Another letter for you."

Brand motioned for his butler to come in. "Thank you, Richards."

The older man nodded, then left the room.

Brand glanced down at the address, and his breath hitched. He knew the handwriting. From a hundred notes exchanged in his youth.

Charlotte had written him.

His pulse skipped as he broke the seal and unfolded the missive.

Dear Lord Wilshore,

Writing this request is the last thing I want to do, because I know you are occupied with your own affairs. But I have been working on my father's ledgers and have found some things amiss. This particular matter has to do with the property line, so you see, I need to discuss the matter with you—the owner of Wilshore Estate. Please let me know at your earliest convenience when we might discuss the matter.

Sincerely,
Mrs. Charlotte R. Ashford

He gazed at her signature for a moment too long. The

name of Ashford jolted him to the reality of his present life. Charlotte wasn't writing a note about a treasure hunt or meeting for a horse ride. She was writing as a widowed woman trying to sort out her mother's financial affairs.

And ... this was the very opening he needed. It was fortuitous, really. He had, at his fingertips, the information that could potentially restore Rochester Estate. He wasn't sure what this matter was concerning the property boundaries, but there was no time like the present to find out. He could settle this all quickly and report to his sister that he'd done his neighborly duty, then he'd get back to his life before Charlotte showed up.

"Richards," he called from the study as he gathered up the correspondence from his solicitor. "I'm going to Rochester Estate. I don't know when I'll be back."

Richards appeared almost immediately, as if he'd been hovering just outside the door. "Will you need the carriage, sir?"

"No, it's a fine day, and I'll walk."

Brand shrugged into his jacket, then snatched his hat and strode out of the house.

It was not a fine day after all. In fact, a light drizzle had begun, but Brand didn't have far to go if he cut through the paths connecting the properties. The rain was light and nearly warm, making him think of the warm summer rain of India. England still had a long way to go to match those temperatures, but Brand was reminded all the same of the humid warmth of Calcutta.

By the time he knocked on the door of the Rochester manor, his jacket was fairly damp. He'd have to shrug it off if he wanted it to dry properly. When the door opened a sliver, it was clear that he'd caught Charlotte by surprise. She was wearing a morning dress, but her hair was down around her shoulders, the dark waves tumbling as he'd remembered from her youth.

"Lord Wilshore," she said, her gaze widening right before she dropped into a curtsey.

"Mrs. Ashford," he said, taking off his hat. "I received your letter."

"You have," she said, her tone faint. "And you decided to come over straightaway?"

"I did."

Their gazes clung to each other, and Brand wondered what she'd been occupied with these past two weeks. Certainly her daughter, as well as the ledgers she'd spoken of. Had she gotten rest? Had she gone to that widows society? Had she been into town and visited their old haunts . . . ?

Charlotte lifted her chin. "It's not the best time, sir. My daughter is fussing this morning, and my mother has kept to her room these past two days." Lowering her voice, she added, "She is very distraught over what I've found in the ledgers. She doesn't even want to discuss them."

Brand took in the whole of Charlotte's appearance. Her muslin dress had seen better days and should probably be altered, since her figure seemed too full for the slim lines. Pale violet lined her eyes, and the hand clasping the door had bitten nails. It was a habit she'd had as a young girl, when she was anxious. It seemed that habit had returned.

He made a decision on the spot. "I have news that cannot wait. If your mother can't join us, you can be the messenger."

Charlotte bit the edge of her lip, and Brand forced himself to focus on her brown eyes. The depth of weariness in them made him want to saddle his horse and ride until he arrived at the Rochesters' solicitor's office. He had a thing or two to say to the man.

But right now, Charlotte was still hesitating, so Brand

said the one thing he thought might gain him entrance. "I don't mind a fussy child. If she's anything like my sister was as a toddler, she'll just need a bit of distraction."

Charlotte's brows slowly lifted. "And you're offering to be that distraction?"

"I am."

Something changed in Charlotte's eyes then; the weariness seemed to fade, and the paleness of her cheeks warmed to a soft pink.

As if on cue, a wail came from somewhere inside the house. Charlotte's skin pinked even more. "I need to get her. We can do this another time if you prefer."

Brand put his hand out to stop her from shutting the door on him.

Charlotte puffed out a breath. "All right. But you've been warned."

Brand hid a smile as he walked into the barren hallway. How much work could a child be who couldn't even walk? His memories of when his sister was young were dim, but he did remember she was very bribable.

The wailing was coming from the drawing room, and Charlotte had already disappeared into it. So Brand followed. He paused in the doorway to see Charlotte picking up her daughter and trying the soothe her.

The little child—Emily, if he remembered correctly—was rosy-cheeked, and large tears stained her face. Her crying completely stopped the moment her brown gaze landed on him.

"This is Lord Wilshore, Emily," Charlotte said, as if a baby could understand an introduction. "He's our neighbor."

Emily blinked at him. "Papa?"

Charlotte gasped, and her face flamed red. "No, Emily, this is *Lord Wilshore*." Her eyes connected with Brand's, and he could see the horror in them. "I'm so sorry. She's never said that word before, even though I've tried to teach it to her."

"Papa!" Emily said louder, lifting her dimpled arms with excitement.

Brand sensed that Charlotte was about to run from the room screaming.

"It's all right, Charlotte," he said. "She's learning words. It's nothing to fuss over."

Charlotte exhaled. "I can't apologize enough. I was teaching her before we left the vicarage, when I took her to visit Daniel's grave, but she'd never say it." Her words had quieted to a whisper, while Emily seemed to fixate on the watch hanging from his waistcoat.

"Do you want to see this?" he asked, lifting it from the miniature pocket.

"Mama!" Emily said.

"That's how she asks for something," Charlotte explained. "I guess it's because I get everything for her."

"As any mother would," Brand murmured, taking a step closer and holding up the watch.

"You don't have to give her that," Charlotte started to say, but she was interrupted by two things.

First, Emily latched onto the watch like a hunting dog to his prey. And she suddenly decided that she didn't want to be held by her mother anymore and practically launched herself at Brand. He grasped the child close so that she wouldn't topple.

"Oh," Charlotte said. "I guess she wants you to hold her. I can take her—"

"It's fine," Brand said. The child weighed next to nothing, yet her solidness told him she was healthy. With one hand she clung to his shoulder, and with the other, she examined the watch as if it were the most fascinating thing she'd ever seen in her life.

He felt Charlotte's incredulous gaze upon him, but he kept his focus on Emily. She resembled her mother quite a bit, and that fact made him curious as to what Daniel Ashford had looked like.

"Don't put it in your mouth, Emily," Charlotte said, stepping closer and reaching for her daughter.

"I've got it," Brand said, tugging the little girl's hand gently so that the watch didn't end up on her lips.

"I'm so sorry," Charlotte said. "She's a sweetheart most of the time, but her sleeping habits have been off since we came to Somerset. I don't know what it is."

Brand nodded. With Charlotte's close proximity, he could swear he smelled lilies. Had she already spent time in the gardens this morning? "How old is she?"

"She'll be one in a couple of weeks."

Emily looked up at him, her brown eyes wide with wonder. She reached for his chin and, in the process, let go of the watch.

"Whoops," Brand said, catching the watch just in time. He pocketed the thing, and Emily used her tiny fingers to touch his sideburns.

"Emily," Charlotte said.

But Brand smiled. "I've a lot more hair than your mother, don't I?"

He didn't need to look at Charlotte to know that she was blushing furiously.

"Papa," Emily said.

"No," Brand said. "I'm not your papa. But you can call me Brand."

Charlotte released a quiet gasp, but he ignored her.

"Can you say Brand?"

Emily stared at him hard, as if she were trying to read the innermost workings of his mind.

"Brand," he repeated, pointing to his chest.

"Ban."

He grinned. "Right. Ban."

"Ban," Emily repeated, patting his face.

Brand chuckled. "You keep your mother on her toes, I can see." His gaze cut to Charlotte.

Her smile was faint, softening the worry lines on her face.

"Come, let's sit," Brand said, carrying Emily over to the settee. He positioned her on his lap, then drew out the letters from the solicitor from his pocket.

Charlotte followed, looking a bit dazed. But she sat next to him on the settee, although keeping a proper distance between them.

"Before we speak about what I've brought," Brand said, "tell me about the property lines."

"It's rather odd," Charlotte said. "A letter came from our solicitor about an agreement made over a decade ago between our fathers. It appears that your father sold some acreage to my father, yet the payment wasn't made in full. Mr. Grant says that we owe your family money, and he will take care of the transaction."

Brand knew instinctively this was not true. He didn't even have to consult with his solicitor. "I believe, Mrs. Ashford, that we have a great many things to discuss. And I think this letter I received from my own solicitor will help us begin."

Charlotte pursed her lips as she took the letter from him.

Brand busied himself with entertaining Emily while Charlotte read the letter. He could feel the tension increase from her. The information would be shocking to say the least. Brand himself still wasn't over the revelation, and now, coupled with this claim about the property lines... Mr. Grant had to be stopped as soon as possible.

Charlotte had gone completely quiet, although her gaze remained on the letter. "How can this be true? It would mean that Mr. Grant has been stealing from my family for years."

"Yes," Brand said in a quiet voice. He met her gaze and saw the brimming tears in her deep-brown eyes. "It is hard news, to be sure."

"This is claiming that two-thirds of our income has been spirited away."

"Yes." Brand absently stroked Emily's brown curls, since she'd laid her head on his shoulder and seemed to be relaxing into sleep. "And potentially more, according to Mr. Grant's claim about the property dispute with my family."

Charlotte closed her eyes and exhaled slowly. When she opened her eyes again, she turned her gaze upon him. Brand could practically see her questions flitting across her face.

"This is a lot to take in," Charlotte said at last. "I am in shock, I think."

Brand nodded, and it wasn't a conscious act, but he reached for her free hand. Her small hand turned beneath his, and suddenly she was gripping his fingers. Brand's heart thumped hard. This wasn't a romantic gesture, though. *No, not at all,* he told himself. He was a longtime neighbor of the Rochesters, and he'd brought hard news. So this was a measure of comfort. Nothing more.

"What should I do, Brand?" she whispered.

He didn't miss the fact that she'd called him Brand and that he'd called her Charlotte a moment ago. Something had changed between them. A barrier had shifted. It hadn't completely fallen away, but there had been movement.

"We will consult with my solicitor, Mr. Wright, and you will need to hire a new one," Brand said.

Charlotte nodded. "I know who I'd like to hire."

This surprised him. "Oh?"

"Mr. Norton," Charlotte said. "He works for Lady Joanna as well."

Brand studied Charlotte's face. "You're in earnest? You know that Lady Joanna is quite the eccentric. I don't know if it's a good idea—"

Charlotte tugged her hand from his. "I've met the man, and I have been impressed with him. The decision has been made. By me."

Brand blinked. "All right . . . I didn't mean to imply that you don't have the right to make such a decision, but there is talk in the county about Lady Joanna and her offbeat ways."

She merely held his gaze. "Such as?"

He hadn't exactly wanted to be in a position of defense. "Her society is teaching young widows to step outside tradition. For instance, a group of them went to visit Factory Row last week. They were given a full tour and created quite a disturbance among the workers."

By the way Charlotte was looking at him, he could only make one assumption. "You were there? You were with them?"

"I was." She folded her hands atop the letter. "When a husband dies, he doesn't leave any instructions. A woman is left to fend in a man's world, and unless she has educated herself on accounts and ledgers, terrible things might happen." She held up the letter he'd brought over. "Like this. My mother has been grossly cheated."

Emily was sound asleep on his shoulder, her breathing even, her small body completely relaxed. First, he needed to have his hands free so that he could review the ledgers. And second, he didn't know how he felt about Charlotte attending the widows society. There had been other rumors . . . of the rules Joanna had set forth upon joining. The young widows had pledged not to remarry unless certain demands were met.

He had no idea what those demands were, but the very idea bothered him. It shouldn't, since Charlotte was beyond his business. Except for one's duty to a neighbor.

"Show me where to lay your daughter down," he said, "and we will go over these ledgers."

9

CHARLOTTE REACHED FOR her daughter, but Brand stood, still cradling her against his shoulder.

Charlotte stood as well. "I can take her." Her voice was hushed, and Brand replied in kind.

"She might be disturbed," he said. "Lead me to her room, and I'll set her down."

Charlotte swallowed. Not only would bringing this man into the private quarters of the house be more intimate, but he'd see the whole of the house's ruin. Yet she knew that look in Brand's eyes. He was not to be dissuaded.

She rose from the settee and walked out of the drawing room, Brand following. She turned toward the staircase and walked up the stairs, knowing she couldn't hide the creaking that should be repaired as well. Her mother's room was to the left, and Charlotte's to the right of the landing.

Emily should be sleeping in the nursery, but Charlotte wanted her closer, especially since they had no money to hire a nursemaid.

"Through here," Charlotte said, opening the door to her bedroom.

Brand passed by her, walking into the room. His height and broadness made the bedroom seem miniature.

"There," she whispered, pointing to the crib on the other side of her bed. At least she'd made her bed this morning, and the room was in a decent state of cleanliness. But the furnishings consisted only of a bed, a crib, and a wardrobe. There was no dressing table and no bookcase, and the hearth remained empty.

As she watched Brand set her daughter down in the crib, Charlotte tried not to let her heart expand, for if it did, she'd surely only feel pain. And longing. She moved to his side and draped a blanket over Emily. Her daughter looked angelic in her sleep, with her long lashes, flushed cheeks, and rosebud lips.

And she was standing much too close to Brand. His presence seemed to be everywhere, and she thought of how he'd grasped her hand moments ago. Offering comfort as a friend, of course. But it had only flamed the suppressed longing inside of her that she refused to identify.

"Thank you," she whispered.

Brand lifted his gaze from Emily, his blue eyes meeting hers. His eyes were gray in the dim light, and she wished she could read his thoughts. Did he see the starkness of the bedroom? Did he understand her growing desperation to provide for her child?

"You're welcome," Brand said, still holding her gaze.

Charlotte ignored the urge to take his hand, to lean into him, to embrace him. It was as if the years had fallen away between them and they were as they used to be. When they'd shared stolen embraces. When they'd held hands when alone.

She stepped away from the crib, from the man in her bedroom. Without looking back, she moved to the doorway and walked into the hall. Brand followed and pulled the door halfway closed. "Do you want it shut?"

"No, that's fine," she said, nodding toward the partially open door.

They stood facing each other in the dim corridor. The narrow space made Charlotte feel smaller next to Brand's larger size, and she had to tilt her head to meet his gaze.

"Charlotte . . ." he began, his voice a low rumble.

He'd called her Charlotte twice today, and the word from his lips had found its way to her heart. Did this mean he forgave her? Did this mean they could be friends?

"Was it difficult?" he asked.

She blinked, and he must have seen the confusion in her expression.

"How did you fare through losing your husband, then delivering a child?"

Oh. The question was so personal, so intimate, but this was her childhood friend Brand. And his blue-gray eyes were filled with something she couldn't name. Not even her mother had asked such a thing. Of course there were the gushing sympathies in Thea's letters, but Charlotte had never spoken of her experiences aloud.

"I went to hell and back, twice," Charlotte said, hearing the tremble in her voice. "Emily has been both my saving grace and solace. There is nothing . . . nothing I regret about her."

Brand's jaw tightened, but his gaze was gentle. "She is a beautiful child."

Charlotte's throat burned, but she would not cry. Not now. There were important and dire things to accomplish.

They were still in the dim hallway, yet Charlotte couldn't move. Couldn't walk away. "I should have never disparaged Daniel." She lowered her gaze, her confession hot in her chest. "He was a good man. His mission was important, and I have belittled it."

Brand didn't say anything for a moment, but his gaze hadn't left her. "It wasn't all right that he neglected you."

Her gaze snapped up. How could he know this? Had she been so transparent?

"Relationships are always complicated," Brand said softly, and she noted a small gleam in his eyes. "But whether or not your marriage was wonderful, you have lost much. And now you are facing a momentous task."

He moved closer, lowering his voice again. "Charlotte, let me help you. If only to make amends for the difficult things we have both faced."

Charlotte's eyes stung now. Here was the man she'd known and loved. Gone were the anger, sorrow, and regret. He was extending the olive branch. "But my hasty actions only brought on more grief, and it seems I continue to pay for them. Over and over. Here I am widowed, and now I am nearly destitute with a helpless child and a mother who refuses to face reality."

"Let me help you," Brand repeated, his gaze searching her face. "You are my sister's best friend. We are neighbors. And I do not want to see your family wronged."

She could not say no to such an offer. "Thank you."

The edges of his mouth lifted, then he raised a hand as if he was about to touch her jaw. Something shifted in his eyes, and he dropped his hand. Another pause, and he turned to walk down the hallway.

Charlotte gazed after him, her pulse jumping. Had he been about to . . .

No.

She followed him down the stairs, where they settled into the drawing room again, the ledger between them. They spent the next two hours going over the accounts of the Rochester household. Her mother had done one thing right. She'd recorded the amounts she'd gotten for the sale of their furniture and other belongings.

As the morning drew on, they went through every line on the ledger, and Charlotte's heart only expanded with

Brand's patience. At one point, she lit a few candles since the room had grown dim with the gathering clouds outside. She became a tad chilled, but she didn't want to excuse herself to fetch a shawl, in case Brand made a comment about how there was no fire to be laid. In truth, there was only a small store of wood outside the kitchen, and Charlotte didn't know when there would be funds to bring on a man of work to do such chores.

Brand was different than his youthful self, yet some things were the same. Interacting with him as a full-grown man had made her impressed with his maturity and expanse of knowledge.

She had changed too. No longer was she the young woman with youthful dreams of happily ever after—back when the only thing keeping them apart was Brand's parents, who didn't approve of a match between them. Both were gone now, yet Charlotte had thrown up newer, more significant barriers. A needy widow with a child. The last thing Charlotte ever wanted to do was encroach on another's charity.

Emily awakened nearly two hours later, when Charlotte and Brand were well into the pages of the ledger.

"I should get her," Charlotte said. "She gives only a moment or two of warning before she goes into full hysterics." She wouldn't be surprised if Brand took the opportunity to make his excuses and leave.

Instead, he only nodded, and she rose, then left the room.

By the time she returned with a fresh-eyed Emily, she found Brand kneeling before the hearth, laying a fire.

"Oh," Charlotte said. "You don't need to trouble yourself."

Brand looked over his shoulder. "It's no trouble. And I'll have more wood sent over tomorrow. You're nearly out."

Charlotte didn't say that they'd been nearly out for weeks, and who knew how long before that.

Brand had shed his jacket, and she looked away from his broad shoulders stretching the shirt across his back.

"Ban!" Emily said.

Charlotte was truly stunned. Emily had remembered the name he taught her.

Brand turned again, his left brow cocked. "Brand."

Emily grinned. "Ban."

"That's right." He was smiling, too, as he stood and moved toward them.

Brand stopped close to her, then grasped Emily's outstretched hand. "Did you sleep well, child?"

At that moment, Emily yawned, big enough to make her eyes water.

Brand chuckled, and the sound of his laughter was like a wave of warm water.

"I should feed her," Charlotte said, mostly because she had to put some distance between herself and the man standing so close to her. Without his jacket, his proximity felt so much more . . . intimate. And she could smell the woodsy scent of him from laying the fire.

"Mama!" Emily pointed at the crackling fire in the hearth.

"That's fire," Charlotte said. "No touch. It's hot."

Emily's nose scrunched as she stared at the orange flames, and in truth, Charlotte was a bit mesmerized too. She'd been cold for weeks inside the drafty manor.

"Would you like to stay and eat with us?" Charlotte asked Brand, her heart thumping at her bold invitation. "But if you need to go, don't let us keep you."

His blue gaze shifted from Emily to Charlotte's. "I'll stay. We've not finished the ledgers yet, and tomorrow, I think, we need to arrange a meeting between both of our solicitors. Then let Mr. Norton take matters into his own hands, if he is the one you trust."

"He is."

Brand nodded. "Very well, then."

"All right," Charlotte breathed. "I'll get supper started. We, uh, don't have a cook right now."

Brand didn't seem taken aback. In fact, he said, "I can hold her while you work."

Charlotte knew she was staring, and she probably shouldn't be so openly shocked.

His mouth only curved as he reached for Emily. "Should we help your mother cook?"

Charlotte blinked. What was going on here? She was passably domestic, and certainly Brand had never cooked a thing in his life.

But here he was, walking with her toward the kitchen, carrying *her* child. For once, Charlotte was grateful her mother was keeping to her rooms, because this lengthy stay with Brand was something she didn't want to feel guilty over. She was enjoying absolutely every moment of it.

The kitchen was the warmest part of the manor, with the live coals in the stove heating the room. Brand set to work stoking the coals to life while he talked to Emily about not touching the stove.

She seemed to be listening to every word he spoke, as if she was trying hard to understand. Charlotte began slicing potatoes. "I'm sorry this is not your usual fare," she said. "We keep our meals simple with such a small household."

At least she could offer cold ham and warmed potatoes, along with leftover pudding from the evening before. She'd taken it upon herself to oversee the meals this past week as her mother's isolation had increased.

"Simple is often better, don't you agree?" Brand said as he moved about the kitchen, searching for something. "Do you have wine?"

She eyed him as he set two wine glasses on the table.

"There's wine in the high cupboard." She didn't say it was the lone bottle in the house. She was more than happy to share it with her guest.

Still working while holding Emily, he poured wine into the two glasses, then set the bottle back in the high cupboard.

"You can finish it off," Charlotte said.

His blue-gray eyes connected with hers from across the table. "I need to keep all my wits about me. It's not every day I'm in such lovely company."

She knew her face was about to flame, so she turned to the potatoes to give them a final stir in the boiling pot. She hoped he'd attribute the blush growing on her cheeks to the steam from the potatoes.

Moments later, the potatoes were cooked and the ham laid upon the table. She spooned the potatoes into a serving bowl, then sprinkled on diced herbs. Next she was about to fetch plates, but she saw that Brand had beat her to it.

"You are well versed in domesticity," she said, teasing him but also curious.

"I've not spent all my days as a pampered baron," he said, his amused tone telling her that he didn't mind her teasing.

"You've never been pampered, in my opinion," she said as she took her seat. "But I am surprised at your ease with such work."

Emily reached for her, and Charlotte was only too happy to take her daughter back. Charlotte didn't want Brand leaving the house with bits of food on him from the baby's mess.

Brand's brows had lifted. "You mean laying a fire and pouring some wine?"

Flushing, Charlotte shrugged.

"Basic life skills are necessary even for a man of my station."

"I agree, and I didn't mean—"

"I know what you mean," Brand cut in. "Truthfully, I've learned things the hard way." His voice was no longer teasing. "After the shipwreck, I didn't exactly travel first-class back to England."

Charlotte didn't know where he was going with this, but she'd heard nothing about his journey after the shipwreck, so she was intrigued.

"When I swam back to shore after the wreck, I passed out," Brand said. "If it hadn't been for a stray dog licking my face, I don't know if I would have awakened before the tide came in. I was so exhausted, you see, and strangely enough the dog gave me motivation."

Charlotte didn't know what she'd thought his experience had been, but it wasn't this.

"I had lost everything," Brand continued after taking a swallow from his wine glass. "And sure, I was obviously English, but looking like a vagabond, with no identification papers or money or anything of value with which to trade, I had to find a job." He lifted his shoulder. "Or starve."

"Could no one vouch for you?"

"I didn't wash up on the shore of Calcutta, where I might have been recognized by other British," he said. "We were quite a distance away, and no one could vouch for me."

Charlotte's mind shifted through multiple scenarios. "What did you do?"

"I found a job as a dock worker, then I eventually got hired on a ship—which sailed to England, of course."

Her mouth nearly fell open. "You were a dock worker and a sailor?"

"Yes."

Charlotte couldn't settle her thoughts on something like this happening to him. "Brand," she said quietly. "What an ordeal."

"I can't disagree on that account."

"How did you manage?" she asked. "Was it so very awful?"

His blue gaze held hers for a long moment. "Parts were certainly awful. Some experiences I hope to someday completely forget about. But how did I manage?" He paused. "By knowing you were waiting for me at home."

10

BRAND FOUND HIMSELF once again, for the second day in a row, standing outside the door of the Rochester manor. Today, he'd not be secluded inside the house with Charlotte and her daughter, but they'd be traveling to Mr. Norton's office. From there, Mr. Wright would join them, and they'd continue to Mr. Grant's.

Yesterday could not be repeated—well, at least not the intimate talks and confessions that had occurred. Yes, Brand was still determined to help clear up the estate matters, as long as it was in his power to do so. Yes, he planned on being a concerned neighbor. But . . . spending most of yesterday with Charlotte and her young daughter had told him one thing.

He was still not over her. Not even close.

Perhaps he didn't love her like he had, because the hurt and disappointment had left a deep scar . . . but what he felt and what he saw in her was the perspective of a different, older Brand.

They'd both changed. And not exactly by choice. Brand through no fault of his own, and Charlotte through a series of decisions prompted by her own fears and insecurities.

So now what?

Now he would do his duty, both by his sister and as a

neighbor to the Rochesters. Then life would move forward for both of them. In which directions, he didn't know yet.

The door opened, and there stood Mrs. Rochester. "Lord Wilshore, it's so good of you to fetch us."

"I'm glad to see you recovered, madam," Brand said. In truth, her complexion was pale and the violet beneath her eyes pronounced.

Mrs. Rochester dipped her head and murmured a thank you, then she pulled the door a bit wider as another woman appeared behind her.

Charlotte wore a dress of pale yellow, and in her arms, she held little Emily.

"Ban!" Emily said, and Brand wouldn't have been able to stop his smile if someone had doused him in cold water. Which was probably what he needed right now to recenter his thoughts, because the child was quickly nestling her way into his heart.

"Yes, I'm Brand."

Mrs. Rochester's thin eyebrows shot heavenward, and he supposed this was a surprise. But he did not comment on it and instead reached a hand out to snag Emily's grasping fingers. Her dimpled fingers latched on to his, and she gave him a smile, showing her eight teeth.

Brand chuckled. "She woke up happy."

Charlotte's smile only warmed him further. The yellow dress made her appear as spring itself, and he'd be blind to not notice how the elegant upsweep of her dark hair exposed the gentle curve of her neck.

"It is fortunate she is so cheerful," Charlotte continued, "for I have fretted over bringing her to the appointment."

"And I have told you not to worry." His gaze shifted to her deep-brown eyes. "There will be plenty of able-bodied adults to care for a small child."

"And I thank you for your confidence," Charlotte said, her voice soft.

Mrs. Rochester's head bobbed back and forth as if she was incredulous about their conversation thread. But Brand didn't meet the woman's gaze.

"Shall we be off, then?" he said. "My solicitor will meet us at Mr. Norton's office, and then we will all travel together to Mr. Grant's place of business."

"And Mr. Grant does not know we are coming?"

"He does not." Brand stepped aside so that the ladies could exit the house. "It is better this way. He'll not have time to prepare a defense or . . . to run."

Mrs. Rochester gasped. "You think he would run? But that would be so . . ."

"Dishonest," Brand finished for her. "He's already proven that." He nodded toward the waiting carriage, which would have plenty of room for the four of them. Mr. Norton would need to ride with Mr. Wright in a second carriage, though.

The women headed toward the carriage, and over Charlotte's shoulder, Emily continued to grin at him.

Despite the seriousness of the situation at hand, he couldn't help but return the darling child's smile. Ah, what it would be to view the world with such innocence and have no trouble trusting all those surrounding you.

As the women climbed into the carriage with his helping hand, he caught the scent of lilies from Charlotte, and something else he could only describe as sunshine.

Maybe it was the yellow dress, or maybe his mind was spinning out nonsensical thoughts.

Settled into the carriage, Brand tried to keep his thoughts and conversation much more elevated than what was actually going through his mind. Mrs. Rochester clutched the household ledger tightly in her hands while Charlotte pointed out the window with Emily as they rumbled along the road.

Soon enough, they'd teamed up with Mr. Norton and Mr. Wright, both men of advanced age—but both were in spritely health. And both the women seemed tenser on the second leg of their journey. Mrs. Rochester kept her gaze averted and focused on the window to her left, and Charlotte kept her attention on her child, who was acting rather sleepy now.

By midmorning, they arrived at Mr. Grant's place of business, which was effectively a shared office at the back of a general store. An odd location to receive clients, but Mr. Grant probably only paid house calls. Not today.

Brand opened the carriage door without waiting for the driver, then he handed down the women. Before Charlotte moved past him, she whispered, "You're carrying a firearm?"

"Yes."

Her face had lost some color.

"I'm not going to let Mr. Grant continue this farce and attempt to flee with no consequences."

Charlotte eyed him. "All right," she said at last.

"If your daughter gets too heavy, let me help you," Brand said, changing the subject as the two solicitors joined them.

He was looking forward to seeing Mr. Grant's expression when the whole lot of them showed up at his office. And if Brand had to use a gun, then so be it.

"This way," Mr. Wright said, having done the most research out of the entire group.

They followed Mr. Wright along the storefront, then turned the corner. There was no sign or indication that the door he knocked on belonged to one Mr. Grant.

But only a moment passed before it was swung open from the inside. Mr. Grant was a short man, not young nor old—in fact, it was hard to determine his age. His impressive eyebrows were like wings slanted over his deep eyes, and Brand fully expected him to take flight.

"Hello, Mr. Grant," Charlotte said, speaking first. "I'm Charlotte Ashford, daughter of Mr. and Mrs. Rochester."

Mr. Grant's gaze flew to Mrs. Rochester. "Y-you are here. Mrs. R-rochester? To w-what do I owe this pleasure?" His eyes flitted to the men, surprise and curiosity soon morphing to wariness.

"My lord?" he said, deferring to Brand since his dress marked his rank above the others.

"Lord Hildebrand Wilshore," he said, extending his hand. The two shook, then Brand added, "This is my solicitor, Mr. Wright, and the Rochesters' *new* solicitor, Mr. Norton."

With each word, Mr. Grant's face lost one more shade of color. "What can I, er, help you gentlemen with?"

"Do you have a place where we can sit and talk?" Mr. Wright said, taking over the conversation.

Mr. Grant's eyes darted about before he said, "Of course. The quarters will be quite cramped with . . . all of you. But there is shopping close by, so that the ladies might occupy their time?"

"The ladies will join us for the meeting," Brand cut in.

And somehow they all filed in and fit into Mr. Grant's small office. He continually tugged at his neckcloth.

Mr. Wright displayed the reports he'd gotten from his contacts. "Please read over these, and then we'll be happy to hear your explanations."

Mr. Grant made a great show of putting on a pair of spectacles before reading. If a man's face could ever go white, Brand was now a witness to it.

"These are very accusatory statements," Mr. Grant said after a full minute. He looked up to meet Mr. Wright's gaze. "Who brought this to you?"

"I sent out for it at the request of Lord Wilshore," Mr. Wright said.

"And as the newly appointed solicitor for the Rochesters," Mr. Norton cut in, "I'm here to transfer all funds due them into my care. We will accompany you to the bank."

Brand was pretty sure that Mr. Grant had nearly swallowed his tongue.

"There are multiple ways we can do this," Brand announced. "We've come with all evidence of the amount that you hold for the Rochesters. If that amount is found in its entirety, then we won't get the authorities involved. And whatever scraps of reputation you survive on will remain intact."

"Or . . ." Mr. Wright said. "If the money *isn't* found, then we passed a river not too far from town that looks deep enough to hide many things."

Mr. Grant blinked. Then he slowly removed his spectacles. "If you will but excuse me for a moment, I will make inquiries at the bank as to the current availability of the amount you are requesting."

"No one will be excused," Mrs. Rochester said, straightening in her chair, her chin lifted. The color was high in her cheeks, and her eyes were bright with determination. "This matter will be settled in my presence. My husband worked his entire life to provide well for his family. What you have done to our estate and with my funds is appalling."

Brand nearly clapped with bravado.

Mr. Grant dipped his head. "This way, if you please," he said in a rasped tone.

But Brand was no fool. As the man reached to open the door, Brand shifted aside enough for the man to pass, but he was right on his heels. Which turned out to be a fortuitous thing when Mr. Grant broke out into a run.

Brand was a half second behind him, and with his longer frame, he easily caught up. Grabbing Mr. Grant's coat and tugging hard brought him to a halt, skidding on his knees.

"Taking a shortcut to the bank?" Brand hooked one arm around the man's throat, then brandished his firearm. Somewhere behind him he heard a gasp, followed by a startled cry that sounded like Emily.

"Leave me be!" Mr. Grant shot out. "The money was invested and lost by Mr. Rochester. I swear on my life."

"You're a fool to gamble your life on this statement." Brand shoved the man to the ground, where he quailed in fear. "We have more than enough evidence against you. You're not even worth the effort of a trial. A judge will simply sentence you on the spot."

Mr. Grant's small eyes grew twice their size.

"You cannot shoot me," Mr. Grant cried out.

"I can," Brand said, squaring his shoulders and keeping his aim dead on. "But I won't if you return the money. If it's not at the bank, then where is it?"

Everyone was silent, even little Emily, as Mr. Grant surveyed the men looming over him. Defeat had stolen across his face, and perspiration glimmered on his brow. "Very well." His eyes slid shut. "I will take you to the bank, and whatever funds I have there are yours."

11

ALL EYES WERE on Charlotte as she told her tale of the renegade man of business who'd stolen from her family for years. The Society of Young Widows was holding another tea, this one with the intention of planning a masquerade ball that would raise funds for sending Mrs. Steel's eldest daughter to finishing school.

But Lady Joanna, knowing somewhat of Mr. Norton's adventures, had asked Charlotte to share with the other women.

"So you see," Charlotte concluded, "Mr. Norton's advice on checking family ledgers was in fact how my mother's estate was restored." She smiled at the stunned expressions of the women in the room.

Lady Joanna nodded in her regal fashion, then clapped her jeweled hands together. "Well, then. What do they say? All's well that ends well?" She gave a benevolent smile to those gathered. "Which is why we are all here today. We're to plan a sensational ball that will turn out the pockets of everyone in all of Somerset."

The women smiled and tittered, while Charlotte pretended she was interested in the planning. In truth, she was wondering if Lady Joanna's *all's well that ends well* declaration was something she'd ever believe.

Yes, the funds of her mother's estate had been recovered. And yes, repairs were well under way. Emily was healthy, another blessing. The early summer weather had brought the meadows into full bloom, and Charlotte had enjoyed many mornings of gathering and pressing flowers. She had even created her own stationery, with pressed flowers glued upon the corners. Thea visited almost every week, and they spent hours together, talking and enjoying one another's company.

But there was something missing, something that had left a gaping hole in her life. Something that had felt like a promise but in the end had faded away into nothing. Absolutely nothing.

It had been nearly a month since she'd seen Lord Wilshore.

Sure, Thea chattered on about him and how he was busy with travels about England and such, but Thea's words only made Charlotte miss him more.

Yes. She missed him. Deeply. Not the young man she used to know and used to be in love with and dreamed of marrying when he returned from India. But she missed the man he'd become. The caring man, the man who'd been through many hardships and heartaches, the man who'd been at ease with her daughter, and the man who haunted every quiet thought she had throughout the day and night.

After the meeting with all the solicitors, Charlotte had written a thank-you note to Brand, which she assumed he'd received. He'd never replied, but why should one reply to a thank-you note? To thank her for sending a thank-you note? No. She'd been sincere in her gratitude and hoped he hadn't found it tedious.

As Charlotte listened to the discussion about the preparations for the masquerade ball, she paid careful attention to the guest list that Lady Joanna was proposing. It seemed that every gentlewoman and gentleman in the county would be invited.

"Lord Wilshore," Lady Joanna read from her list. "His sister and brother-in-law, Lady and Lord Blackdene."

Charlotte straightened at the mention of their names. Surely Thea would love attending such a ball, but it was anyone's guess whether Brand would come. Was he even in Somerset now? Charlotte had kept enough self-control to at least not spy on his home and grounds. Although, she couldn't deny that her visits to the meadow were in hope that he'd appear with his dogs again.

But as the days passed, inching closer to the masquerade ball, she neither saw nor heard anything from the Wilshore Estate. Thea had written more than one gushing letter about her excitement for the ball and had insisted that they go together. Charlotte's mother had already agreed to watch over Emily the entire evening, so there was no pressure to return early.

Still, Charlotte's stomach danced with nerves. She'd never been to a masquerade ball, and her dancing skills were certainly out of practice. And . . . it had been a long time since she'd been in a man's arms. Her husband had showed little affection, so Charlotte's last truly affectionate embrace with a man had been with Lord Wilshore. Years ago.

No matter. The goal of the masquerade ball was not to dance the night away with a man with whom she'd fall in love and live happily ever after in wedded bliss. That would be against Lady Joanna's rules of young widows, anyway. Marrying a man for love would only spell disaster. Marriage should be a practical arrangement, one that benefited both parties, and women should never be left in the dark about household or financial matters.

When the evening of the masquerade ball arrived, Charlotte was nearly finished with her toilette in her bedroom when her mother entered.

"Say goodbye to Mama," her mother said, holding little Emily.

"Hello, my sweet." Charlotte smiled at Emily's toothy grin. Charlotte was grateful that her daughter had taken so well to her grandmother. The two were inseparable sometimes.

"Bye-bye, Mama!" Emily pronounced.

"Bye-bye," Charlotte repeated. "You be good for Grandmother, all right?"

"Mama!" Emily said, which could pretty much mean anything.

Her mother's gaze took in the whole of Charlotte's blue-silk dress, pinned-up hair, and cane fashioned into a shepherdess staff. Perhaps it wasn't the most original costume, but Charlotte already had most of the items to make it work.

"You look beautiful, Charlotte," her mother said, sincerity in her tone.

Charlotte would be forever grateful for this new relationship with her mother. This softer and humbler side of her mother had drawn the two women closer as they shared the hardships of the past and pushed forward together, with the same goal of providing a good home for Emily.

"Thank you, Mother," she said. "I'm as nervous as a fox during hunting season. I already feel like I have two left feet."

Her mother's gaze filled with compassion. "Just think of all you have endured and how strong of a woman you are. All you need to do is enjoy the evening. Don't think of anything else. Emily and I will be here when you return."

Charlotte smiled, then moved to kiss her mother's cheek.

"Kiss!" Emily declared, patting her own cheek.

Charlotte laughed. "All right, I'll kiss you too, sweet baby."

Her mother swept Emily out of the room, wanting to avoid Emily watching Charlotte actually leaving the house. She might put up a fuss at that point. So Charlotte took a final look in the mirror, making sure that everything was in place. The only thing left to do was put on her mask, which Thea had created for her and would be bringing in the carriage. Charlotte had told her the color of her shepherd costume, so it should match fine.

A rap on the front door caught her attention, and she snatched her gloves and went down to meet her friend.

Thea's husband stood there. He was an older man, his hair nearly all gray, but he carried himself with a stately elegance. "My wife says it's too much of a bother to get in and out of the carriage more than once, so I am here to escort you to the carriage."

Charlotte smiled. Lord Blackdene was a very somber man, but he was kind to the core. And, frankly, indulgent of his wife's many whims.

"Thank you for the escort." She pulled the door closed behind her, then took the man's offered arm. "What is your costume about?"

Lord Blackdene didn't look much different than he usually did as far as his clothing, since he wore a navy coat, a plum waistcoat, and an expertly tied cravat. "I am some prince or other; you'd best ask my wife."

Charlotte held back a laugh. When Lord Blackdene opened the carriage door, she gasped at the sight of Thea. "You're stunning," Charlotte said.

And she was. Thea wore a burgundy gown with massive bell sleeves, a flat bodice, and voluminous skirts. Upon her head was a glittering crown. "I am Queen Mary II, and this is

William III, Prince of Orange." She smiled at her husband as he took his seat next to her. "Or he will be as soon as he puts on this crown and spotted fur cape."

"It's too warm of an evening, and the ballroom will be stifling," Lord Blackdene grumbled, but remarkably he let Thea fuss over him, and in moments, he was wearing said cape and crown. Thea smiled triumphantly.

"Here are the masks." Thea opened a hatbox to reveal three intricately decorated masks.

Lord Blackdene groaned. "I suppose there's no way I can get out of wearing that?"

Thea smiled prettily up at him, and his gaze softened.

Inwardly, Charlotte sighed. It was plain they adored each other, something she'd never had in her own marriage. But she was truly happy for her friend. She took her own mask, a delicate blue-and-silver one, then tied it on carefully. By the time the carriage arrived at Lady Joanna's, Charlotte was as ready as she'd ever be.

"It's gorgeous," Thea said, looking at the house, lit up by torches on the outside, with windows glowing from the candle chandeliers on the inside. "The only thing that would make this night more perfect was if my brother could have come."

Charlotte nodded but kept her gaze upon the approaching house. She felt Thea looking at her, and Charlotte wasn't about to give away one speck of emotion.

When it was their turn to alight from the carriage, Lord Blackdene handed them both down, then escorted them to the front doors. Lady Joanna stood at the front of the receiving line. Even though she wore an elaborate mask of peacock feathers, there was no doubt the auburn-haired woman was her.

She must be playing the part of a water nymph, because her dress was a mixture of blue and green, and the train was at least three feet long.

"Welcome, welcome," Lady Joanna said. "All guests are to report to the ballroom and must select a number. Dance partners will be assigned to each other randomly by one of the Young Widows, and each progressive dance will require a pledge of money." She looked pointedly at Lord Blackdene. "I hope you are feeling generous tonight."

"I certainly am, my lady," he said immediately.

Lady Joanna gave him a pleased smile, then turned to the next guest.

Charlotte followed the moving crowd into the ballroom. The orchestra was already playing, and couples were dancing, apparently assigned together. New arrivals were swept up and steered to a partner, then directed to the dancing floor.

"Let's assign ourselves to each other," Lord Blackdene told Thea.

She laughed and said, "That's not how it works."

But her husband spirited her off anyway, and within moments, they'd joined in the dancing.

Charlotte's gaze moved about the room. The costumes were beautiful and dazzling and quite breathtaking. She studied the dance steps of the quadrille and hoped that she might have a bit of reprieve before she was partnered with a man.

That reprieve didn't come, because a woman latched onto her arm. "Come this way, dear," she said.

Charlotte was pretty sure it was Mrs. Givens. She barely had time to rest her shepherdess staff against a wall before Mrs. Givens drew her to stand before a gentleman.

"This gentleman has pledged a dance, so we need you to fulfill that pledge," Mrs. Givens said, motioning toward a man with deep-auburn sideburns peeking beneath a black mask. His long cape and gold-colored waistcoat made Charlotte guess he was pretending to be a Spanish matador.

"Hello, shepherdess," the man said, with a quirk of his mouth.

"Good evening." Charlotte curtseyed.

Her heart thumped as she moved through the dance steps with the matador. At first, every step brought a shudder of nerves, but about halfway through the number, she began to relax and enjoy the music, the dancing, the whole of it. Since the steps only repeated over and over, it wasn't hard to improve her skills quickly.

For the next dance number she was paired with a man disguised as a priest. "We seem to be paired perfectly," the thin blond man said. "A priest and a shepherdess."

Charlotte smiled. "Then perhaps we shouldn't be dancing the waltz."

The priest chuckled, his laugh a bit breathy. "But then how will we know if we are suited?"

Suited for what? Charlotte didn't ask, because she didn't want this vein of conversation to continue. She was grateful when the waltz ended and the next dance paired her with a man dressed as a Turk. He was quiet, and Charlotte didn't mind. She was pretty sure that if her identity was revealed as a widow who was a member of the lower class of gentry, most of these men would have never asked her to dance in the first place.

She caught glimpses of Lady Joanna as she flitted from person to person. She never danced but ensured that everything was running smoothly and that the pledges kept coming in.

The evening wore on, and Charlotte found that she was looking forward to the next waltz and the slower pace that would bring.

When finally the waltz number started up, Charlotte watched as Mrs. Givens approached, intent on pairing up all the remaining bystanders. But before Mrs. Givens reached her, a man touched her elbow. She turned to face a sailor. Well, he wasn't a true sailor, but he looked as if he'd walked off of one of London's great ships.

His dark-gold hair beneath a sailor's cap was the first thing she noticed, and the second? The blue eyes studying her through the black mask hiding the upper half of his face. But his angular jawline and lips she'd stolen more than one glance of told her this was Lord Wilshore.

He was here. He had come.

For an instant, her breath stalled. Did Thea know her brother was here? How had his plans changed? But before she could come to any conclusions, he spoke. "Is your dance card full, ma'am?"

She blinked, then swallowed. "We don't have dance cards, it's a—"

His hand grasped hers and tugged her fingers upward.

All of Charlotte's words fled.

"Then I need to make good on my promise from long ago."

Charlotte stared at him. This tall man with broad shoulders, whose handsomeness couldn't be concealed by a simple black mask or the roughness of a sailor's costume, which she sensed was no costume but clothing from his sojourn across the ocean. Was he referring to . . . that promise she'd given up on?

"There you are," Mrs. Givens said, interrupting Charlotte's spinning thoughts and cooling her growing blush. "You've been paired with the gentleman in the Iranian costume."

"She's paired with me," Lord Wilshore cut in.

Mrs. Givens' gaze snapped to him, and she narrowed her eyes as she looked him up and down. "You, sir, will be paired with the milkmaid woman in blue."

"I think not," Lord Wilshore said. "You can double my pledge since I've already chosen my partner."

Before Mrs. Givens could gather her wits or come up with a response, Lord Wilshore drew Charlotte toward him by her hand, then deliberately linked their arms.

Charlotte's mind buzzed, her feet seemed to be floating, and she wasn't entirely sure how she found herself in the arms of Lord Wilshore.

12

BRAND HAD TALKED himself out of attending the masquerade ball at least a dozen times. But the invitation had been burning a hole in his mind for the past three hours. He'd watched the clock in his study pass the hour mark of when the ball was to start. Then he watched the hands of the clock pass the next hour mark.

Charlotte was there, or Mrs. Ashford, as he had to think of her. Thea had written him more than once to attend if he was back in Somerset. He'd not committed either way. And now . . . here he was, waltzing with Mrs. Ashford in his arms.

Blast. She was no Mrs. Ashford to him. She was Charlotte, she'd always been Charlotte. And tonight, he was determined to let her know what she meant to him. Whatever course their relationship might take after this would be determined. But Brand could not agonize another month, not even another day, over whether or not Charlotte Rochester Ashford would ever consider him. Just as he was. Just as she was.

Her steps were tentative, and he guessed she hadn't danced much at public events, being a vicar's wife. Another dark cloud settled over his mind. He had to stop thinking about her being married. About her in the arms of another man. About her kissing...

"Is this an authentic sailor uniform?" Charlotte asked in a quiet voice.

He pulled his gaze from the soft curls framing her face. There was never any doubt that the shepherdess in blue was Charlotte. He'd seen her the moment he'd entered the room, as if she were a magnet he'd been drawn to.

"Yes," he replied. Her brown eyes were beautiful, set off by the mask she wore. Not that he was surprised. Everything about Charlotte was beautiful. How she protected her mother. How she cared for her daughter. How she had apologized when she'd disparaged her husband, a man who had been less than a husband to her. "It was the only thing I could come up with on short notice."

It hadn't been entirely short notice.

Her fingers pressed against his arm, her touch light, but he felt it all the same as if her bare fingers had branded his skin.

"You look like you've just walked off a ship," she said, her mouth lifting at the corners.

"Not the gentleman you're used to?" he said. "Do I offend?"

"Nothing like that, Lord Wilshore," she said. "A gentleman such as you could dress as a chimney sweep and capture the notice of every woman in this room."

Brand's heart skipped ahead. "Are you flirting with me, Mrs. Ashford?"

The beautiful pink staining her neck was answer enough.

"With a sailor?" she said. "Surely not."

He chuckled, and although he was skirting the edge of propriety, he pulled her closer. Her scent of lilies made him want to close his eyes and breathe her in.

She did not stiffen, nor did she draw away. In fact, she

released a soft sigh. "It is good to see you again, Lord Wilshore. You have my eternal gratitude for aiding my mother with such a delicate matter. I only wish there was a way to repay you."

"I have been repaid," he murmured.

Her eyes widened behind her mask.

"How?"

He couldn't stop his smile. "By having the assurance that my neighbors are well and no longer suffering."

Charlotte's exhale was soft. "You are too generous."

Brand couldn't look away from the deep pools of brown that were her eyes. "I am trying valiantly to make up for my shortcomings," he said. "Your opinion will go a long way in that."

The waltz ended, and couples began to lead off the dance floor, forming new pairings and waiting for the next number to begin. Brand released Charlotte but kept ahold of her hand, not leaving the dance floor.

"You know my opinion is very high of you, my lord," she said.

"Is it?"

The music began, a quadrille, and slowly, Brand moved her into the formation. Their conversation was cut off because the steps of the dance pulled them apart, but in the small moments when they stepped close again, Charlotte said, "My opinion of you has never changed."

"Not even when I refused to hear your confession?"

She blinked, then stepped away with the dance. Once they were close again, she said, "Not even then. But I fear your opinion of me has been shattered."

He let that statement part them until the dance steps brought them together. "Nothing has been shattered. If anything, it has only grown stronger."

Charlotte stopped, even though others about them continued in the steps. Heads turned, but Brand didn't care.

"Truly?" she whispered.

"Truly," he confirmed. He held out his hand to lead her in the group circle. When her gloved hand touched his, he felt the trembling there.

He wanted nothing more than everyone and everything to disappear so that he could pull her into his arms and never let her go. But he'd known it was important to her to regain her strength as a woman, to know that she could stand on her own two feet. Only then might she accept him once again. So he'd waited. But he could wait no longer.

The dancing continued, and they no longer spoke. It seemed that gazes and glances could speak things of the heart. As the quadrille ended, Brand held out his arm to Charlotte. The flush of her neck and her increased breathing told him she was in need of refreshment. Two dances down. One to go.

"Would you like refreshment, Mrs. Ashford?" he asked formally, even though his thumping heart was anything but formal.

"Yes, thank you, Lord Wilshore." Her return of his formality only made him smile.

Her lips twitched as they walked arm in arm to the refreshment table.

After pouring Charlotte a glass of what seemed to be lukewarm lemonade, Mrs. Givens approached, her gaze intent on him. A bit of frenzied anger lurked behind the woman's sharp green eyes.

Before she could open her mouth and order either of them about, Brand handed Mrs. Givens a glass of lemonade. "I hope you're taking time to enjoy yourself as well, ma'am."

Mrs. Givens took the glass because it was right in front of her. "Why, I don't—"

"Double my pledge again." Brand drained his glass, then grasped Charlotte's hand.

"But sir," Mrs. Givens complained. "You've danced twice already. Think of your reputations."

This gave Brand pause. He turned to face Charlotte. "Do you want to stop now?"

Charlotte's chin lifted. "I think you promised me three dances, my lord."

"And I always keep my promises."

Her laughter made his chest swell, and he led her back to the dance floor. The next dance had already begun, and every step that brought them close made him smile and her blush. He didn't care about the fuming Mrs. Givens on the side, watching them. She'd get her money. Who could be cross about that? Midnight was still an hour away, and the dancing would continue well past that.

But the number was drawing to a close, and Brand could only think of the second half of his promise. "Would you like to get some air with me?"

There was no hesitation, only a breathless reply from Charlotte. "I'd love that."

So that was how he found himself walking through the back gardens of Lady Joanna's immaculate estate. Torchlight guided them through the winding paths. Other couples were about, so there wasn't complete privacy, but there was enough for Brand to finally shake off the prying eyes of the crush.

Having Charlotte nearly to himself was good enough for now.

"The stars seem so numerous tonight," Charlotte said when they reached a small gazebo.

The pressure on his arm from her small hand was a comforting thing. He halted in his step outside the gazebo, and they both looked up into the heavens. "It's a fine thing to realize that wherever you are in the world, you can look into the night sky and know that others are looking as well. It makes one feel less alone, I suppose."

"Is that how you felt on that ship?" she asked.

"I was alone, certainly." He raised a hand and pulled off his mask. "But when I looked at the sky, I felt less alone. I imagined that you were also looking at the same night sky, and somehow you'd know I was coming back to you."

"I'm sorry, Brand," she whispered.

"Life has happened to us both," he said with a shake of his head. "I don't tell you that to make you regret anything. I tell you that because I want you to know my feelings for you are the same now as they were back then."

Her mouth parted in surprise, and he lifted his hands to untie her mask. As it fell away, her luminous eyes glimmered up at him.

"I've had no word from you for weeks," she said. "You've all but disappeared. How could I know anything?"

His throat tightened. "I was waiting."

"For what?"

"For you to be sure."

"Me?" Her pretty brow wrinkled. "I am already sure, Brand. I just didn't know if you'd have *me*. I knew I had no right to ask anything of a man I'd hurt so deeply."

"Charlotte," he whispered. "You were hurt first, and keeping score does no one any favors. Perhaps we can heal that pain together."

A tear fell and trailed along her cheek. Brand smoothed it away with his thumb. "Three dances. Do you remember?"

"I do," she said, another tear falling, but a smile had bloomed.

He cradled her face, her skin soft and delicate beneath his fingers. "Three dances and a kiss. Then you'll be mine."

Her hands moved up his chest, tentatively, and then her fingers brushed his neck. Warm. Tender.

He leaned down, cradling her face in his larger hands. "You're about to kiss a sailor, Charlotte, do you approve?"

"Wholeheartedly."

Her lips were as soft as he had dreamed, but he had not expected the fire in his veins as she pressed close and let him claim her mouth. Her hands tangled in his hair, and his sailor hat fell off. But no matter; she was in his arms, and she was kissing him as intensely as he was kissing her. Surely she'd not shared such a kiss with her husband, but just to make sure, Brand kissed her with every ounce of love he possessed. He did not want her to doubt; he did not want her to question what he felt for her.

His heart thumped wildly as she tugged him toward the gazebo, effectively putting them in the shadows should anyone approach along the path. And then he was sitting on the bench, and she was on his lap, still kissing him. He cradled her close, slowing down the fire between them until it became a low simmer.

"Charlotte," he rasped. "I cannot celebrate your misfortune, but I am determined to create a life with you now that you are free."

Her chest heaved with her breathlessness, and her fingers slipped down his neck and across the rough fabric over his shoulders. "Brand, I have never been free. My heart has always been in your keeping."

Their gazes held, and he was the one with tears in his eyes now. "Will you marry me, my dearest Charlotte?"

She blinked rapidly, then wrapped her arms about his shoulders, burying her face against his neck. "Yes," she whispered against his skin. "Yes, yes, yes."

He grinned as he held her tightly against him, and if

anyone had walked by at that moment, he wouldn't have moved an inch. "I love you, darling," he said when his emotions allowed him to speak.

Her hold only tightened, and her next words were as shaky as he felt. "I love you too."

They sat in the gazebo long after it was proper to do so, missing the midnight removal of masks and all the other dances following as they stayed locked in each other's embrace. Many more kisses were stolen, for each one aided in ebbing away the pain of the past, replaced by new hope, growing happiness, and rekindled love.

13

"Blast," Brand murmured as the banging continued on the front door. He'd gotten home from the ball in the wee hours of the morning. For some reason Richards had waited up for him, so the man was likely still asleep.

What time was it anyway?

Much too early to be awake, that's what time it was. Brand had been enjoying the remnants of his delightful evening with Charlotte. They'd spent over an hour in the garden, then they'd gone in to supper after everyone had removed their masks. Brand had asked her to dance again, but she'd said there was no way she could dance with him four times, even if they were engaged.

And since he refused to dance with anyone else, he had pledged more money. He and Charlotte had then played whist with Thea and Lord Blackdene. Well, *they* had played and competed, while Brand lost every hand due to his mooning over Charlotte. He hadn't even minded his sister's teasing.

Knock. Knock. Knock.

"I'm coming," Brand hollered. He shoved his legs into some trousers, then tugged on his shirt. Not bothering with a cravat, he slipped his arms through his jacket sleeves but didn't take time to tuck in his shirttails. Or put on shoes.

He hurried down the staircase, then strode across the cold stone floor. The knocking continued, firm and persistent.

"This had better be important," Brand grumbled before swinging the door open, only to be hit by the glaring morning sunlight.

And the sight of... eight women.

The two carriages standing in his driveway had apparently delivered the women. He squinted against the sunlight to make out the identities of each. Lady Joanna was among them, several inches taller than the rest and looking like she was a countess of a foreign land in her pale-green gown and more jewels than his entire estate possessed.

The other ladies looked familiar, but he only knew the names of Mrs. Steele, a rather round blond woman, and Mrs. Fletcher, a friend to Thea. They were all... widows.

Brand's greeting stuck in his throat. If he wasn't mistaken, these women were members of the Secret Society of Young Widows. And they were all at his doorstep.

Brand cleared his throat. "To what do I owe this pleasure?"

No one spoke. It seemed that everyone was staring at his chest. Brand looked down at the gaping collar of his shirt. No cravat meant there was plenty of skin showing. He folded his arms and stared them down. "Don't tell me you ladies have never seen a man early in the morning in a state of undress."

Someone gasped, he wasn't sure who. Another woman blushed a fiery red, reminding Brand of holly berries. Two of the women lowered their gazes. But Lady Joanna merely clucked her tongue and said, "We understand this visit is early and unexpected, but can you please put on a cravat, Lord Wilshore? We've an important matter to discuss."

Brand stared. Then he remembered his manners, or what was left of them. "Of course. Come in, and make yourselves comfortable in the drawing room. I'll be but a moment." He stepped back, opening the door wider. Then stepped back again.

The women followed, all of them keeping their gazes averted as they passed by him on the way to the drawing room.

"It's just there," he said, pointing, although no one seemed to need any directions. With a shake of his head, he shut the door, then returned to his rooms, where he made a half-decent job of tying a cravat. Then he pulled on his boots and tucked in his shirttails. It would have to do.

By the time he returned downstairs, the gaggle of women in his drawing room had most certainly made themselves at home. Lady Joanna had taken up residence before the hearth, and the other women were sitting on the various wing-backed chairs and settees.

All heads turned as he entered.

"Much better, Lord Wilshore," Lady Joanna declared.

If Brand were a man with a weaker constitution, he might be feeling a little ill right now. As it was, he was merely curious. And put out. He wanted to return to his dreams of Charlotte and remember her touch until he could see her again. Which he planned to do very soon.

"Sir?" a male voice said behind him.

Brand turned to see Richards. "Ah, there you are."

Richards's eyes had rounded. "Do you require anything for your guests? Perhaps refreshment?"

"Oh, we aren't here for scraps," Lady Joanna cut in. "Please, don't trouble yourself, sir."

Richards nodded, then bowed. He turned and left the room, when Brand wanted to beg him to stay. But there were some things he apparently had to face himself. Which in this case meant eight women.

He faced Lady Joanna again. "How might I be of service?"

"We've come to speak to you about the rumors," Lady Joanna said. "Mrs. Givens told me that you refused to relinquish Mrs. Ashford last night in order to dance with others."

Brand cast the apparent Mrs. Givens a quick glance and noted her lifted chin and her pursed lips. "That is correct."

"You understand the rumors that fly when a man dances exclusively with a woman he is not related or married to," Lady Joanna continued, walking toward him where he still stood near the drawing room door.

"I am aware."

She stopped, her gaze moving in a slow perusal. "And what, pray tell, possessed you to single out Mrs. Ashford?"

"We have been friends our whole lives," Brand said. He'd tied his cravat a bit too tightly, and it was possibly off-center.

"She is like a sister to you, then?" Lady Joanna prompted.

Brand blinked. "No, not a sister." He looked at the other women, who seemed to be hanging on his every word. "Last night, Charlotte and I became engaged."

Mrs. Steele gasped. Another woman leapt to her feet and clapped.

Lady Joanna frowned. "You proposed, and she *accepted*?"

"Yes," Brand confirmed.

"Marriage is a lifelong commitment," Lady Joanna said. "It is not a matter to trifle with."

"I understand that fully," Brand said.

"And a woman in Mrs. Ashford's situation should not marry into a difficult situation," Lady Joanna continued. "She has a child to think about, and she's already been through hard trials. A woman's heart is not to be dallied with—"

"Madam," Brand cut in. "I've loved Charlotte as long as I can remember. Circumstances pulled us apart, but now that we've overcome obstacles, there is nothing that I won't do for her." He surveyed the other women. "All of you have been her champions, that I know. You have been her protectors. She has found friendship among you, and I don't intend to interfere with that. But I want you to know, Charlotte will be cherished and cared for until the end of my days."

The women smiled, but Lady Joanna's frown didn't soften. "What about *after* all your days? What happens to her when you die?"

Brand couldn't have been more surprised if Lady Joanna had slapped him. "What happens? I hope she would continue to live many more healthy years . . . if I were to die before her."

"This, Lord Wilshore," she said, pointing at his chest, "is precisely why we've come."

Brand's eyebrows shot up.

"We've come to ensure that Mrs. Ashford—the future Lady Wilshore—and her daughter, Emily Ashford, will both be provided for after your death. She will not become a destitute widow a second time. It is part of the vow we all make when joining our society." The woman set her hands on her hips. "We have a contract for you to sign that we call the Continuation of Care contract. Mrs. Givens?"

Mrs. Givens rose. Her cheeks were flushed on her rather pointy face as she crossed to Lady Joanna.

In moments, Brand held a contract in his hand spelling out the details of an agreement he was expected to sign. He read through the terms of the contract. *Impressive.*

A loud knock sounded from the front door.

"Blast," he said, jolting from his concentration. Then, to the women, he said, "Apologies." Who else could be here? More society women?

"My lord," Richards said, appearing in the doorway of the drawing room, "a Mrs. Ashford is here to see you."

Brand spun to see the woman in question enter the room on the heels of the butler.

"Charlotte. By all means, join us." Brand didn't give a fig that he'd addressed her by her Christian name in front of a roomful of people.

Charlotte looked as if she'd slept as little as he, although she was beautiful in her disheveled state. She'd worn a simple cream-colored day dress, and her hair fell down her back in a long braid. She looked as if she'd spent time in the meadows among the flowers and grasses. Brand had no doubt that she smelled as fresh as a summer morning.

He wanted to tug her into another room, away from all of her friends, and kiss her properly.

Charlotte's gaze widened as she surveyed the company in the room. "What's this?"

Lady Joanna straightened to her full height. "We are here to administer the Continuation of Care Contract."

It was Charlotte's turn to frown. "Ah." Her gaze flew to Brand. "And you are going to sign this document?"

"I am," he declared. "Right now, in fact." He strode over to the desk near the bank of windows, and with a flourish, he dipped a quill into the inkpot, then signed his name to both pages of the contract.

After blowing the ink dry, he handed it to Lady Joanna.

"Anything else, madam?" he asked.

Lady Joanna titled her head, her dark-green eyes steady on him. "That will be all, for now."

"Very well," Brand said, with his own tilt of his head. "If that will be all, I have something to discuss with my fiancée in private."

The women on the settees and chairs tittered, and all eyes shifted to Charlotte.

And, bless her heart, she merely clasped her hands

together and said, "That's right. Thank you all for coming over to present my betrothed the contract. I am greatly indebted to you."

If that wasn't a dismissal, Brand didn't know what was.

And if there was ever a miracle, this was it. The women left his drawing room, loaded themselves back into the two carriages, and vacated the property.

"I am sorry about that," Charlotte gushed the moment the door shut behind them.

Brand only smiled. "I must say, waking up to very loud knocking was quite unpleasant, but now . . ."

Charlotte's brows lifted. "And now?"

He walked toward her, one slow step after another until he stood only a handspan from the woman he'd spent the past few hours dreaming of. The morning sun had deepened in color, splashing the drawing room in patches of gold.

"And now . . ." he said in a soft voice, "I've changed my mind."

"Have you?" she whispered, swaying toward him.

Brand lifted a hand to curl his fingers around her braid. He brought the hair forward over her shoulder. His fingers lingered, brushing against the delicate skin of her neck.

Charlotte's lips curved.

"You may knock on my door any time of the day or night," he whispered. "Until we are married, that is."

Her eyelashes fluttered as she studied his face. "Oh, and what happens after we are married?"

His fingers danced across her jaw, then slid along her cheek. "When we're married, we'll be on the same side of the door. Thus, no knocking required."

She smiled, and he could not wait another moment, not even another heartbeat. He closed the distance and pressed his mouth to hers.

He'd thought their first kiss last night had been divine, but here, now, in the budding morning light of the silent drawing room, her sweetness invaded his every sense, his every emotion. They didn't embrace, which was a wise thing, but kept the kissing light.

And the only reason he drew away was to breathe. "To what do I owe the pleasure of your company this fine morning, my dear Charlotte?"

"I saw the carriages passing by and recognized them as Lady Joanna's." Her fingers played at the nape of his neck. "I thought I'd come rescue you."

"I am a fortunate man then, darling." He kissed her again, and this time lingered quite a while. "Will you marry me?"

She laughed and drew away, her eyes sparkling up at him. "You've already asked, Lord Wilshore. And I've already consented."

"Ah, I thought I might have been dreaming all of last night." A grin tugged at his mouth. "I'm so pleased to know it was no dream at all."

"Oh, it is definitely a dream." She slipped her arms about his neck and pulled him close. It appeared she wasn't quite finished with kissing him either. "One I hope will last for many, many years."

Brand couldn't agree more. And he'd sign any contract it took to keep this woman in his life. But first things first. He had his fiancée in his arms, and the day was just getting started.

Heather B. Moore is a *USA Today* bestselling author. She writes historical under the pen name H.B. Moore; her latest are *Ruth*, and *Deborah Prophetess of God*. Under the name Heather B. Moore, she writes romance and women's fiction; her latest include the Pine Valley Novels and Prosperity Ranch Novels. Under pen name Jane Redd, she writes the young adult speculative Solstice series, including her latest release *Mistress Grim*. Heather is represented by Dystel, Goderich & Bourret.

www.ingramcontent.com/pod-product-compliance
Lightning Source LLC
LaVergne TN
LVHW021757060526
838201LV00058B/3125